RESCUING GABRIELLA (SPECIAL FORCES: OPERATION ALPHA)

BRAVO SERIES BOOK 3

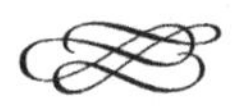

ANNA BLAKELY

Dear Readers,

Welcome to the Special Forces: Operation Alpha Fan-Fiction world!

If you are new to this amazing world, in a nutshell the author wrote a story using one or more of my characters in it. Sometimes that character has a major role in the story, and other times they are only mentioned briefly. This is perfectly legal and allowable because they are going through Aces Press to publish the story.

This book is entirely the work of the author who wrote it. While I might have assisted with brainstorming and other ideas about which of my characters to use, I didn't have any part in the process or writing or editing the story.

I'm proud and excited that so many authors loved my characters enough that they wanted to write them into their own story. Thank you for supporting them, and me!

READ ON!

Xoxo

Susan Stoker

This book is for two of my closest friends, Angie S. and Nancy G. From day one, you've both been there for me. Whether it be to offer your support, share your suggestions, read over my messy, unedited manuscripts, or to talk me off the ledge when I'm convinced I need to throw out what I've written and start over...you've both always, always been there.

You truly have no idea how much your support and belief in my writing means to me. It still blows my mind that I get to wake up every day and live my professional dream, and I couldn't do this without you two. (Well, maybe I could...but it wouldn't be near as much fun! LOL)

I love you both so hard!

XOXO
Anna

PROLOGUE

With his shoulder resting against the wooden doorjamb, Zade King stared down at the stunning, redhead sleeping in his bed.

Taking advantage of the uninterrupted moment, he wondered for the umpteenth time in less than a handful of days how he'd gotten so lucky.

He'd come to Grand Isle, Louisiana two weeks ago in hopes of finding a sense of peace he'd suddenly found himself to be lacking. Meeting Gabby had been the most delicious of surprises.

Physically, he'd already healed. It was his head—and his heart—that had been in a desperate search for solace.

So he'd decided to put some distance between himself and his team, hoping the time away would bring with it the answers he needed.

Having been a Marine, Zade knew better than most how useless he'd be to his teammates if his head wasn't in the game. With that in mind, he'd taken two extra weeks off to regroup and reflect on what had happened and figure out a way to move past it.

He'd also used the time alone to really think about what he hadn't yet accomplished in his thirty-one years…and try to decide if his priorities were in need of a change.

The doctors had cleared him for full duty sixteen days ago, but Zade wasn't ready to get back in the field. Not mentally, anyway.

Most Marine's he knew—hell, most *men* he knew—would never admit something like that. Not to themselves or anyone else.

But Zade wasn't like most men.

As a result, he'd taken more shit from the guys than he cared to admit, but it was simply the way he was built. Since he was a kid, Zade had never been shy about sharing his feelings. He was pretty much an open book, and like it or not, what you see is what you get.

If he hadn't come here when he did, Zade's teammates would've seen much more than he wanted them to.

So he'd left.

Thankfully Gabe Dawson—Bravo's team leader—had not only understood Zade's need to get away, but also fully supported it. Dawson was a former SEAL and knew the importance of being mentally ready before stepping back into the fire.

Speaking of fire…

Zade placed the cardboard drink carrier with two full cups of fresh coffee onto the small dresser to his left. Next to it, he dropped the bag of fresh pastries he'd bought at the tiny bakery up the street from his rented beach house.

With one of the lidded to-go cups in hand, he walked over to where the woman of his dreams lay. The mattress dipped from his weight as Zade placed one knee beside her and leaned down.

Using his free hand, he gently wafted the aromatic steam toward her gorgeous face in hopes the scent of freshly brewed beans would break through her subconscious.

Gabby's eyelids fluttered, their naturally long lashes lifting from her cheeks as a set of emerald green eyes found his.

Zade's heart kicked against his ribs, just as it did every time she looked at him. "Mornin', beautiful."

She smiled, her drowsy eyes filling with genuine happiness. "Hey."

Her voice's natural raspiness was even rougher from the hours she'd spent resting. The sexy sound made his greedy cock twitch with desire.

Ignoring it, for now, he tipped his head toward the dresser at the foot of the bed. "I brought you some breakfast. Thought you might want to start with the coffee, first."

With a deep inhale, Gabby scooted herself up to rest against the bed's headboard. Swiping some of her long, auburn hair from her face, she held the sheet in one fist and cleared the sleep from her throat before taking the cup from his hand.

With an appreciative nod, she said, "Thank you."

Zade watched as she closed her eyes and savored that first sip, the tip of her tongue running along her plump bottom lip to catch a drop before it fell onto her chin. A low moan escaped from her throat, mimicking the way she sounded when he'd slid into her welcoming heat just hours before.

Now achingly hard, his greedy dick pressed against his boxer briefs, ready to tear through those and his thin, mesh gym shorts in order to return to the promised land. But Zade was more than a little sweaty from his run on the beach and needed a quick shower before that could happen.

When Gabby opened her eyes again, one corner of her mouth rose into a knowing grin. "I recognize that look."

"Yeah?"

She nodded, the green in her eyes darkening with desire. "I would've thought you got enough of that last night." Her lips quirked. "And the night before."

Zade carefully took the cup from her hand and set it on the nightstand before bringing himself closer and taking her lips between his. With a teasing nibble, he cupped one side of her beautiful face and whispered, "No such thing as enough when it comes to you."

Beneath his, Gabby's perfect mouth spread into a full smile. "I know the feeling." In a bold move, she gently bit his bottom lip as her hand slid down over his rippled abs, straight into the elastic waistband of his shorts.

Closing his eyes, Zade slid his tongue into her mouth. She tasted of coffee and seduction, her soft, warm fingers wrapping tightly around his hot shaft.

Hissing in a sharp breath, he slid his fingers into her thick hair, fisting it at her nape as Gabby began moving her hand up and down in slow, deliberate strokes.

"You like that?" She nipped at his chin.

"You know I do." Zade kissed her again. "But I've been running. Need to shower."

"Later." Gabby squeezed his cock a little harder to literally hold him in place.

Pulling his head back slightly, he raised a brow at the gorgeous temptress. "You sure?" He looked down at himself. "I'm kind of sweaty."

With a playful smirk, she shrugged a bare shoulder. "You're just going to get sweaty again, anyway, right?"

Zade shook his head, but grinned. "Damn, woman. I love the way you think."

Within seconds, he'd stripped off his boxers and shorts, covered himself with one of the condoms from the box he'd left on the nightstand the evening before, and had the sheets ripped away from her delectable, naked body.

After kneeling on the bed at her feet, Zade gently tugged on her ankles, pulling her until she was lying flat on the mattress. Before he could make the move, Gabby gave him a sly grin and spread her legs wide, allowing him all the access he needed.

His mouth watered at the sight of her glistening sex, but his impatient dick had him climbing the length of her body. Before he could give it a second thought, Zade was pushing himself inside her velvet heat, a guttural moan rumbling from deep inside him as Gabby's smoldering core sucked him in.

The sensation was unlike anything he'd ever experienced before. Being with Gabby this way, making her body come alive beneath his, was the most incredible, indescribable feeling in the world. Of course, from the second he first saw her, Zade knew everything with this woman would be different.

He began pumping himself in and out, using the tantalizing rhythm they'd created together. With his elbows keeping his weight from crushing her, he brought his mouth to hers and began to feast.

For the next several minutes—or hours, he wasn't sure—their bodies danced together as one. Their movements were slow. Deliberate. And unbelievably satisfying.

"Zade," Gabby panted his name as she tore her lips from his. With her eyes closed, she tilted her head back against the pillow and lifted her lean but supple hips upward to meet his. "God, you feel so good."

A rush of heat filled his cock, and Zade felt himself become impossibly harder. Her encouraging words spurred him on, and he knew he wasn't going to last much longer.

"So do you, sweetheart," he promised. "Better than anything I've ever felt before."

In response to his claim, Gabby's inner muscles clenched

tightly around him. Even through the condom's thin barrier, he could feel the rush of hot liquid coating him as he continued thrusting himself in and out of her drenched channel.

A sudden and familiar tingling began spreading from his lower spine upward, his balls tightening with their impending explosion.

"Ah, hell, Gabby." Zade's chest heaved between thrusts as he tried to hold off. "I'm not gonna…last…much…longer."

Knowing what he needed, Gabby started to slide her hand between their bodies, but Zade stopped her. Though the thought of her getting herself off was hot as hell, he wanted to be the one to get her there.

Gently swatting her hand away, Zade put his weight on one elbow and used his free hand to reach down to where they were connected. Gathering some of her essence onto his fingertips, his body jerked when he inadvertently touched his sensitive shaft in the process.

Determined to get her there first, he did everything he could to hold off his own climax as he brought his fingers to her swollen clit. Rubbing in small, tight circles, Zade pushed himself in and out of her body while at the same time paying close attention to the bundle of nerves begging for his touch.

Gabby cried out, her body jerking below his, and when her thighs began to tremble, he knew she was almost there.

"Oh god, Zade. I'm close. So close."

Zade's hips reflexively thrust harder. Faster. His body demanding he give it the release it so desperately needed.

"I can't hold off any longer, sweetheart." He moved his fingers faster. Pressed a little harder. "Come on baby. Let go. Now!"

A loud, keening cry tore from the back of her throat as she fell apart beneath him. Gabby's entire body arched, her pussy clamping down onto his cock with incredible force, sending Zade into his own amazing orgasm.

With a loud roar, her name echoed off the tiny room's paneled walls as he began spilling his hot seed into the tip of the condom. His movements became jerky, almost uncontrollable as the powerful climax rolled through him from head to toe.

Minutes later, with their bodies depleted of all the pleasure they could possibly share, Zade held on to the condom as he pulled himself out of her trembling body and lay there, panting and sweaty beside her.

"Just when I think...it can't get...any better..." He barely managed to breathe out.

Despite his eyes being closed, he could hear Gabby's smile in her rough voice as she finished for him. "It does."

Chest swelling from primal pride, Zade turned to face her. A set of heavy-lidded, satiated eyes stared back into his. "Glad you feel the same."

She smiled lazily. "How could I not?"

Because he could, Zade leaned up and pressed his lips to hers. Before when he'd kissed her, he'd been hungry. No, not hungry. Starved. Now that he'd temporarily whet his carnal appetite for this woman, he wanted to take his time. Savor every drop.

When the deep, emotional kiss finally ended, Zade used his fingertip to brush some hair from her face as he looked down at her. "Come to Texas with me."

The presumptuous question was out before he could stop it. Yet, he didn't regret it for a second. At least, not until he saw her eyes widen with surprise.

"I-I'd love to, Zade. But I can't."

"Why not?" he pressed. "You said your school doesn't resume from spring break for another week." He leaned up onto his elbow while running his fingers along the slope of her flat belly. "Come on, Gabby. Come to Dallas with me. You can even stay at my place, so you won't have the expense of a hotel," he added quickly, "but only if you're comfortable with that. If not, I'll pay for a room for you while you're visiting."

"I'd love to, but..." She shook her head.

His big heart fell, and he started to pull his hand away. "You don't trust me enough? I get it. It's probably too soon for you to—"

"No." She grabbed his hand to stop him. "It's not that. I mean"—she glanced down at their naked bodies—"if I didn't trust you, I wouldn't have spent the last three days with you."

That made him feel a little better. "Then what is it?"

"Actually, I got a phone call while you were running. My mom and dad want me to come stay with them in Chicago for a few days before I have to go back to work. I already told them I would."

Okay, that made sense. She'd told him that first night about how close she was to her parents and sister. "When do you get another break?"

"Not until school's out in mid-May."

That also made sense. As an elementary teacher, it wasn't like she could take off whenever she wanted. Damn, he wished she could.

Taking a chance, and trying hard not to sound as desperate as he felt, Zade said, "All right. What about this summer?"

A slight show of panic crossed her face, and he rushed to put her at ease. "I'm sorry, Gabby. I know we just met, and I don't mean to come off pushy or anything. I just..." He sighed, giving her his boyish smile. "There's a connection between us. And I don't think I'm the only one who feels it."

She smiled up at him, her hand cupping his jaw. "No." Her

red hair swooshed against the rough pillowcase. "You're not the only one who feels it."

"Thank Christ." Zade leaned down and gave her a hard, short kiss. "So is that a yes to summer?"

Gabby's smile grew wider, but there was a flash of something odd that crossed over her. It was gone as quickly as it appeared.

"I'd love nothing more than to spend the summer with you."

It was his turn to smile. "Good. I'm going to go wash up." He kissed her again, because he could. "Wish the shower in this place was bigger than a Cracker Jack box. I'd haul you in there with me."

She chuckled, causing her perky, perfectly proportioned breasts to jiggle, and damn, if he didn't feel his lower body starting to stir again.

"You're insatiable, you know that?"

Zade leaned down and took one of her rose-colored peaks between his lips. With a flick of his tongue, he let the tip move back and forth before swirling around the hardening nub.

She moaned, and he felt her fingers grab ahold of the hair on the back of his head, her body telling him she was every bit as hungry for him as he was her.

Knowing she was probably a bit sore and that he really did need that shower, Zade reluctantly released her breast with a 'pop'. Her heavy-lidded eyes smoldered back at his with such intense emotion it almost felt as though she was committing his face to memory.

The same way he had hers with every glance they'd shared.

"Don't move from this spot."

Her thin brows turned inward. "Why not?"

He shrugged. "If we only have one more night before I fly back to Texas, I want to spend every second I can with you."

An emotion Zade couldn't quite place filled her mesmerizing stare. "I feel the same way."

His heart swelled as he kissed the tip of her cute-as-hell nose before hopping off the bed. "Guess I'd better hurry." He winked at her from over his shoulder as he made his way to the bathroom.

From behind him, Gabby laughed. The sweet, feminine sound was laced with that natural rasp he'd almost instantly fell in love with.

That's not the only thing you love.

The thought took him off guard as he disposed of the used condom and started the shower. Standing under the too-short showerhead, he thought about how crazy it was to even be thinking that way.

They'd known each other three days, for crying out loud. And, as much as he appreciated the thought, love at first sight was a myth. Wasn't it?

For the entirety of the shower, Zade analyzed what he thought he was feeling for this woman. Was it possible to be falling in love with someone he barely knew?

Physically, he knew all sorts of things about Gabby. What she liked. What turned her on. What made her writhe beneath his touch, and what made her scream his name in ecstasy.

But other than the basic, where are you from type questions, they'd spent most of their time together in bed. Something completely out of character for him.

Through the years, Zade had met plenty of women who were fine with a little no-strings fun. Same as most guys he knew. Until Matt, his teammate and friend, reconnected with his childhood sweetheart, the guy had been the poster boy for casual, one-night-stands.

Either way, male or female, it wasn't Zade's place to judge. After all, sex was as natural as eating or sleeping. A basal need for both men and women alike. So he didn't care what other people did.

Personally, however, sex meant more to Zade than most. And he wasn't ashamed to admit it.

Whether it be his upbringing or some innate characteristic, he'd always regarded sex as something special. Personal.

Since high school, he'd been the butt of jokes from his friends. Later, in the military it got even worse. Even his Bravo teammates would sometimes razz him about being the emotional one on the team, but he didn't care.

Zade lived his life the way he wanted. The way he felt was right for him. And he didn't give two shits what anyone else thought.

Despite the fact they'd only known each other a few days, Zade knew in his heart his time with Gabby meant more to her than a simple weekend fling. He'd seen it in her eyes. Felt it in her ravishing touch.

His cock twitched as he ran his lather-filled hand over it and below. He had a feeling he and his hand were going to become even more acquainted over these next couple months, until he could see Gabby again.

Thankfully he'd stored up every enticing, delicious memory he could in only three days' time. They'd have to hold him over until her school let out for summer break. Speaking of memories...

Time to make some new ones.

After a quick rinse-off, Zade stepped out of the shower and dried himself off. Foregoing the clothes—because, why bother?—he wrapped the towel around his waist and headed for the door. He started talking as he turned the knob.

"I was thinking, if you want, we could try that little diner on the east end of Highway One the bartender told us about the other..."

He stopped short when he noticed the empty bed. With a quick glance, he noticed her coffee was still on the nightstand, and the bag of pastries was still where he'd left it on the dresser.

Assuming she'd gone in search of something cool to drink, Zade sauntered down the short hallway in that direction. He frowned when he found the kitchen empty.

Spinning around, it took less than a second to scan the adjoining living room which was also empty. An uneasy feeling began to claw its way into his gut, but Zade pushed it back.

Not one to borrow trouble, he calmly made his way back down the hallway to the rental's second bedroom, thinking maybe she'd gone in there for some reason. But it was empty, as well.

With a bit more urgency, Zade went outside to the back deck. Still, no Gabby. Officially worried now, he raced back into the house, hollering her name as he double-checked each room again.

Only this time, when he'd made it back to the bedroom, he noticed something he'd missed before. Something that left his stomach churning and his heart lying in pieces on the floor.

Gabby's things were gone. Her clothes. Her shoes. Her bag. Everything. And on the nightstand, next to the coffee he'd brought her, was piece of paper. It was folded with a large Z written on the top flap.

Jaw clenched, Zade slowly shuffled over to where it lay. Swallowing against the painful knot already forming in his throat, he picked it up and read it.

. . .

Zade,

These past three days have been the best I can ever remember. You gave me hope at a time when I thought there was none. I'll never forget that or you. Thank you.

Love,

Gabby

Zade plopped his towel-covered ass down onto the mattress. A note. She'd left him a fucking note.

Christ, King...you're such an idiot.

Crumbling the paper in his tightened fist, he knew it was ridiculous to be this upset over a woman he'd just met. But damn if he could help it.

He could've sworn Gabby was different. Someone he'd had a real connection with. A woman who'd miraculously come to care about him as much as he had her. Boy was he wrong.

You pushed her too far.

That tiny voice was right. He never should've mentioned coming to Dallas for the summer.

Even so, she could've said no. The least she could've done was wait until he was out of the shower to say goodbye. Hell even some fake-ass story explaining her sudden departure would have been better than the freakin' cryptic note she'd left behind.

Maybe that was the whole point. Maybe she'd been planning to slip away undetected the entire time.

After running his free hand over the scruff on his face, Zade pinched the bridge of his nose and tried not to chew his own ass out for having been so stupid. It was hard as hell not to. The woman had completely fooled him.

As crazy as it was, his heart physically hurt from the

sudden void she'd left. Gabby had seemed so different from any other woman he'd gotten to know romantically.

She'd seemed so real. So genuine. The looks she'd given him and the way she'd been...Gabby had made him believe she'd started to care about him, too. And like a dumbass, he'd fallen for it. Hook, line, and sinker.

Another thought crashed its way through causing Zade to hop up and go to the dresser where he'd also left his wallet. Fully expecting it to be empty, he was surprised to find all his credit cards and cash still present and accounted for. It was both a relief and confusing as hell.

If she hadn't spent the weekend planning to scam him, then why? It wasn't because she actually gave a damn about him. That was obvious. If she had, she wouldn't have ghosted him the way she had...right?

Opening his fist, Zade smoothed the crinkled paper and read the written words again. The logical part of his brain said to forget her. Told himself Gabby had been lying when she said she wanted to see him again after their time here was over.

Zade continued to sit where they'd made love more than once, doing his damnedest to accept the sultry woman had simply used him for a weekend of great sex. That she'd gotten her fill and then left without giving him a second thought.

But there was another part of him, the emotional part that seemed to be Zade's perpetual driving force, that refused to believe he'd meant nothing to her. At least he hoped he'd meant something.

Her words rang through his head again.

You gave me hope when I thought there was none.

Suddenly, his heart ached for a different reason. He thought of the guarded way she'd looked at him the first night they met. How shy and almost closed-off she'd seemed when he'd finally gotten up the nerve to approach her at one of the local bars.

At the time, Zade assumed she was simply weary of a strange man trying to pick her up or take advantage of her. His assumption was further solidified when, as time went on and they talked some more, she'd begun to relax.

Looking back, Zade couldn't help but wonder if what he'd first read as trepidation had actually been...hopelessness.

So many questions began rolling through his mind, but as he got himself dressed and began packing for his trip back home, there was one that stood out over the rest.

What happened to make you lose hope, sweetheart?

It was a question Zade intended to ask Gabriella Smith, the second he saw her again. And come hell or high water, he would find her.

Because he and Gabby? They weren't even close to being done. Not by a long shot.

CHAPTER 1

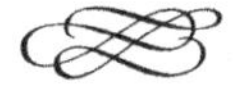

One month later...

"No!"

The sound of gunfire was deafening inside the car. Warm liquid splattered the entire right side of Zade's face as he struggled to keep his composure. He closed his eyes, his heart racing as he said a silent prayer.

This is it. I'm going to die now.

He couldn't believe it. Didn't want to believe it. After all his years serving proudly as a United States Marine, and more recently as a member of one of the country's most elite black ops security teams, he was going to die here? Like this?

Sweat beaded on Zade's forehead, his chest heaving with shallow breaths as he thought about his mom and dad. His two younger sisters. And the man who'd just been ruthlessly executed in the seat beside him.

Zade thought of his R.I.S.C. family...especially his buddy Matt. His stomach churned knowing his last act on this earth was to fail one of his best friends and the woman he was supposed to protect.

He heard her scream. Saw that bastard take her from the back seat, and he couldn't do a fucking thing to stop it.

Zade yelled. He pleaded. But it was too late. Seconds later, he was looking down the barrel of the assassin's gun as the man pulled the trigger...

"No!"

Zade sat straight up in bed, gasping for air as he looked around his darkened bedroom. He forced himself to swallow a choking breath, trying with herculean effort to bring his racing pulse back to a healthy, even beat.

With a curse, he ran a hand over his sweaty face before throwing the covers off and walking to the bathroom. His legs trembled the entire way.

Flipping the switch on the wall, Zade's eyes squinted together, reflexively protecting themselves against the harsh light. Blinking quickly, he gave his vision a few seconds to adjust before turning on the faucet.

Cupping his hands below the running water, Zade waited until they were nearly overflowing before leaning down and splashing it over his face. He repeated the action a few more times before turning the faucet off and grabbing the nearest hand towel.

For several seconds, he stood still, pressing the terrycloth tightly against his face. Breathing in and out slowly, Zade waited as the final remnants of the recurring nightmare's effects dissipated from his body.

The same damn dream had been preventing him from getting a good night's sleep since the day of the shooting several weeks ago. The only exception to this were the nights he'd spent in Grand Isle...with Gabby.

Zade's chest tightened as he thought of the woman he'd been searching for. She'd made him smile. Brought him laughter. And Gabby had—for a few days, at least—replaced his nightmares with wonderful dreams. And somehow, during their short time together, she'd also managed to give him hope for a future he'd begun to think was uncertain.

Zade knew she wasn't perfect—no one was. Like his, her body housed a few scars. He'd seen them, kissed them but hadn't asked about their cause. Though she tried her best to hide it, he'd also sensed a hint of darkness buried behind those stunning green eyes.

There hadn't been enough time for him to delve into those parts of her world, but he would. He just needed to find her first.

Since his return to the team, Zade's down-time between jobs had been eaten up by his efforts to figure out who and where she really was.

He'd tried calling the school in Chicago where she told him she taught third grade. They'd never heard of her. Zade then spent countless hours looking up every single Gabriella Smith known to man and had still come up empty.

From everything he'd found so far, the woman he met in the tiny bar on Grand Isle didn't seem to exist.

But Zade knew she was real. As real as the note he kept folded in his wallet.

After his online searching had yielded no results, Zade thought of the note. He had Nate run the paper for prints. Not surprisingly, they'd come up empty.

Zade had handled it too many times. Read it over and over again on the flight home...and since. In turn, he'd inadvertently replaced any prints Gabby may have left with his own.

For now, the note and his memories were the only things he had to prove her existence. Those and the love he'd only just begun to feel before she vanished. Even so, Zade refused to give up hope.

With every resource imaginable at his fingertips, it was only a matter of time before he figured out who the woman claiming to be Gabriella Smith really was. Until then, he needed to get his head out of his ass and back with his team, where he belonged.

Right on cue, Zade's phone began to ring from its place on his nightstand. Knowing there was only one reason someone would call him so early in the morning, he tossed the towel onto the sink's countertop and quickly made his way to his phone, stubbing his toe on his bedframe as he went.

"Shit!" Pain shot up his toe and into his foot as he began hopping on the other one. Muttering several low curses Zade grabbed his cell and answered it.

"King," he ground out, leaning down and rubbing his tender toe.

"Bad time?" Gabe, his team leader, asked.

"No." Zade straightened his spine and breathed through the pain. "Just stubbed my toe. What's up?"

"Bravo's been called up. We're meeting with Ryker and Matthews in an hour. Bring your go-bag."

He drew in a silent breath. "Copy that."

There was a pause before Gabe said, "I know this isn't your first op since coming back, but King...This one could get ugly. You good to go?"

Zade understood what his leader was asking. He needed to know if Zade's head was clear enough to execute the mission and have his brothers' backs.

"Yeah, Dawson," he assured the other man. "I'm good."

"All right, then. See you in an hour."

After ending the call, Zade took a quick shower before grabbing his large, black duffle from the closet floor and double-checking its contents to make sure he had everything he needed.

Once that was finished, he zipped it up tightly and got dressed in a pair of jeans, black T, and his combat boots before making his bed and heading out.

The twenty-minute drive to R.I.S.C.'s downtown office gave him the time he needed to prepare for whatever lie ahead. Knowing his teammates were counting on him was one hell of a motivator for getting his head on straight.

R.I.S.C.—which stood for Rescue, Intel, Security, and Capture—was the private security company Zade started working for after ending his time with the Marines. All former military, each of their operatives brought something special to the table. Unique talents and strengths that, when combined, made them damn near unstoppable.

Headed by former Delta Force operator, Jake McQueen, it consisted of two teams: Alpha and Bravo. Both teams worked black ops missions for Homeland Security, as well as taking on the occasional private sector client.

Zade thought about the guys he worked with now. As these things went, they'd only been a team for a relatively short period of time, but they were brothers. He'd recently let down one of those brothers in spectacular fashion.

His thoughts turned to Matt and everything he'd been through lately. A twinge of familiar guilt struck. The man nearly lost the woman of his dreams because Zade had failed to protect her.

He knew Matt didn't blame him for what had happened to Katherine—Matt's childhood sweetheart and the love of his life—but Zade couldn't help but feel responsible.

The woman had been taken on his watch. She'd been held captive and damn near died because he hadn't been able to do the one thing he'd been assigned to do.

With a tightened gut, Zade thought back to his nightmare. No, not a nightmare. A memory.

Once again, he saw Katherine being pulled from the car

as he remained trapped. Useless. The exact opposite of what a R.I.S.C. operative should be.

Whether it be as bodyguards, rescuing hostages, or taking out the enemy to ensure the safety of the United States and its citizens, Zade and the others were the best at what they did. At least he'd always thought he was.

Goddamn it, King. Cut that shit out.

From behind the wheel, Zade blew out a breath and shook his head because that tiny voice was right. If he allowed self-doubt to crawl its way back inside, he would be of no use.

To his team, or himself.

With that in mind, he pulled into the parking garage next to the building where his office was located. After parking the truck in his reserved spot and taking a few deep, cleansing breaths, he pulled the key from the ignition. Grabbing his bag from the passenger seat, he slid its wide strap over his shoulder and got out.

Securing the vehicle, he began making his way through the concrete structure to the sidewalk out front. Ignoring the slight, intermittent ache pulling at his now-healed collar bone, Zade put on his game face and went to work.

Their office was on the top floor of the building, overlooking downtown Dallas. Once in a while, they'd meet up at Jake's very private and secure ranch located about an hour from the city. Since Jake's wife, Olivia, had recently given birth to their first child, he was keeping most R.I.S.C. business away from there, for the time being.

"Good morning, Zade," Gracelynn Carter—Nate's wife and the company's PR rep and office manager greeted him as he walked through the door. "How's the shoulder?"

"Great." Zade smiled back at the pretty blonde. He'd be even better if everyone would quit asking about his shoulder.

"That's fantastic. Trevor and the others are already in the

conference room. Agent Ryker got held up, but he just called to say he's on his way in now."

"Sounds good."

"Oh, and Lexi sent some goodies with Trevor, so I hope you didn't stop for breakfast."

Okay, so that did put a little perk in his sour mood. Lexi was married to Alpha team medic, Trevor Matthews and owned The Gardens—one of the city's hottest restaurants. In addition to being super sweet, the tiny bit of a thing was also one hell of a cook and an amazing baker.

"Awesome. Thanks, Gracie."

"No problem."

With a slight tip of his head, Zade gave the sweet woman a parting smile and made his way down the long hallway. When he entered the conference room, he found exactly what he expected.

Trevor Matthews—Alpha Team's medic and Jake's second in command—was sitting to his left, at the head of the long, oval table. He'd temporarily taken Jake's place as the man in charge so Jake could take some paternity leave.

Gabe was in his usual seat across from where Zade stood. The former SEAL greeted him with a head nod and continued drinking his coffee and talking with Trevor about whatever they were already discussing when he'd walked in.

Standing by the table in the back were Kole, Nate, and Matt. The three men talked and laughed as they filled their plates and cups with pastries and coffee. Nate, in particular, looked more than a little happy, and Zade didn't have to wonder about the reason why.

A few weeks ago, right before the op where Zade had gotten shot, Nate and Gracie had eloped in Vegas. Zade was still getting used to the fact that Nate was now a married man, but he was damn happy for his friend. Especially after everything he and Gracie had been through.

In a situation somewhat similar to Matt and Katherine's, Gracie had been under Nate's protection when Nate had been shot and left for dead, and she'd been kidnapped. Thankfully the computer genius recovered from his wound and was able to play an active role in saving Gracie from the asshole holding her hostage.

Zade thought about the pain he'd witnessed his friends suffer as a result of the pure terror they'd felt thinking their women would be lost to them forever. Both men had gone through hell, which made Zade wonder if it was even worth it.

The image of Gabby's smiling face entered into his mind's eye. Despite her deception and sudden disappearance, his gut tightened at the thought of something like what happened to his teammates' women happening to her.

Maybe I'm better off not getting romantically involved with someone.

"Hey, look who finally decided to join us," Kole, the team's other sniper, smarted off.

Zade rolled his eyes. "The meeting hasn't even started yet, dickhead."

"Hey, man. Good to see ya." Nate tipped his chin and motioned toward the platter that was already half-empty. "Lexi sent these, so you'd better get 'em while you can."

"Glad I got here when I did." He grabbed a plate. "Another couple minutes, you greedy bastards would've taken them all."

Standing on the other side of Nate, Kole shook his head. "We would've saved you one."

"Gee, thanks Jameson," Zade feigned his appreciation. "That's mighty generous of you."

Balancing his loaded plate, Kole came over to him. Squeezing one of Zade's broad shoulders, the guy grinned.

"Anything for you, brother." Almost as an afterthought, Kole quickly removed his hand and apologized. "Shit. Sorry, man."

He resisted the urge to growl. "Wrong shoulder, dumbass. And I'm fine." To reiterate this fact, he forcefully slapped against the area where he'd been shot. "See? Good as new."

"Damn." Kole frowned while scratching his short, sandy blond hair. "Who pissed in your cornflakes this morning?"

"No one. I'm just sick of everyone treating me like I'm gonna fucking break or something. I've been back for a damn month. In that time, we've worked two ops. Pretty sure I did my damn job without incident either time, yet you dickheads are still treating me with kid gloves."

"We're just worried about you, Zade," Matt chimed in. The man's brown eyes illuminated with guilt, pissing Zade off even more.

"And that's another thing," he bit out sharply as he pointed his finger toward the other man. "Quit with that shit, right now."

A set of dark brows arched as the former pararescueman blinked. "The fuck did I do?"

"You've had that same guilty-as-sin look on your face ever since all that shit went down." A constant reminder of Zade's failure. "I told you that day in the hospital it wasn't your fault. So stop acting like you let me down."

If anything, *he'd* been the one to drop the ball.

Rather than say anything more, Matt wisely turned away and walked to his seat.

With an expectant look, Zade dared the other two men to say more, but like Matt, they remained silent and took their places around the table, as well.

Shit. Zade closed his eyes and let out a silent breath, feeling like a complete ass for the way he'd reacted. Mainly because he knew Matt was right. His teammates were only showing their concern, and instead of being grateful that they cared, he'd bitten their damn heads off.

With a plan to apologize later, Zade used the plastic tongs Lexi had provided to pick up two raspberry Danishes and a cinnamon roll before filling one of the disposable cups to the rim with what he prayed was strong coffee. Avoiding eye contact with the others, he walked around the front end of the room, behind where Trevor was sitting, to take his usual spot next to Gabe.

The big guy leaned in. "Rough morning?" he spoke low enough only Zade could hear.

"Rough night," Zade admitted.

His team leader gave him a sideways glance. An assessing glance. "Had a lot of those lately?"

Knowing the man was studying him too closely, Zade shrugged it off with what he hoped to be a plausible explanation. "My hospital stay threw my sleep cycle off. You know it's impossible to sleep in one of those places. Nurses constantly coming in to check vitals and shit. Body's still trying to get back into a routine, that's all."

With a slow swig of his coffee, Gabe finally nodded. "It becomes more, you let me know, yeah?"

Zade looked at the other man. "It won't, but thanks, anyway."

With the rim of his cup at his lips again, Zade's team leader muttered, "I'm sure you're right."

Frustration rolled through him, but rather than pop off, Zade shoved a large bite of pastry into his mouth. He took his time chewing to deter himself from saying anything more. The last thing he wanted to do was piss off Dawson and get benched for this next job.

Thankfully, Homeland Agent Jason Ryker chose that same moment to enter the conference room. Followed by...Ghost?

What the hell?

Keane "Ghost" Bryson was the leader of a Delta Force team they'd worked with on two separate occasions. Those guys had been instrumental during the mission to save Gracie, and also when they'd traveled to Iran to rescue Kat.

By now, Ghost and his teammates almost felt as though they were an extension of Bravo. However that still didn't prepare Zade for the man's sudden appearance on their turf. And from the looks on their faces, the rest of Bravo were just as surprised.

"Ghost!" Kole stood and held out his hand. Parroting Zade's thoughts, he said, "What the hell are you doing here?"

Their unexpected guest shook Kole's hand. "Jameson."

Trevor also stood to greet the other man. "Damn good to see you again, brother."

As former Delta Force themselves, both Trevor and Jake had actually worked alongside Ghost even before R.I.S.C.'s existence.

Matt joined in on the greetings. "Hey, man. I know we've emailed, but I never got a chance to thank you face to face for helping us get Kat out of Iran." Instead of a simple handshake, the two men embraced in a quick half-hug.

And another rush of guilt slammed into Zade.

"No need to thank me again, Turner." The six-one Captain shook his head. "You'd do the same for one of us."

Matt gave the man a curt nod. "I know if Kat were here, she'd want to thank you, as well."

A corner of Ghost's lips turned upward. "How is the doc?"

Though she wasn't a medical doctor, Matt had dubbed Kat with the nickname 'Doc' when the two had been reacquainted. She was a brilliant-as-hell scientist who'd since been hired to run an entire lab funded by the government for the sole purpose of aiding the U.S. Military.

"Kat's great." Matt smiled. "Construction on the lab is in

full swing. For now, she's been working out of a temporary space until it's completed."

"Good for her. Still can't believe the shit she helped create. Can't wait until it's available to all U.S. black ops, not solely the military."

"She's pushing for it, trust me."

Zade watched his teammate's face light up the way it always did when he talked about his woman. A narrow slice of jealousy ripped through Zade's system.

Despite all they'd been through, Nate and Matt—and nearly all the guy's on Alpha Team—had found a way to make a relationship work. Real relationships. Marriage. Kids. The works.

I want that, too.

After only three days with Gabby, Zade had found himself wanting it all with her. Now he had no idea if he'd ever even see her again.

From beside him, Gabe spoke up next, greeting Ghost from his seat. Zade and Nate followed, Agent Ryker purposely clearing his throat the second they were finished.

"Now that we've made the rounds, I'd like to get started." Dressed in his typical black suit and tie, the dark-haired man waited at the front beside Ghost while Kole and Matt found their seats again.

From what Zade understood, Jason Ryker had been R.I.S.C.'s Homeland handler almost since its conception. As head of his own covert department at the agency, Ryker routinely turned to them for assistance with particularly sensitive or difficult missions. Ones the government couldn't officially become involved with.

Zade's gut tightened, knowing this time would be no different.

"What's the matter, Ghost?" Nate smirked. "Your team need our help this time?"

A round of low chuckles filled the room. Ghost smiled back at Nate. "As much as it burns my ass to admit it...Yes. We do."

The laughter died down quickly. The guy's answer making them all sit a little taller.

"Really?" Kole sounded as surprised as Zade felt.

The entire team shared a look before bringing their unified focus back to the front of the room. "What's going on, Trevor?" Zade looked to their interim boss.

With a somber expression, the dark-haired man began to explain. "As you know, the human trafficking business is at an all-time high around the globe. My most recent data shows young men and boys make up about thirty percent of the sex-trafficking victims, leaving young women, mostly mid-to-upper teens, to make up the other seventy. As with the males, these young women and girls are being brought here from other countries, either by force or under some sort of false enticement."

"I've done a lot of reading on this sort of thing," Nate spoke up. "These assholes use fake dating sites or social media profiles to lure these girls in. Some even going so far as to buy one-way plane tickets for the victims. These guys troll around for those most vulnerable and then swoop in like some sort of twisted Casanova. The girls think the guy they've been 'talking to' is their white knight, when really they're the Devil in disguise."

"You're exactly right, Carter," Ryker agreed. "And equally as bad are the men who pose as headhunters for fraudulent modeling agencies. They know exactly what to say to entice them into either coming into our country for job interviews or, if they're already here, these predators will oftentimes go to them."

Locking eyes with the Homeland agent, Gabe leaned his elbow onto the table's smooth surface. "So what's our involvement with this? Are we looking at a rescue, infiltration...what?"

"Neither, actually," Ghost answered for the other man. "This is a takedown mission. A big one. From what we know, the target we're after uses young, attractive, American men to lure young women into their trap. By the time these girls realize what's really happening, they're already on their way out of the country and in Mexico. My team's been asked to be on-call for when this op moves over the border into Mexico. And trust me. It will."

"Okay..." Zade's voice trailed off as he waited for an expanded explanation.

What he got from Ryker was, "The sex-trafficking operation we're looking at is larger than any we've shut down in the past."

Zade's gut tightened. Though he didn't know specifics, Zade had heard stories about the ones Homeland had gone after in previous years. None of those cases had been a walk in the park for the agents and operatives involved, and now they were being asked to work with Delta to take down one that was bigger than those?

Hot damn.

The thought of ending something so horrific and dehumanizing as a sex-trafficking ring was enough to put a kick back in Zade's sluggish steps. Nothing made him more enraged than the thought of some bastard preying on the weak or vulnerable. Especially if the victims were female.

It wasn't that Zade thought women were weaker than men. He'd served with enough kick-ass female Marines to know better. Plus, respecting women had been engrained in him as a child, and again later in the Corp.

Between what his parents had taught him growing up and the three core values the Marines lived by: honor, courage, and commitment, Zade's personal code of conduct had never allowed him to stand by while a woman was being hurt. Verbally or otherwise.

Did that mean he was excited at the thought of tearing down an ungodly organization like the one Ryker had described? Hell yeah, he was.

"So who are we looking at for this?" Zade directed the question to either man.

When Ryker gave Trevor a nod, the GQ-looking operative used a small remote to activate the room's interactive board on the wall behind him. Both Ryker and Ghost stepped to the side to avoid blocking anyone's view.

A man appeared on the screen, his image somewhat blurred. He was wearing sunglasses, his face partially obstructed by his sideways stance, and it was clear the photo had been taken without the guy's knowledge.

"This is Hector Andino. As of right now, he's the biggest player in skin trade. Has been for the past two years. In addition to at least a hundred females from other countries, we believe Andino is also responsible for the disappearance of over fifty American women and girls over the past year."

"Not to sound condescending"—Gabe began—"but if you know Andino's your guy, why hasn't he been caught?"

"Same reason Javier Cetro got away with his shit for so long. We start to get close and the bastard takes off. Shuts down his operation, relocates, and lays low until he feels safe to start up again."

"Cetro..." Zade let the name fall off his tongue. "Why does that name sound familiar?"

A shadow fell over Trevor's face. "He was the bastard who took Liv a while back."

Liv was Olivia McQueen, their boss's wife. From what Zade understood, the guy kidnapped Olivia not once, but twice. The second time he tortured Liv and would have killed her had Jake and Trevor not shown up when they did.

"My point in mentioning Cetro was to make you understand how good Andino is. The man knows how to play the game."

"Actually, he's a fucking master at it," Ghost added grimly. "I earned my nickname with good reason." He pointed at the large screen. "But this guy's every bit as good me, if not better. One minute, he's there. The next, he's nowhere to be found."

"Sounds like you're speaking from personal experience," Matt commented.

Ghost nodded. "My team was assigned a surveillance op a few months back. Our instructions were to watch Andino from a safe distance and gather as much intel on the guy and his lackies as possible, but we were under strict orders not to make contact." He looked over his shoulder at the man's picture. "Hollywood snapped that pic, along with several others. Over a period of two weeks, we were able to use facial rec to get positive I.D.'s on not only Andino, but also a handful of his men."

Hollywood was another member of Ghost's Delta team.

Curious, Matt asked, "So what happened?"

"Don't know." A muscle in Ghost's jaw bulged. "From everything we saw, he was working to set something up."

"A sale?" Nate asked, sounding disgusted. Not one member of Bravo could stomach the idea of a business such as the one this Andino guy supposedly ran.

"We thought so. In the days before he took off, Andino held a few shady, closed-door meetings with his minions, but we couldn't risk getting too close to figure out what they were discussing. Then one night, poof! The bastard and his men slipped away without a trace."

Just like Gabby. Ignoring that train of thought, Zade looked over at Ghost. "Any chance he made you or one of your guys?"

Ghost narrowed his eyes in a playful glare. "I'm going to pretend you didn't ask that, King."

"Sorry, man." Zade raised his palms. "Had to ask."

With a sideways smirk, the well-trained captain shook his head. "Wasn't us, but something sure spooked the guy. Whatever it was, we were left with nothing but a bunch of pics and a shit ton of speculation."

"Could've been any number of things," Ryker pointed out. "Delta isn't the only group who's been watching Andino and his men. Hell, before their assignment, we were actually close to getting an agent on the inside, ourselves."

"Close?" Nate looked at the Homeland agent quizzically.

"Same thing. A deal was about to be made, or so we thought, but Andino never showed."

"Not to be the Debby Downer of the group"—Matt leaned forward in his chair and rested his elbows on the table— "but if Delta couldn't get to Andino and your guy also failed, what makes you think we'll have any better luck?"

"Same reason we always do." Ryker smirked.

"Because Delta's rules don't apply to us?" Matt raised a knowing brow in Ghost's direction before returning his focus back to the Homeland agent.

"It's true, you and your guys can get closer without fearing the types of repercussions we could face."

Matt snorted. "Meaning, if shit hits the fan, it's our asses on the line, not the government's."

"Same story, different bad guy," Kole quipped. "We take all the risks while Uncle Sam gets all the glory."

Ghost's mouth spread into an unapologetic grin. "All part of the job, right boys?" The comment garnered a few eye rolls and muttered curses. "But it's more than that. We can't risk Andino or any of his associates recognizing one of my men from our previous surveillance attempts. We don't think it would happen, but there's too much at stake to risk it."

Gabe sat up a little straighter. Addressing Ryker, he got down to business. "Fine. Let's say you locate Hector Andino again and we go in. Then what? We run surveillance, make contact, go under to set up a buy…what's our main objective, here?"

"It's possible you'll end up doing all of those," Ryker answered honestly. "At this point, we want to start with surveillance, but we have to play this thing close to the vest. We've lost Andino twice now. Word around town is he's prepping for one hell of a sale. His biggest yet, as a matter of fact."

Zade's stomach became a pit of dread. "How big are we talking?"

"Over thirty girls," Ghost answered for Ryker. "Give or take."

Ryker's nod confirmed the other man's statement. "Something tells me, this guy gets spooked again, our asses will be left high and dry. Bottom line, gentlemen…we can't risk losing Andino a third time. Too many innocent lives are at stake, and every time he slips through our fingers, more girls are at risk of being taken and sold."

Andino had girls in his possession right this second? Zade's entire body itched to get out there and stop the bastard.

They needed to quit talking and start acting. Now.

"How do we find him?"

Ghost took the lead and answered the question. "There's been some chatter in the past couple of days. Andino's supposedly been spotted back in La Paz."

"Back?" Kole asked. "He go there often?"

"Andino owns a nightclub there. Actually, Andino controls nearly *all* of the real estate there, as well as the people." To the entire group, Ghost explained further, "For those who are unfamiliar, La Paz is the capital of Baja California Sur, which makes up the southern half of the long peninsula on Mexico's west coast. Word is Hector Andino's been hanging out at his nightclub more frequently, lately. We haven't been able to prove it yet, but Agent Ryker and my commander both agree the best course of action would be to send your team in first for confirmation of Andino's presence and go from there."

"You want us to go to Mexico and hang out at a nightclub?" Matt looked around the table. "As far as assignments go, I guess that doesn't sound too bad."

"That's what I was thinking." Nate shot Kole a look, the spark of a new idea shining in his widened eyes. "Hey, we could have a belated bachelor party for you. You know, since you and Sarah both shit all over my idea for one before you two tied the knot."

Kole rolled his eyes. "It's a nightclub, not a strip club. Besides, it's a little late for a bachelor party, seeing as how I'm already married."

Nate sighed. "I wasn't talking strippers, dumbass. Even if I wanted that, and let's be very clear, I do *not*, Gracie would have my ass. I just meant we could use the situation to liven it up a little. You know, hanging out with the guys."

"We aren't going there to party," Zade reminded the two men.

"No, but it sure would help our cover if it *looked* like we were." Nate eyed Zade closely for a few seconds. The way he was staring made Zade nervous as hell.

"What?"

"You're still single," Nate pointed out the obvious.

"And?" Zade asked, afraid of the answer he'd receive.

A wide grin spread across Nate's face. "It could be *your* bachelor party."

"A guys' getaway." Matt nodded. "I like it."

Zade shook his head. "I'll pass, thanks."

"Actually." Gabe looked over at Zade. "That's not bad."

"I agree." Trevor looked over at Bravo's team leader. "Given La Paz is one of the world's most dangerous cities due to cartel activity, it's likely you'll need a plausible explanation as to why you're there. A bachelor party weekend seems as good as any."

"You're single, too," Zade quickly reminded Gabe. "Why can't this be your bachelor party?"

The man looked back at him as if he'd lost his damn mind. "Not happening."

"Why not?"

"'Cause I'm the team leader and I say so."

Great. The guy chose *now* to pull rank.

Nate laughed. "Look at it this way, Zade. Maybe you'll find a sweet senorita to help take your mind off Gabby."

His friend's attempt to make the situation better failed.

Fucking. Miserably.

Matt, Kole, and Gabe all looked at Nate with confused expressions while Zade glared over at Nate with a look that he wished could kill.

"Hold up. Who's Gabby?" Kole shot Zade a look.

Before Zade could formulate a response, Matt's lips curled into a half-grin. "You sly dog. You been holding out on us, King?"

Nate's a dead man. "No."

Matt didn't buy it for a minute. "So what's Carter talking about?"

"Nothing." Zade slid Nate another death stare. "It's nothing."

"Sorry, man." Nate looked chagrined. "I forgot they didn't know about her."

"So there *is* a 'her'." Kole smirked from across the table.

"No. There's no 'her'." *Not anymore.* "Can we please focus on the job?"

When the others attempted to continue their razzing, Gabe held up a hand to stop them. "King's right." He waited for the guys to quiet down before speaking again. "We'll definitely stand out in a crowd, so we need a plausible story as to why we're hanging out in the city and at Andino's nightclub." He turned to Zade and smiled. "Congratulations, King. Can't wait to celebrate your upcoming nuptials."

Fuck. Me.

Zade knew it was only a cover, but he also knew his team. These guys were going to have way too much fun with this shit.

He could see it now. They'd buy him drinks, play it up with the ladies. Hell, knowing them, they'd probably take things too far and even try to get a few of the ladies to give him one last hoorah before his fake big day with a non-existent bride.

An instant and harsh pang settled in his chest as he thought of the woman he wanted to be with for real. Like the other jobs Bravo had taken on recently, part of him wanted nothing more than to stay here and continue his search for Gabby.

But that wasn't an option. For one, Zade had already let one of his teammates down before and refused to let that happen again. And two, like Ghost said...there was too much at stake to let Andino disappear again.

With that in mind, Zade re-focused on the conversation around him. Soon, with help from Trevor, Ryker, and Ghost, a solid plan was put into place.

They'd fly to La Paz the next morning, get settled in, and begin the mission.

Zade just prayed they'd be able to put an end to Hector Andino's reign of terror in time to save those innocent girls.

CHAPTER 2

Please, Gabriella. Please do this for us.

Those whispered words, pleading words, rolled through Gabriella's mind. They were words she couldn't stop hearing. Words that gave her the strength to continue on.

For the third night in a row, Gabby sat alone at the small, round table. She sipped her drink and pondered the answer to the question she'd asked herself a billion times since coming here.

You had to be crazy to think this would work.

She'd purposely chosen this spot that first night because it was in the far back corner of the club. Hidden in the shadows, it gave her the perfect vantage spot to see pretty much everything happening in the busy club.

From here, she could see the people dancing, the bar on the opposite side of the room, and those sitting at the other tables identical to hers. For the past few nights, she'd seen everything from couples dancing to fighting, to practically making love right there on the dance floor.

There'd been not-so-discreet drug deals, money

exchanged for other services Gabby had no desire to become privy to...you name it, she pretty much saw it. Unfortunately, she'd come up empty on the one thing she needed. The reason she was here in the first place.

The one person she'd risked everything to find.

That familiar sinking feeling began to settle in. The one threatening to convince her she was already too late. Gabby ignored it.

For weeks, she'd been searching. Down every street. Every dark alley. She'd even gone to the places she'd vowed never to return to. Places she'd tried desperately to forget.

Each time she thought she was close, she hit a dead end. In Chicago. Atlanta. New Orleans...

Taking another, miniscule sip, Gabby silently ordered herself not to think about New Orleans. If she did, she'd think about how excited she'd been. How, even though part of her had known it was a long shot, she'd convinced herself that time would be different. She'd find what she'd spent weeks searching for, and everything would go back to normal.

If Gabby allowed herself to go there, she'd recall just how hopeless she'd felt when her lead turned out to be worthless. How *she'd* felt worthless and how those feelings of self-doubt and deprecation had sent her running to Grand Isle. Unable to go back home and admit to the only people to ever care about her that she'd failed them. Miserably.

Once those thoughts settled in as they always seemed to do, Gabby would remember Zade. Sweet, sexy Zade.

The incredible man had given her the escape she'd so desperately needed. And though he had no way of knowing, he'd offered her the most precious gift anyone could have given...A moment in time where she could forget what had happened.

It started out as a one-time thing. A way to relieve the unsurmountable stress that had been threatening to destroy her sense of being.

When they'd first met, she'd given Zade a fake last name, a phony story of a family that didn't exist, who'd given her the most wonderful childhood a kid could ever ask for. None of it had been real.

Nothing except the feelings she'd begun to develop for a man she'd just met. It was crazy. Stupid, even. He could've fed her full of shit as easily as she had him, but Gabby's instincts were usually pretty spot-on. Something told her the muscular, private security expert was the what-you-see-is-what-you-get type.

He was also the caring, thoughtful, and blow-your-mind-in-bed type. Sure, he'd given her the most incredible orgasms she'd ever experienced, but that wasn't why she hadn't stopped thinking about him.

It was because, for a beautiful moment in time while hiding away on that tiny island, Zade King had somehow made her start to believe everything would be okay. That she was actually worth something.

God, when he'd asked her to come back to Texas with him, she'd been so tempted to say yes. To forget her old life and pretend she hadn't failed the one person who'd been there for her when she needed them most. To start a life with the man who, after only three days, she knew she could love.

So she ran. As fast and far as she possibly could.

As much as she wanted it, there was no way she could continue on with the fantasy. Because that's all it had been. Zade had practically offered her the moon, and what had she done? She'd reverted back to her self-protecting ways and had lied to him...about everything.

Gabby may not have had the chance to get to know him

like she wanted, but of one thing she was certain. A man like Zade deserved someone much better than her.

Allowing herself a bigger swig that time, Gabby used the slow burn to bring her thoughts back into focus. Enough time had been wasted chasing down false leads. She sure as hell couldn't afford to waste any more by thinking of impossible dreams.

The club's DJ changed the loud music mid-song, taking the beat from a loud, thumping rhythm to a sexy salsa. Gabby sat there, watching the dancers merge into duos, their hips swaying back and forth as their feet moved seamlessly, refusing to accept she'd hit another dead end.

This most recent lead had to pan out. It *had* to. For her, there was no other choice.

I can't fail them. I can't fail her.

Three hours later, while nursing her second drink of the night, Gabby was about to give up and call it a night when the door to the club opened, and her growing disappointment came to a sudden and abrupt halt.

Three men entered the club together, the one in the middle giving off a particularly strong vibe. One of strength and power. Importance.

Though it was dark out, he wore sunglasses, but when he turned and looked over the crowd, he reached up and removed them.

Holy shit.

She'd spent weeks and nearly every cent of her savings trying to track down the man who'd taken Sam. Had cashed in every single favor ever owed to her. Even stooped so low as to contact several slimy, crooked characters from her past. Ones she thought might be able to help.

All in an effort to find him.

Now here he was—standing twenty feet away. And Gabby had no idea what to do next.

Her mind became a whirl of ideas. Some bad. Some *really* bad. Others downright suicidal.

But Sam was counting on her. So were Sam's parents. They'd offered Gabby a life at a time when it seemed hers was all but over. Risking that life to save their only daughter was the least she could do.

Through the underground grapevine, Gabby had heard more than once that the powerful man who'd just graced the club with his presence had a weakness for redheads. Especially beautiful, American redheads with green eyes.

Check, check, and check.

Growing up, Gabby never had much. Nothing, really. Nothing but her looks. She learned at an early age how to use her big, green eyes to her advantage.

Whether the occasion called for puppy dog eyes, an innocent smile, or the look of a seductive temptress, she'd pretty much mastered them all. She'd also mastered the art of deception, which was why it had been so easy to lie to Zade.

No. Do not start thinking about him, now.

Going with the only thing she could think of, Gabby took a swig of liquid courage and stood. Before she could change her own mind, she pulled at the too-tiny skirt she'd purchased for this specific occasion, straightened her shoulders, lifted her chin, and put on her most confident face before walking toward the man and his two sidekicks, now standing at the end of the bar.

Forcing herself to not look in his direction, she put a little extra sway in her step. Knowing the three-inch heels she'd chosen were doing exactly what they were designed to, Gabby allowed her hips to move with sensual purpose.

Despite the obvious looks she was receiving from most of the men she passed—and some of the women—she kept her expression casual, almost disinterested. The crowd around her moved to the beat of the loud Latin music, and she had to fend off a couple of wannabe suitors as she crossed the final few feet separating her from the bar.

After giving her order to the busy, almost frazzled waitress, Gabby reached back and pulled her long hair over one shoulder. She hoped the move would grab Andino's attention, and he'd notice her.

Letting her body move to the music while she waited, Gabby did her best to act bored as she turned her head and glanced around. Her heart thumped against her ribs when she saw Hector Andino staring back at her, and it took every ounce of strength she had not to glare at the sick jerk.

Instead she gave him a slight tilt of her full, red lips before checking out the dancers on the floor behind her.

"Senorita!"

Gabby spun her head back around when she realized the waitress was trying to get her attention. The young woman slid the glass her direction.

"Thank you," she told the woman loudly. "Keep the change."

With a half-hearted, "Gracias," the woman grabbed the bills from Gabby's hand and went about taking care of her other customers.

She wanted so badly to turn and see if Hector was looking at her again, but Gabby forced herself to focus instead on the strawberry margarita in her hand. Stirring the pink drink with her finger, she quickly swiped up a bit of the salt from the rim, licked it off her fingertip, and took a drink.

The big toe on her right foot bounced up and down in nervous concealment until finally she couldn't take it anymore. With another, what she hoped to be casual glance, Gabby looked to her right. Her heart dropped into her stomach.

He's gone.

Cover forgotten, she spun around, her eyes doing a thorough sweep of the dance floor and tables behind. She didn't bother looking to her right, toward the hallway housing the men's room, because he would've had to walk past her to get there. There was no way she would've missed that.

Gabby wanted to scream with frustration. Hector Andino and his goons had already left the club, and she hadn't said a single, solitary word to the man.

With her funds running low, she only had another night, maybe two before she'd run out of money and have to go back home. If that happened, Gabby knew in her gut she'd lose her chance at finding Sam forever.

No. She would *not* give up. Not when she'd come this close.

With her small clutch in her hand, Gabby squared her shoulders and headed for the door. She'd come back tomorrow night, and when she did, she wouldn't wait for Andino to make the first move.

When she saw him again, and she prayed she would, Gabby was going to approach him. Approach him, come on to him…she'd do *whatever* it took to gain his trust.

Swallowing back bile from the thought of what that could possibly mean, she knew it would be hard. But at least it would be her choice.

Gabby kept telling herself that. She was *choosing* to do this.

For Sam.

For Anna and Everett.

For the only family she'd ever known.

Sam and her parents had saved Gabby all those years ago, and she'd go to Hell and back for them. She looked at her reflection in the bar's large mirror.

Welcome to Hell.

Her stomach churned at what the next step in her plan most likely entailed, but time was running out for Sam. Gabby knew it. Could feel it deep inside her bones.

But she was ready and willing to pay any price to get Sam back, and prayed what she had to offer would be enough.

CHAPTER 3

"How can Ryker be so sure Andino will be here?"

Zade studied the club's entrance through their SUV's tinted windows. They could see out, but no one could see in. The glass was also bullet resistant.

Essential upgrades when traveling to one of the continent's most dangerous cities.

"According to Ryker's asset," Gabe began explaining while scanning the area for threats, "Hector is planning to stop by here tonight. Guy claims Andino spotted some chick he wanted to hook up with but got a text and had to leave to take care of a sudden business matter before he could talk to her. Rumor has it, he's making an encore appearance tonight to see if she's there again."

"See, that's what I don't get," Kole stated from his spot between Nate and Matt. His tone was laced with skepticism.

Shifting in the front, passenger seat, Zade looked at his teammate from over his shoulder. "What?"

"Guy as powerful as Hector Andino could have any woman around this place." A muscle in Kole's jaw twitched. "Whether they consented or not."

Sitting behind Gabe, Nate looked over at Kole. "Your point?"

"Nothing, I guess." Kole shrugged. "Other than there must be something special about this chick if Andino's making plans to come here to look specifically for her."

Nate softened his expression a little too much as he patted Kole's shoulder. "I guess it's true what they say, Jameson. Everyone deserves a chance at love. Even a sick fuck like Hector Andino."

The guys all chuckled. Even Kole's lips curved upward a bit as he rolled his eyes and shook Nate's hand away. "Fuck off, Carter. You know what I meant."

"You know what *I* don't get?" Zade spoke up again. "How is it Ryker's asset can give us intel on Andino's social life, but the guy doesn't know squat about his business plans?" He looked at the others. "Does that seem strange to anyone else, or is it just me?"

"Not strange at all," Gabe answered from behind the wheel.

Zade's brows pushed inward as he glanced over at his team leader. "How do you figure?"

Shrugging one of his wide shoulders, the big guy looked over at him. "From what Jason told me, the asset was new to Andino's crew. Guy by the name of Manuel Rivera. He joined up with Andino less than two weeks ago."

"Shit," Matt muttered from his seat behind Zade. "Homeland didn't waste any time turning him."

Gabe's eyes slid to the other man's. "That's the whole reason they were successful at making the guy an asset."

"Makes sense." Zade nodded in agreement. "I mean, from what Ryker said they've spent the past two years trying to get convictable intel on Andino from deep inside."

Matt shook his head. "His men are too loyal."

"Or too scared," Zade added. "Either way, those guys

aren't gonna roll on Andino easily. But a newbie's a different story. Rivera hasn't had enough time invested to be that loyal or scared...yet. Especially if Homeland's offering him a good enough deal."

"Damn, King." Matt's lips curled into an impressed smirk. "When did you get so fucking smart?"

"I've always been smart, asshole." Zade raised a brow at his friend. "You've just been too busy runnin' your mouth to listen."

Matt flipped him off even as his shoulders shook with silent laughter.

"King's right." Gabe looked back at the club. "Jason's asset was easy to turn because he's green. Also explains why Rivera's privy to general knowledge, such as Andino's social schedule, but nothing pertaining to the asshole's business. A guy like Hector Andino isn't going to start spilling trade secrets to a newbie. That kind of trust takes time."

With a loud sigh, Nate sat back in his seat. "Which means this job could take us a while."

"Don't care how long it takes." Zade gritted his teeth as he thought about what a monster Andino was. "Just so we figure out the bastard's next set-up so we can stop him from selling more innocent girls."

"Well." Gabe pulled his keys from the ignition. "We sure as hell aren't going to do that sitting out here." He gave Zade a sly smile. "Is the groom ready to party?"

Zade's face went flat. "You're seriously sticking with that shit?"

Gabe smiled, but it was Nate who said, "Hell yeah, we are. Let's go celebrate the end of your single days, brother."

Zade sighed. *Fanfuckingtastic.*

The five men paid the cover charge and entered the club. They'd barely made it two feet inside when Zade felt two strong hands dig into his shoulders.

"Remember, brother," Matt spoke loudly enough for others around them to hear. "These are your last days as a single man. Time to let the good times roll!"

Lips curling into a fake as shit smile, Zade looked at his friends and forced himself into character. "Bring it on, boys!"

With several whoops and hollers, the group of men strolled to the bar and ordered their first round. Once their drinks were in hand, they made their way to a table located at the back in a dark corner. The perfect spot for people-watching.

It was still fairly early, so the crowd wasn't as dense as Zade assumed it would become. Still, the music was loud as fuck, and he was glad they were sitting far enough away from the speakers they could talk without having to shout.

Things would end very badly for them if others overheard what they'd been discussing in regards to their target.

For the next two hours, they continued to 'party'. The men danced and flirted. Told dumbass jokes and laughed. Downed a few drinks to appear legit, but then took sporadic turns in the bathroom to empty their glasses, or inconspicuously dumped their drinks into a nearby trashcan as they walked by.

Each guy on the team could hold their liquor with the best of them, but even someone with as high a tolerance as theirs could only hold out for so long before the alcohol started to affect their ability to think clearly.

Speaking of...

"I need to hit the head." Zade stood.

Gabe glance down at his half-filled glass. "Don't forget your drink."

He shook his head. "Need to go for real, this time."

"Copy that." The other man tipped his beer bottle to his lips and pretended to swallow.

"Be right back." Zade was halfway across the dance floor when someone grabbed both cheeks of his ass and squeezed.

The hell?

He spun around to see a sort-of pretty, very intoxicated woman smiling back at him.

"Can I…help you?"

The woman's smile grew even wider. "You are American. Even better." She leaned toward him, as though she intended to kiss him.

"Yes." Zade took a step back, just out of her reach. "I'm American."

"And muy hermoso." She ran a long, red fingernail down the center of his chest.

"Thanks, but I'm engaged."

"So?" She rose a thin, perfectly plucked brow.

"*So*…I'm with someone." He tried to turn away, but she dug those fucking nails into his bicep.

"I have not seen any chicas with you tonight."

She'd been watching him? "That's because this is my bachelor party."

Zade motioned behind her, to his friends sitting at the table. They were staring back at them, each one grinning from ear to ear. Matt and Kole both raised their drinks to him as though they were giving him their freaking blessing or something.

Thanks a lot, assholes.

"Your amigos seem eager to see us together." She turned back to him.

"My *amigos* are drunk as shit and have apparently forgotten I have a fiancée waiting for me back at the hotel."

As if the thought of him cheating turned her on even more, the stranger closed the distance between them and pressed her ample breasts against his chest. Wrapping her arms around his neck, she let her legs relax, her body half-hanging from her grasp.

Speech slightly slurred, the pushy woman said, "What your fiancée doesn't know won't hurt her."

"I'm flattered." Zade reached back and lifted her arms high enough to slide out of her hold. "Really, I am. But I don't cheat."

It was a good excuse to go with his cover. It was also the truth.

Finally free, he wasted no time removing himself from the incredibly uncomfortable situation. Zade's Spanish was sub-par at best, but he had no problem understanding most of the words being thrown at him from the woman's mouth.

He definitely heard the word 'burro' loud and clear.

The woman had called him a jackass because he *didn't* want to cheat on the woman he was supposedly engaged to.

Weren't women supposed to think loyalty and commitment were good qualities in a man? Not that he knew anything about women, apparently.

The image of a certain redhead filled his mind's eye. He saw Gabby smiling up at him from the bed they'd shared. Could hear her laughing at one of his lame jokes.

No. You cannot think of Gabby. Not now.

With a shake of his head, Zade finally made his way into the men's room. Relieved to find he was alone, he took a moment to clear his head of anything not pertinent to Bravo's mission.

That meant there could be no more thoughts of Gabby. Not while he was on the job, at least.

When this assignment was completed and he and the team got back to Dallas, he'd pick back up with his search for the mystery woman. Until then, his focus needed to be on finding and stopping Hector Andino.

After taking care of his business, Zade washed his hands

and splashed some cold water on his face for extra clarity. Using a paper towel to quickly dry himself, he tossed it into the trash before exiting the small room and heading back to the guys.

"What happened to your lady friend, King?" Kole taunted.

Nate snickered. "Yeah, man. Saw her get a handful. Looked like she had a good grip."

"She got *two* handfuls, asshole." Zade scowled at his friend. "And thanks for helping me out, by the way. Really appreciate it."

"Are you kidding?" Nate laughed even harder. "No way in hell was I stopping that shit. Only thing that could've made it any better would've been some popcorn."

The others laughed. Zade did not.

"Cheer up, King." Kole smirked. "Hot chicks are supposed to paw you. It's your bachelor party, remember?"

Zade glared at his friend. "One, she was far from hot. And two, this isn't a real party. *Remember*?" He picked up his glass and took a large gulp.

Gabe leaned over so he didn't have to yell. "Easy man. You know what happened last time you hit that stuff too hard."

"Christ." He slammed the glass down. "First you want me to act like a bachelor, then you don't. Which is it, Dawson?"

Everyone at the table stopped laughing and swung their heads around. Gabe's dark eyes widened slightly as they stared back at him, clearly not expecting such an asshole response from one of his guys.

Shit.

Zade hadn't meant to say that so loudly. Shouldn't have said it at all.

"Wanna try that again?" Gabe's voice had turned low, and a muscle in the former SEAL's square jaw jumped.

"Sorry." Zade inhaled deeply before letting it out. He

began tracing the rim of his glass. "Guess I'm not feeling like myself tonight."

"Just tonight?" Matt quipped.

Zade scowled. "What's that supposed to mean?"

"He means you've been a grumpy-assed bastard ever since you got back from your little vacation." Kole gave him an unapologetic shrug.

"Have not." Zade frowned.

Have I?

"Uh...yeah, you have." Kole stared back at him. "Come on, Zade. Even you have to admit something's been off with you, lately."

"They're right," Nate joined in. "You're usually Mary Fucking Sunshine, but lately we've all been walking on eggshells around you because we never know what's gonna set you off."

Fuck.

Zade sat back in his chair. He removed his black ball cap long enough to run a hand over his hair before replacing it. Pulling the bill until it was back in its rightful position, he sat up straight once more.

Then Zade did something he almost never had to do. He swallowed his pride and apologized.

"I'm...sorry." He made sure his eyes met each of the other men's, ending with Gabe's. "I've been trying to work through some shit, but clearly I haven't done a very good job of it."

"Not your fault, man." Matt gave him that same guilt-ridden expression Zade was sick to death of seeing.

"Not yours either, Turner. My...issues have nothing to do with what happened when Kat was taken."

Okay, well maybe that wasn't completely accurate, but he sure as shit wasn't going to tell Matt that.

Gabe studied him more closely. "If not that, then what?"

Zade's hesitation lasted all of two seconds. It was all the time Nate needed.

"It's her, isn't it?"

His eyes narrowed as Zade glared at his friend. A biting retort was on the tip of his tongue, but he clamped his mouth shut.

In the recent past, these guys had dealt with their own troubles when it came to their women. Some more than others.

These were his friends. They'd listen and, most likely, understand.

So why keep all that shit buried inside?

The tiny voice in his head was right. It was time to come clean.

"Yeah." Zade nodded. "It's her."

Kole took a swig of his beer. "Who is this mystery woman? Better yet, what the hell did she do to you?"

The thought of admitting he'd been played for a fool suddenly didn't seem like such a good idea.

Chickening out, Zade responded with, "I thought we were supposed to be pretending to have a good time while we waited for Andino to show."

"We can talk and watch the door at the same time."

To prove his point, Kole's eyes slid toward the door and back while he took what was supposed to look like another long draw from his beer.

"Yeah, man." Matt was still looking over at him. "Come on. Spill it."

Fuck it.

Letting out a loud sigh, Zade finally gave in. "I met someone while I was at Grand Isle. We hit it off from the get-go. Spent that entire last weekend together, and even talked about her coming to see me in Dallas over the summer."

"Sounds great." Matt nodded. "So what happened?"

"She..." He paused, sliding a sideways glance in Nate's direction. "She ghosted me."

Kole's brows arched high as he blinked. "She what?"

"She took off. One minute, everything was great." Better than great. "The next, I get out of the shower, and she's gone."

Understanding filled Gabe's eyes. "And you haven't heard from her since."

"Not a word. She left me a note, but that was it."

"What'd it say?"

Zade shrugged it off. "Thanked me for a good weekend, wished we had more time together. Yada, yada."

There was a bit more to it than that, but he didn't feel like sharing all of Gabby's last words to him with the team.

"Damn, man." Matt sounded sincere. "That sucks. I'm sorry."

"Wait, what did Nate say her name was..." Matt tried to remember. "Gretchen...Gertie..."

"Gabby," Zade said her name aloud for the first time in weeks. "Gabriella Smith is how she introduced herself. But that's not her real name."

Matt frowned. "How do you know?"

"Because we've tried to find her," Nate answered for him. "The Gabriella Smith Zade described to me doesn't seem to exist. There's no record of her anywhere. And you know if there was, I'd find it."

The man spoke the truth. Nathan Carter wasn't only a badass in the field. He was a wiz when it came to computers and finding shit.

"I don't know what you're complaining about." The comment came from Kole. "You're single. I'm assuming she was single. So you had a little, no-strings vacation fling. What's the big deal?"

The big deal was, it wasn't just a fling. Not for Zade,

anyway. Apparently that's all it was for Gabby, however. Or whoever the hell she was.

Christ, man. You gonna host this pity party the rest of your life or actually try and have a life?

For once, Zade decided to listen to that tiny voice of reason. It was right, and so was Kole. He'd had fun with Gabby while it lasted. Now it was time to forget about her and move the hell on.

"You know what, Kole?" Zade looked at his friend. "You're right. It was fun and now it's over. No harm, no foul. Right?"

"There's the spirit!" Kole reached over and tapped the top of his beer bottle to his. "Just because the rest of us have happily settled down with the love of our lives doesn't mean you have to be."

Gabe cleared his throat.

"Oh, sorry, Dawson," Kole offered their team leader a chagrined smile. Returning his focus to Zade, the sniper amended his statement. "Just because some of us have been lucky enough to find 'the one', that doesn't mean you have to. You're young. You're single. Enjoy it, man."

Despite the sliver of pain Zade could've sworn had flashed behind Gabe's eyes, the former SEAL nodded. "Turner's right, King. One piece of advice, when the time comes that you *do* find the woman you want to spend the rest of your life with, grab on tight and don't let her go. Second chances are a hard fucking thing to come by these days."

The other man's words seemed to have come from experience. One that, from the look Gabe was trying damn hard to hide, was not a pleasant one.

"Preach, brother." Matt snorted, and the emotion in Gabe's eyes vanished. "Most mornings, I wake up next to Kat, and for the first few seconds I think I'm dreamin'."

Refusing to think about how close Matt and Katherine

came to losing their second chance—*because of me*—Zade decided to ask Gabe about his words of wisdom.

"Sounds like you're talking from experience, Dawson. Care to elaborate?"

And while you're at it, maybe take the focus off of me.

"Nothing to elaborate on." Gabe shook his head. "Merely offering some advice."

"Yeah, but based on what?" Matt's eyes narrowed as they looked over at their team leader.

The experienced man arched a brow. "Based on none of your damn business, Turner."

Rather than seem intimidated, Matt offered Gabe a slow smile. "Copy that."

"All right, enough of this touchy-feely shit." Nate sat back in his chair. "We've been here damn near three hours and Andino is still a no-show."

"Carter's right." Kole took a sip of his drink. "And I have yet to see the super-hot redhead Ryker's asset claims has been hanging around here lately. I'm starting to think this entire operation's a bust."

Gabe grinned. "I thought snipers were supposed to be masters at having patience."

"Oh, I have patience." Kole shrugged. "Just ready to get the show on the road, that's all."

Nate nodded. "I'm with Kole on this one. I prefer to take the bastard down sooner, rather than later."

"And we will," Gabe assured them all. "We just have to trust the intel we've been given. That intel says he's on the prowl for a foxy redhead in a tight skirt."

Matt grinned. "You mean like the one walking through the door right now?"

At the guy's words, Zade turned his head toward the club's entrance...and forgot how to breathe.

"Damn." Kole nodded in appreciation. "If I wasn't already

married to the woman of my dreams, I'd definitely offer to buy that one a drink. But, hey...you're single, King. Why don't you go cozy on up to the bar? Woman who looks like that, in a skirt like *that*...I bet she could do all sorts of things that would make you forget about..."

"Gabby," Zade barely choked out her name.

"That's right." Kole snapped his fingers. "Why do I have such a hard time remembering her name?"

Zade shook his head, his heart hammering inside his chest. "No. I mean, *that's* Gabby."

The table rumbled with a collective, *"What?"*

"You sure?" Gabe swung his head back around to face him.

Zade gave the man a shaky nod. "I'm sure."

I'll never forget that face. Or that body.

"What the fuck?" Matt frowned. "You're telling me, the same mystery woman who hooked up with you in Grand Isle before vanishing into thin air is here? In La Paz?"

Gabby hadn't noticed them yet. Something Zade was grateful for because he couldn't take his eyes off her. He nodded woodenly. "That's exactly what I'm saying."

"Hector Andino is supposed to be coming here tonight in search of a beautiful redhead," Nate reminded them all. "Now, the same woman who ghosted our boy shows up, and *she's* beautiful with red hair? Can't be a fucking coincidence."

Matt scowled. "She must be involved with Andino."

No!

Zade's refuting thought was instant and unwavering.

"How the hell do you figure that?" He turned away from Gabby—*Jesus, she's here!*—and lowered his ballcap to conceal his face. "I met her over a month ago. We didn't even know about Andino until two days ago."

"Doesn't matter." Matt shook his head. "The same chick

you hooked up with winds up here, the same night *we're* here? No way that's a fucking coincidence."

"Look, man." Zade scooted closer to the table. "I get what you're saying, and yeah, this whole thing reeks of a set-up. But I'm telling you, it's not possible."

His Gabby couldn't be involved with a man like Hector Andino. His Gabby was sweet and loving. Caring and passionate. His Gabby was...

Not his Gabby.

Gabe leaned his elbows on the table. "Did you tell her who you were, King? Who you worked for?"

"She knows my name, but all I said was I worked for a private security company."

Nate shook his head. "It would take all of two seconds to do a Google search and find out which company that was."

"Even so," Zade continued to argue his point to his teammates, "I had zero ties to Hector Andino or any of his operations when I met her.

"So you're saying her being here is a coincidence?" Kole asked. It was clear the man was not convinced.

"I'm saying, there's no way she can possibly know what we're doing here."

"Unless she bugged your shit while she was shacking up with you," Nate piped up again.

Zade nearly growled. "She didn't bug my shit, Carter."

"Then why is she here?" Kole leaned in, working to keep his voice down. "Think about it, Zade. We may have just gotten this job, but you heard what Ghost and Ryker said the other day. The government's been after Andino for a while. No, our team didn't get involved until now, but it's still possible the idea of bringing Bravo on board was pitched to one of the agencies early on."

"So what?" Zade looked back at his friend. "You think

Homeland has a mole and they slipped information to Hector Andino?"

It was possible, but highly unlikely. Jason Ryker ran a tight-as-fuck ship over at Homeland. If someone was leaking sensitive government intel, the man would be all over that shit.

"I think what Carter's trying to say"—Gabe jumped back in—"is if the woman you know as Gabby *is* in bed with Andino, it's possible she targeted you."

Jesus. Zade couldn't believe they were seriously having this conversation.

"Makes sense." Matt shrugged. "She gets close to you to see if you'll slip up and give away anything pertinent to the case she thinks you're working. When she realizes there's nothing to find, she splits."

Zade was shaking his head before Matt even finished. "No. I'm tellin' you, it wasn't like that."

"So what was it like?" Kole asked with a challenging tone. "I know you don't want to hear it, but there has to be a reason she connected with you in Grand Isle, Zade."

She connected with me because we had a connection. A real, deep, electrifying connection.

"Sorry, man." Kole gave him a sympathetic look. "But if you'll take a second to think like an operative instead of a guy who got played, you'll see I'm right."

Zade glanced over to where Gabby was standing. Thankful she was looking in the opposite direction from their table. Kole's words were harsh, but it didn't make them any less true.

Was it possible? Did his desire for this woman cloud his judgement so badly he hadn't seen the truth about her? Had she been playing him for a fool all along, and he'd missed it?

His heart still said no, but the operative in him couldn't help but think maybe that's exactly what had happened.

"I don't know what's going on." Zade tore his gaze away from her to face his team. "But I damn sure intend to find out."

He started to stand, but Gabe wrapped one of his strong hands around Zade's forearm. "Wait."

"For what?"

Zade didn't want to wait. He wanted to sprint his ass over to where Gabby stood and ask her what the fuck was going on.

"If this woman *was* trying to play you in Grand Isle, we need to know why."

"That's exactly why I'm going over there. I'm going to find out what she was doing there."

What she was really doing while she was with me.

Gabe kept his grip tight and shook his head. "Not like this."

Zade stared at the former SEAL as if he were crazy. "Are you kidding me right now? I've been looking for this woman for the last month. She shows up here on the exact same night *we're* here, and you seriously expect me to sit on my ass and wait?"

"No one's sitting on their ass, King. If she's involved in Andino's business and you approach her, chances are she'll get spooked and take off. That happens, we run the risk of losing our best shot at getting to Andino."

Damn it, Zade really hated that the man was right. With another sideways glance in Gabby's direction, he sat back down.

"Fine. We'll do this your way. How do you want to play this?"

Gabe's brown eyes zeroed in on his. "What would we do if this were any other op?"

Zade thought for a moment. *Shit.* "You want to interrogate her."

Nodding, Gabe said, "We need to find out what she knows and why she targeted you. See if she can be of use to us."

A ball of dread settled in his stomach. "And if she can't?"

The seasoned operative's square jaw tightened. "Either way, we hand her over to Ryker when we're finished. Let him and his boys figure it out."

"Jesus." Zade shook his head and sat back in his chair. He ran a hand over the scruff covering his jaw.

He couldn't believe this was happening. Were they really talking about putting the woman he'd come damn close to falling for through a black ops interrogation? Could he actually turn her over to Homeland Fucking Security?

Zade's chest tightened, and his stomach churned. He'd participated in hundreds of interrogations. Most were fairly uneventful, but it was the others rolling through his brain now. The ones where they had to persuade their subjects to give up the intel.

That shit still gave him nightmares.

The outcome of Gabby's questioning would depend solely on her cooperation. While Bravo would never resort to physically harming a woman, Zade had no idea what would happen to her once they turned her over to Homeland.

As sick as it made him to think she'd be involved in something as horrifying as human trafficking, he knew even the most beautiful of women could be the Devil in disguise.

Adjusting his ball cap again, he covertly glanced at the woman in question once more before looking back at Gabe.

There was only one way he was ever going to learn the truth about Gabriella Smith, which was why Zade heard himself saying, "All right. Let's do it."

CHAPTER 4

This was it. Her last chance.

Gabby took a sip of her third club soda, her heart racing with nervous anticipation as she looked around the bar. If she didn't make contact with Hector tonight, she'd be forced to go home empty-handed.

The thought of that happening was soul-crushing.

Thanks to another sleepless night, she'd gotten here later than planned. The place was already crowded, and Gabby prayed she hadn't missed the man she was hoping to meet.

She could tell from the brief glance Hector Andino had given her last night, he was interested. *How* interested, she wasn't sure.

Hopefully enough to make an encore appearance.

The night before, after his sudden disappearing act, Gabby had taken a chance and struck up a conversation with the bartender. Since Hector owned the place, she thought maybe his employee would pass along her strong desire to meet him.

Acting as if she wanted to hook up with the dangerous man, Gabby had laid it on thick. Told the young woman how handsome she thought Andino was. How she'd give *anything* to be introduced to him.

After that little performance, she'd left and gone back to her hotel. Once there, she'd stayed up half the night, worrying herself to the point of physical sickness.

Gabby had laid in that bed and cried, terrified her weeks of questions, cashing in old favors owed, and traipsing all over the country—and here, to Mexico—were all for not. That Sam's fate had already been sealed.

When the tears had all dried up, she'd spent the rest of last night tossing and turning, telling herself she was crazy to think she could do this on her own. Of course, then she reminded herself there was no one else to turn to.

With the exception of Shoemaker's financial support, Gabby was alone in this. Just as she'd been during most of her twenty-six years.

When her thoughts threatened to turn to Zade, Gabby had quickly shut them down. It was a waste of time to dream about a man she wanted but could never truly have.

One she could see herself loving but would never see again.

You might be wrong about that. Maybe I'll see him again. Someday, once this was all over and Sam was back home where she belonged.

Which was something that would never happen if she didn't get her head out of her ass and focus on why she was here.

Pushing all that aside, Gabby took another drink and looked back toward the door. Hector still hadn't shown, and though she hated to run the risk of missing him, her need to visit the ladies' room was becoming too strong to ignore.

Setting her glass down, she quickly made her way along the bar toward the narrow hallway at the back of the club.

Once inside the crowded bathroom, she waited in line, hurrying when it was her turn to go.

After taking care of business, Gabby washed her hands, only bothering to half-dry them before rushing into the hallway. She was so busy focusing on getting back to the bar, she didn't see the man coming up behind her.

Or the syringe in his hand.

Feeling a sharp prick on the side of her neck—almost like she'd been stung by something—Gabby stopped suddenly and slapped a hand to the area.

"Ouch!"

Her fingers met bare skin, but the stinging persisted. A few seconds later, a cool, burning sensation began spreading through her neck and into her shoulder.

What the hell?

She didn't know what she'd been stung by, but whatever it was, it *hurt.*

Shaking it off, Gabby started walking again…or at least she tried to.

After one, heavy step, she began to feel dizzy. Before she could even try to call out for help, her knees buckled and her legs gave out.

A set of strong arms caught her before she could hit the floor, and Gabby could've sworn she heard Zade's familiar voice tell her he was sorry a second before everything went black.

Sometime later—she had no idea how long she'd been out—Gabby woke with a pounding headache and the worst case of dry mouth she'd ever experienced.

It didn't make sense. She'd only had club soda to drink at the bar. So why did it feel like she'd been on an all-night bender?

A quick flash of memory jolted through her.

She'd been coming out of the bathroom. There was a

sharp stick in the side of her neck. She'd gotten dizzy and was falling.

Someone had whispered something in her ear, and then…nothing.

Oh, God. I was drugged.

Forcing her eyes to open, it took several, quick blinks before everything finally came into focus. The first thing Gabby noticed was that she was still fully clothed.

A feeling of relief rushed through her. Most rapists didn't bother re-dressing their victims. A fact she knew first-hand.

That same relief vanished quickly when Gabby tried to stand but couldn't because her wrists and ankles were bound to the chair she'd been placed in.

"What the hell?" she mumbled to herself.

Panic set in, and Gabby's breathing picked up at an alarming pace. Blood rushed past her ears as she began pulling and twisting, attempting to break free of the plastic ties keeping her in place.

The only thing she managed to accomplish was to rub the skin at her wrists raw.

Needing to get herself under control, she squeezed her eyes shut and tried to calm her racing heart. After several slow, deep breaths, Gabby opened her eyes again and began looking around the small room for something, *anything* to tell her where she was or who had taken her.

Paint was peeling from the plaster walls and water stains marked several spots in the ceiling. The floor beneath her feet was made of worn and cracked tile, and there was one open window centered on the wall to her right.

From where she sat, the only furniture Gabby could see was the chair she was in and a small, wooden table positioned a few feet in front of her.

A bead of sweat ran down the center of her back as her mind raced to make sense of what had happened. One minute she was at the club, the next she's waking up here. Tied to a freaking chair.

Hector Andino.

Gabby closed her eyes again, mentally chastising herself for being so stupid. She'd asked about Andino in hopes he'd come looking for her but not like this.

Her plan had been to catch his eye and make her interest known. Get close enough to him to find out where he kept his girls.

She must have come off too strong when she'd talked to the bartender, and now she was stuck here with no means of escape.

Muted male voices reached her ear from the other side of the door, and Gabby's eyes flew open. A large man entered the room, his muscular build and strong, scruff-covered jaw made him surprisingly handsome.

His intense stare made her nervous as hell.

Evil comes in all forms.

It was a lesson she learned years ago.

"You're awake," the man's deep voice rumbled. Dressed in jeans and a gray T that stretched across a set of broad shoulders, he walked toward her with a bottle of water in his hand. "I'm guessing you could use this."

That he looked and sounded American didn't surprise her. From what she'd learned, Hector Andino employed several men and women from the United States to do his dirty work.

Gabby watched as the man unscrewed the bottle's lid and began advancing toward her. When he brought the water toward her face, she turned her head and pulled away as far as the chair would allow.

The man halted his movements, his head becoming slightly tilted as his brown eyes studied her.

"You think I'm trying to poison you?"

Gabby remained silent.

He sighed and took a big swig from the bottle before swallowing it down. Wiping his mouth with the back of his hand, the man raised a brow.

"Happy?"

Is he serious?

Glaring up at him, Gabby cleared her dry throat, a move that ignited the drumming in her head. "Let's see. You drugged me, kidnapped me, and have me tied to a chair. Not to mention my head feels like it's about to explode. *Happy* isn't the word I'd use to describe what I'm feeling."

Keeping his expression unreadable, the man tipped his chin. "Fair enough. But that pounding in your head is due to dehydration. An unfortunate side effect of the drug you were given." He held the water up again. "This will help."

As much as she wanted to act the martyr, her mouth *did* feel like she'd swallowed half of the Sahara.

With a jerk of her head—damn, she really needed to not do that—he brought the top of the bottle to her lips. Tilting her head back, Gabby allowed him to help her take a drink. She barely held back a moan of appreciation as the cool liquid quenched her parched throat.

After a few more swallows, the man replaced the lid and set the near-empty bottle onto the table behind him.

"Who are you?" Her voice came out stronger than before. "Why did you bring me here?"

"I'll answer your questions, if I'm able." He faced her once more. "But first, you're going to answer mine."

"What do you want to know?"

"Let's start with your name."

"Gabriella Smith." She didn't hesitate to lie. "I'm here with a group of friends who are probably worried sick about m—"

"Your real name," he cut her off.

Gabby looked him in the eye and lied again. "That *is* my

real name. Check my ID." She looked around. "I'm assuming my purse is here, somewhere."

She was certain he already had, which was why she'd given him the same name as the one on the driver's license currently in her wallet. The asshole probably stole what little cash she had left, too.

The man's mouth curved up into a half-smile. "You know, this will go a lot easier for the both of us if you're honest with me."

"Well, why didn't you say so?" Gabby's sarcastic tone filled the tiny room. "After all, making things easier for guys like you *is* my goal in life." She batted her eyes, her lips curling.

Like I'd do anything to help one of Andino's men.

A muscle in the guy's chiseled jaw twitched before he turned away from her. Sliding one hip onto the table, he bent that leg a bit while his other foot remained on the floor.

With his hands clasped loosely in front of him, he stared back at her. "We'll come back to your name. Tell me something different."

"There once was a man from Nantucket…" she recited the first line in a crude joke she was taught years ago.

"Funny." The man didn't smile. "That's one of my favorites, but I'm not in the mood for jokes."

"No?" Gabby let her eyes travel down the length of his toned body. "What are you in the mood for, big guy? Maybe we can work something out."

The words made her want to vomit. Even though the man had that whole Silver Fox thing going on, he worked for a monster.

Like you'd do anything with him even if he didn't.

The voice in her head was right. It had been a month since she'd last seen Zade, but when it came to him, time didn't seem to matter. Since then, handsome men had tried to get her attention. They'd failed miserably.

There was only one man Gabby wanted. One man she *craved*. And it was not the one staring back at her.

Stop thinking about him!

Damn it, the voice was right again. Zade wasn't who mattered, now. Only Sam.

The only thing that mattered was finding her. *She* was the important one, here.

I'll do whatever it takes to save her.

"Appreciate the offer, but I'm not really in the mood for that, either. Pretty sure you aren't, either, so let's start with something easy. Why don't you explain what you were doing in Grand Isle a few weeks ago."

What the hell?

Shocked by the unexpected question, Gabby's eyes widened before she could stop them. With a quick blink and shake of her head, she tried to play it off, but she had a feeling the man had noticed.

Still, she did her best to recover. "I don't know what you're talking about."

"Come on, Gabby," The man used the shortened version of her name. "It's simple. You help me, I can help you."

"It's a little late for the good-cop routine, don't you think?"

The man chuckled, his broad chest shaking as his deep voice rumbled. "Trust me, sweetheart. I'm not a cop, and I'm far from being good."

"Given who your boss is, I believe it." Gabby stared back at him. "Although, Hector Andino does have most of the cops around here in his pocket, so it's hard to know who you can or cannot trust."

His expression didn't change, exactly, but Gabby still noticed the tiny twitch in the corner of one eye. It was almost indiscernible, probably would be to most people. Not her.

The time she'd spent on the streets growing up, Gabby had learned how to read people pretty damn well. Better than most, she could pick up on the slightest ticks and tells, and this man was definitely holding something back.

Something big.

"Grand Isle." His dark brown eyes stared into hers. "What were you doing there?"

Gabby lifted her chin. "I told you, I have no idea what you're talking about. I've never even heard of the place, let alone visited there."

"Is that right?"

"Yep."

She had no idea how this man knew about her trip down south, but that was her story, and she was sticking to it.

Clearly not buying into it, the big guy smiled. "See, that's interesting because my intel says differently."

Gabby shrugged a shoulder. "Guess your intel is wrong."

"It happens." The man nodded. "However, in this particular case, I'm fairly certain the information I was given is correct. My source on this one's pretty reliable."

She kept her blasé expression in place. "Even reliable sources can be wrong."

"They can be," he agreed before turning and walking toward the closed door. "I guess there's only one way to find out."

Now he'd lost her. "What do you mean?"

The man stopped walking and turned back around. His distinguished features somehow gave him both a kind, yet deadly appearance.

"Well, Miss *Smith*. I find the easiest way to get to the truth is to go straight to the source."

Okay...

Unsure of the road she was about to go down, Gabby began grasping at straws.

"If this is about money, I can pay you," she blurted. *Liar.* "It'll take a day or so, but I can get someone from the States to wire it to you. Whatever Andino's paying you, I'll double it." *Big. Fat. Liar.*

Sure, he'd eventually figure out she was full of shit, but hopefully this would at least buy her some time.

"Andino?" The man raised a dark brow as if he'd never heard of the prick.

Gabby rolled her eyes. "Hector Andino. That's why I'm here, right? He ordered you to kidnap me?"

With an assessing glance, he paused before asking, "You really got that kind of money?"

"Would I have offered it, if I didn't?"

Hell yes, I absolutely would, if it meant giving me a better chance at surviving this nightmare.

Without another word, the man left the room, shutting the door behind him. Had it worked? Did the big guy actually believe her?

Gabby blew out a breath and hung her head, praying he did. Closing her eyes, her mind worked to come up with a plausible solution to her very messed up situation.

At least she'd bought herself some time. For what, she didn't know, yet. She also had no clue how the hell this guy knew about her trip to Grand Isle.

There was only one plausible explanation she could come up with. Her actions these past two months must've stirred up a hornet's nest of trouble.

Andino had to have gotten word she was asking around about him and decided to have her followed. It was the only thing that made sense, except...

It doesn't.

If Hector Andino knew she was looking for him—and

why she was looking for him—he wouldn't have had her followed.

He would've had her killed.

So why go through all of this? The drugging, the kidnapping...why go through the trouble of having his bruiser bring her here?

And that was another thing...

Yes, she was tied to the chair. Yes, her wrists were raw and even bleeding in a few places, but that had been of her own doing. Andino's man hadn't laid a finger on her.

Not that she was complaining.

Seriously, though. The guy had brought her water, for crying out loud. Went so far as to drink some himself to prove to her it was safe. He'd even been *gentle* when he'd helped her with it.

She had no doubt the man was as deadly as they came, but there was more to him than he wanted her to see. A light he was working damn hard to keep dimmed.

That and his behavior went against everything Gabby had learned about Andino's men. Working for the leader of the most dangerous cartel in operation, those guys didn't wait patiently for answers. They beat their captives until they got what they wanted.

The bastards sure as hell didn't offer women water. Instead they hauled them off like cattle and sold them to monsters who did only God knows what to them after the fact.

So what the hell was going on?

The question had barely rang through her mind when the door to the room opened once more. Assuming the same man had returned, Gabby opened her mouth to ask him that very question, but her words—and the breath in her lungs—froze.

Someone different had entered the room. Someone Gabby thought she'd never see again.

"Zade?" Shock had her choking out his name. "W-what… what are you doing here?"

Well-worn jeans covered his taut thighs and rested low on his hips. A plain, black T-shirt stretched over a landscape of muscles she was intimately familiar with. God, he was even sexier than she remembered.

At the same time, he seemed almost like a stranger.

Looking more like a hardened warrior and less like the man she'd spent the most glorious weekend of her life with, Zade King shut the door and walked toward her.

"Hello, Gabriella." He glanced down at a tablet he'd carried in with him and back to her. Lips she'd feasted on curled into a humorless smirk. "At least you were telling the truth about your *first* name."

Gabby's heart pounded fiercely against her ribs. "I can explain," she blurted without thinking.

"Oh, you'll explain, all right." He came closer. "You're going to tell me everything I want to know, and then your ass will be transported back to the States."

"The States?" Gabby shook her head. "No. I can't go back. Not yet. Not until I've—"

"Not up to you, sweetheart."

The term of endearment sounded nothing like the loving way he'd used it in the past.

"Zade, please. Listen, I can exp—"

"Explain." Beautiful, cold eyes met hers as he cut her off once more. "Yeah, I got that part."

They stared at each other for several seconds. It was enough time for her mind to race past the magnificent memories she'd locked away and gather her scattered thoughts into one horrifying conclusion.

No. It can't be true.

She couldn't have been this wrong about him. Granted, her choice in men hadn't always been the best, but this was different. *He* was different.

Yet, her current predicament said otherwise.

Gabby's heart shattered as she glared up at him. "You sonofabitch." She seethed. "You played me."

Zade flinched, almost as if she'd struck him. "Excuse me?"

"Andino sent you to follow me, didn't he? Back at Grand Isle. You…you followed me from New Orleans and then set up that whole, accidental meeting in the bar that first night. Then you used our time together to…what? Try to find out what I knew about him?"

Except he hadn't asked her about Hector Andino or the cartel. Not once.

For a second, Zade looked as confused as she felt. Then he threw his head back and laughed.

"Nice try, Gabriella. Take the focus off of you by turning it around on me. Classic move, really. But I've been in this business a long damn time. Too long to fall for the innocent act. Besides"—he lifted the tablet—"I've got the truth right here. Well, part of it, anyway."

This business.

Oh, God. Gabby swallowed hard as she thought about what his business truly was. She felt like she was going to be sick.

Opening her mouth, she sucked in a breath and started to ask exactly what business he was in. Unfortunately, the man of her dreams was already busy reciting information from her past.

The same past she'd tried hard to escape, but never quite managed to.

"Gabriella Jaqueline Stevens. Born twenty-six years ago this past April to Kelly Stevens. No father listed on the birth certificate. You entered the foster care system at age eleven after your mom was arrested and sent to prison on her fourth drug charge. Possession with intent to sell, plus a second prostitution charge. You bounced around a few homes." Face void of any emotion, Zade looked up from the screen. "Says here you were a runner."

"Stop," she whispered the order.

Glancing back down, he ignored her and continued on. "According to one set of very well-off foster parents, you falsified a report against their son...your seventeen-year-old foster brother...when you were sixteen. They claim you attacked the boy with a golf club and then ran away. When you were caught, you told the police he..."

Zade stopped himself short, his brows turning inward as if he were reading the horrors of her past for the first time.

He looked back up at her. "You told the police he raped you."

Don't react. It's all in the past. "Zade, stop."

He didn't. Instead, he cleared his throat, the bit of emotion he'd let slip into his cold demeanor, gone.

"In their statement, the boy's parents described you as being a liar and a trouble-maker. Said you made the claim against their son in an attempt to blackmail them for money and explain away your own violent behavior. They said their son's injuries were all defensive wounds, and yours were..." He swallowed tightly before beginning again. "The boy's parents stated your injuries were self-inflicted in order to mimic sexual assault."

His eyes raised to meet hers once more. This time when he looked at her, the anger he'd shown when he first entered the room had become slightly faded.

If Gabby didn't know any better, she'd almost think he felt badly for her.

The last thing I want is his pity.

She looked away from him, a damn tear falling down her cheek when she blinked. "I said, stop."

"You were charged with assault, but because of your age, you went into a juvenile facility for nine months instead of jail. When you got out, you went to live with Everett and Annabelle Shoemaker, two teachers at the high school you attended. They have a daughter a few years younger than you. Her name is"—

"Sam." Gabby looked back up at him, her heart aching with fear for her foster sister. "Look, if you're going to kill me, just do it. Otherwise, you really need to let me go."

"Kill you?" His handsome face contorted with confusion. "Why would I"—

"Isn't that why I'm here?" she cut him off. "Your boss wants to know why I've been asking around about him, right? But why? Does Andino think I'm some kind of narc or something? Because I'm not."

I just wanted to find my sister, which clearly isn't going to happen now. The thought ripped her soul in two.

"So like I said"—she jutted her chin upward toward Zade —"whatever it is you came to do, either do it and get it over with, or cut me loose."

By the time she was done talking, both cheeks were damp with fresh tears. Tears she hadn't even realized were falling.

For the longest time, Zade did nothing but stand there, staring down at her from his spot near the table. He didn't move any closer. Didn't utter a single word.

He did nothing but stare, and for the life of her, she couldn't tell what he was thinking. What he was feeling.

Gabby was about to open her mouth and start screaming at him to do something, to say *something*, but closed it again when Zade sat the tablet down onto the table and began talking again.

"What were you doing in that club tonight?"

The truth was on the tip of her tongue. Part of her wanted to tell him. Wanted nothing more than to talk to someone she could trust about the pain and fear she'd been living with for the past two months.

Actually what she really wanted was to talk to Zade. Not the man staring down at her expectantly, but the sweet, caring Zade she thought she knew.

Too bad he doesn't exist.

"Like I told your buddy..." Gabby lifted her stubborn chin. "I was there with some friends."

"You also told him you'd never been to Grand Isle."

Almost subconsciously, his eyes trailed her body as he spoke. Gabby was shocked to see the same heat she remembered flare to life behind the swirls of brown and green.

He blinked, and it was gone.

Jaw tightening, Zade brought his focus back to her face. "We both know that was a lie."

She could feel her cheeks becoming flushed, wishing she could pull her damn skirt down. "My weekend there had nothing to do with the reason I'm here."

"And that reason would be…" His voice trailed off.

"We've been over this, Zade." She worked to keep her voice steady. "My friends and I—"

"Come on, Gabby," he growled. The man actually *growled*. "We saw you come into Andino's club. Watched you stand at the bar for quite a while. Alone."

Keep your cool.

Neither Zade nor the other man had mentioned Sam, so it was possible they didn't know she was the reason Gabby was here. She didn't want to offer up that information, either, for fear word would get back to the man who'd taken her. If that happened, Sam could be in even more danger than she already was.

"I got there before they did," Gabby continued with the lie. "I was waiting for my friends to show when—"

"Enough with the fucking lies!" Zade's booming voice made her jump. Fists tightening at his sides, he looked both angry and…a little lost. "I want the *truth*. I think I've at least earned that much."

Her brows arched high as anger flooded her veins. "I'm sorry, you've *earned* it? Why, because we slept together a few times? How about this, Zade. How about you tell *me* the truth!"

"Me?"

"Yes, *you*. You want to stand there acting like a freaking Boy Scout demanding honesty from me when you lied, too."

Scowling, he spoke through a set of perfect, clenched teeth. "What the hell did I lie to you about?"

"Uh, your job, for one."

Lord only knows what else.

"I never lied about that."

"You told me you worked for a private security company in Dallas." Gabby glanced around the room. "Does this look like freaking Texas to you?"

Zade swallowed. "I do work for a private security company." His voice didn't waver, his gaze on her remained firm. "It *is* based out of Dallas."

Damn, he was good. Most dishonest people she knew had some sort of tell to give them away. Not this guy.

Of course, he doesn't.

Gabby shook her head. "When you said private security, I thought that meant you installed alarm systems or something."

Her eyes slid over his left shoulder. His shirt hid the scars there.

She'd seen them when they were in bed, together. Had touched them with her fingertips.

Gabby had kissed them, her heart aching for the pain she knew he must've suffered.

At the time, she'd assumed the injury was from his military days. But now…

Her eyes met his. "My fault, I guess. I didn't realize 'private security' meant playing enforcer for a freaking cartel leader."

Zade's dark eyes widened before narrowing in an assessing glance. "You really think I work for Hector Andino."

The statement made it sound as if this bit of news was surprising.

"Don't you?" Gabby shot back, wishing he'd just own up to his shit and move on, already.

Except Gabby didn't *want* to think it was true. Never in a million years would she have put the sweet, gentle Zade she'd briefly known into bed with a man like Hector Andino.

But he was here, and *she* was here. Either Zade or the other guy who'd been in here earlier had tied her to a chair after drugging and kidnapping her.

So there was that.

Gabby watched Zade's wheels turn for several seconds before his brows grew closer together.

"What kind of game are you playing, here, Gabby?" When she refused to answer, a muscle in his strong jaw bulged. "Why were you in Grand Isle?"

She continued to remain silent. Out of preservation or spite, she wasn't exactly sure. What she did know was that her silence had him nearly growling again.

"How did you know to target me?"

"Target you?" Gabby chuckled, unable to keep quiet at that remark. "Now who's playing games, Zade? I didn't target you. *You* targeted *me*."

"The hell I did!" His face turned red, a vein in his forehead becoming much larger than before. Hands that knew every inch of her body flew to his hips as he took a step forward. Fury marred his handsome features. "How long have you worked for Hector Andino?"

"I don't work for that bastard!" she shouted back, her body tensing beneath her restraints.

God, she was tired of all the questions and the games. She needed to get *out* of here.

She needed to find Sam.

"Well neither do I!" Zade yelled back, staring at her with fierce determination.

If she didn't know any better, Gabby would swear he was telling the truth. And if that was the case, then...

"Why are *you* here, Zade?" Her demand was soft. "Why did you drug me and"—Gabby looked down at her raw wrists, refusing to let her fear show—"tie me up? And why are you interrogating me like I'm some kind of criminal?"

You are a criminal, remember?

Looking as honest as she'd ever seen him, Zade locked eyes with her and said, "I'm here because my team was assigned to take down Hector Andino, by any means necessary."

CHAPTER 5

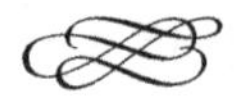

"Your...team?" The smooth skin on Gabby's forehead bunched together. "What team?"

Zade watched her carefully before answering. Though it was almost impossible at this point, he did his damnedest to hide his body's reaction to seeing this woman again.

For weeks, he'd done little else but think about her.

Think about her. Dream about her. Search for her.

And here she was, less than ten feet away from him. Tied to a fucking chair while he *interrogated* her.

Every night since coming back from that island, Zade had fantasized about seeing Gabby again. Though the scenes in his mind would change slightly from one night to the next, at their core, they all consisted of the same, incredible things.

Hot passionate kisses and making love until the sun came up.

But this? Of all the scenarios he'd imagined, *this* was about as far the fuck away from his dreams as he could get.

Gabe thought she was trying to pull one over on them with the whole, 'they-work-for-Andino' angle. Somehow turn the tables on them or some shit. Zade wasn't so sure.

The Gabby he knew wouldn't do something like that. Of course, the Gabby he knew never really existed. Did she?

Using the coms they were all still wearing, Zade had listened in on Gabby's conversation with Gabe. He'd heard the lies she'd told. How easily she told them.

Then he saw her record.

Nate had taken her picture and her prints while she was still unconscious. Using facial recognition software, he'd run her through his system.

A system that shed one hell of a light on who this woman really was.

Struggling to reconcile the woman he'd only just begun to love with the one they'd abducted, Zade had been filled with too many conflicting emotions to make it past reading the first line of her background report.

The one showing her real name and arrest record.

Instead of acting like an experienced operative and reading the entire thing first, he'd immediately barged in here to confront her. Tired of her lies and deception, and feeling like a fool who'd been royally played, it wasn't until he got to the part about her foster brother attacking her that he'd even questioned the validity of the charges.

When he saw her reaction to what he'd been reading aloud—her statement telling how her foster brother had assaulted *her*...had fucking *raped* her—Zade knew in his heart she'd been telling the truth all those years ago.

But was she telling the truth now?

Either way, Gabby had been the victim back then. She'd been assaulted, violated in the most heinous of ways, yet she was the one who'd been sentenced to juvie while the prick who'd raped her walked free.

All because no one had believed her. She'd had no one on her side.

I'm on your side, baby.

The thought was instant. It took no effort on his part and was simply there, despite the circumstances. It was as natural as breathing for him.

I'm going to find the sonofabitch who hurt you and make him wish he'd never laid a finger on my Gabby.

Whoa. That wasn't right.

Until a few minutes ago, he didn't even know her real name. So, no, she wasn't his.

Except when they'd been together on that island, Gabby had *felt* like his. His present and his future. His...everything.

"Zade?"

He blinked, her voice tearing him away from his thoughts.

Shit. He needed to talk with Gabe and the others and figure out what their next step should be. Because all of a sudden, he had the feeling they'd made a massive fucking mistake.

"Helloo..." Gabby turned her voice all sing-songy. "Did you hear what I said? I asked what team you're referring to. And are you guys really going after Andino?"

Her hopeful tone had Zade's eyes sliding to hers. The hope she felt wasn't only present in her voice. It was staring straight the fuck back at him.

She wasn't working *with* Hector Andino. Gabby wanted the man caught as much as he did. Question was why?

Needing to get away from her so he could think clearly and talk it all out with his team, Zade turned and left the room. Gabby's voice followed him as he went.

"You're leaving? Wait! Zade, *please!* Don't leave me here!"

He didn't say a word. Zade simply shut the door behind him and blew out a breath he hadn't realized he was holding. Closing his eyes, he took a second to regroup.

After a few seconds, he pushed away from the door and looked around the room. The abandoned house had nothing but bare, peeling walls and a couple of tables and a few chairs.

One of those chairs was in the room he'd just left.

Leaning against the far wall near an opening that had once housed a window, Matt glanced his way. "Well, that was interesting."

The other men had obviously heard his entire conversation with Gabby.

"That's one way to put it." Gabe stared at him from where he sat.

"Yeah, what the hell, man?" Kole was sitting across from Gabe. The man's face had turned into a deep scowl. "You told her our objective?"

"Relax, Jameson." Gabe looked at the other man. "It's not like she's in any position to run off and tell anyone."

Because she's still in there, tied to that fucking chair.

"She's not involved with Andino." The words were out before Zade had time to think about them.

Gabe's gaze swung back to his. "You sure about that?"

He gave his team leader a single nod. "I'm sure."

"Why?" Nate asked from his spot near the door. "Because she told you so, or because you two bumped uglies a few times?" The computer geek smirked, clearly amused by his own smartass comment.

Remember, he's your teammate. You can't kill him.

"No, jackass." Zade looked over at him. "Because I saw it in her eyes. She's telling the truth."

Kole snorted. "That'd be a first."

An unexpected rage filled Zade as he stormed over to where his teammate sat. "You got something to say, Jameson?"

Kole's shoulder rose and fell in a casual shrug. "Just that she's already proven herself to be deceitful."

"He's right, Zade." Matt stood and walked over to him.

"She lied to Gabe about why she was really in that club tonight. Lied to you about it, too. About all sorts of things, actually."

"Because she thought we were Andino's hired gunmen. As for the rest…she probably didn't tell me the truth about who she really was when we first met, because she didn't want me to know about her past."

He wished she'd felt comfortable enough with him to be honest with him, but it actually made sense to him, now.

Their time together was supposed to be nothing more than a weekend fling. They'd both agreed going in. No strings or talk about a future, which meant…

"We were two, consenting adults having fun and blowing off steam for the weekend. There was no reason for her to divulge her time spent in juvie." Zade gave Matt a raised brow. "Did you share all the shit you did in the past with every woman you slept with?"

He knew the remark would hit home with his friend. There'd been several women in Matt's life before he and Katherine finally found their way back to each other.

Since then, the former playboy didn't so much as glance in another woman's direction. Kat was it for him.

I want that, too.

With Gabby? He thought he did. Now, he wasn't sure.

What he was certain of was that she played no part in Andino's skin trade business.

"If that's all it was"—Matt kept on, bringing Zade's focus back to the subject at hand—"then why have you spent the past four weeks searching high and low for this woman?" The man's question came with a challenging tone. "It may have been fun for her, but you, my friend, fell hard and fast for that woman in there."

No, he'd fallen for the woman she projected herself to be.

That was the fucking crux of the whole damn problem.

Zade didn't know what to believe right now. He didn't know which version of Gabby was the real thing.

The liar?

The lover?

Both?

You know.

Running a hand over his jaw, Zade shook his head. "Look, none of that matters now." Though he'd damn sure be clearing that particular issue up soon. "What's important is finding the girls Andino's planning to sell and getting them back home where they belong."

Zade had two sisters. Some bastard ever even attempted to do something like this to either of them, he'd hunt the fucker down to the ends of the earth if he had to.

The girls Andino had taken deserved nothing less.

"All right, fine." Nate was the first one to relent. "In the meantime, what do we do about Red?"

"Red?" Zade shot his friend a look.

"She has red hair, doesn't she?"

Hell yes, she did. He'd spent hours running his fingers through her long, thick, silken hair.

"I say we have Ryker send in a team to take her back to Texas," Kole shared his opinion. "Let Homeland deal with her."

"*Deal* with her?" Zade glared at the other man. "She's a human being, for Christ's sake. Not some goddamn stray cat."

"Look, man. I get that you have a history with her." Kole's tone was steady and in control. "But it's not like we can keep her tied to a fucking chair while we go searching for our target."

"He's right, Zade." Matt's remorseful gaze locked with his. "Not to sound like a total prick, but if Gabby's telling the truth about not working for Andino, she's of no use to us."

"We don't know that. Hell we still haven't figured out why she's here," Zade reminded his teammates. "There *has* to be a connection. Either to me or Andino. I know I can get her to—"

"Talk?" Kole looked unconvinced. "The woman's been awake for damn near an hour and hasn't given us shit."

He had a point, but it didn't matter. Not to Zade. "She'll talk to me. I just need more time to show her she can trust me. To convince her *we're* not the bad guys."

Kole stood and walked around the edge of the table. "The girls Andino took? They don't have the luxury of time, Zade. Every minute your girlfriend stalls is a minute closer to those other women and girls being sold. It's a minute closer to them being taken against their will…*again*…for God only knows what purpose."

"Pretty sure we can all guess what that is," Nate mumbled.

Ignoring the girlfriend comment, Zade got right up in Kole's face. "You think I don't know that? That I don't care about what happens to those girls?"

"Oh, I know you care. I just think you care more about that deceitful little—"

Zade was moving before he even realized it.

One minute he was standing toe-to-toe with one of his best friends, and the next his fists were filled with the front of Kole's shirt. He shoved the guy backward.

"Watch your fucking mouth!"

"Ah, hell," Nate groaned from somewhere nearby.

Sure, Gabby had lied to them. Multiple times. But he was starting to understand why. At least part of the reason, anyway.

Regardless, he sure as shit wasn't going to stand by and let his teammate—or anyone else—disrespect her.

"Guys." Matt tried pushing himself between Zade and Kole. "This isn't helping."

Neither man relented.

"Stand down." Gabe was suddenly there, his dark eyes shooting lasers at him and Kole. "Both of you take a fucking step back. Now."

With a shove, Zade released Kole's shirt and did as he was ordered. Chest heaving, he ran a hand through his hair as he tried to get a grip and understand what had just happened.

You damn near beat the hell out of your teammate defending Gabby. That's what happened.

"King. Go cut Miss Stevens free."

Kole's eyes flew to Gabe's. "Seriously?"

"I'm with Jameson on this one, Gabe." Nate's gaze bounced between Zade's and Kole's before landing on Gabe's. "Don't you think we should figure out why she's here before we let her go?"

The former SEAL addressed the entire group. "We're not letting her go."

Nate frowned. "Then why—"

"I'll tell you why." The formidable man rested his hands on his hips. "While these two shitheads were bickering back and forth, I got word back from Ghost about Gabby's involvement with Andino."

Zade's heart beat a little harder. When Nate had taken her picture and prints earlier, he'd also sent the info to Ghost and his Delta team so they could do their own checking. Second set of eyes and all that.

"What did Ghost find?" His question came out a hell of a lot steadier than he felt.

Gabe stared back at him, his expression unreadable. Zade held his breath and waited.

"Not a damn thing. She has no known connection to Hector Andino or any other member of his cartel."

Hope flared to life inside him. "So Gabby's telling the

truth." Zade slid an *I told you so* gaze to Kole. "She isn't on Andino's payroll."

Gabe shook his head. "Doesn't appear to be, no."

"I knew it." Zade's shoulders fell with relief.

"I wouldn't celebrate quite yet," his team leader warned. "We still need to know why she's here, in La Paz."

Kole opened his mouth to argue, but Zade shut him down.

"You heard him, Kole. Gabby's not in bed with the cartel."

The young sniper gritted his teeth. "Doesn't mean she's *clean*."

He had a point. Still…

"We'll have a hell of a lot better chance at getting her to talk if she doesn't feel like a damn hostage."

"King's right," Gabe agreed. To Zade he said, "Cut Gabby loose. We'll take her back to the hotel with us. Give her a chance to clean up and get something to eat. She gets a little more comfortable and starts feeling as though she can trust you again, she may let her guard down enough to open up to you."

Zade liked Gabe's plan. He liked that plan a lot. But he needed to tread carefully. Why? Because he was man enough to admit his weaknesses.

He didn't want to get close to her simply to gain intel. Zade wanted to be close to Gabby again, period.

Huge. Fucking. Weakness.

"Think we all could use a shower." Matt sniffed himself. "It's after eleven and it's still hot as fuck in this place."

Ignoring the others' mumbled agreements, Zade returned to the room where Gabby was being held. He tried to ignore the defeat in her red-rimmed eyes as he made his way over to her.

Pulling his knife from his jeans pocket, Zade heard a sharp intake of air over the snick of his blade being released.

"W-what are you doing?" Gabby began fighting against her restraints. "Please, Zade. I swear I'm telling you the truth. I'm not involved with Andino or anyone like that. I swear!"

He froze in place, his eyes locking with hers. The fear he saw there nearly undid him.

Jesus, she thinks I could...

"I'm not going to hurt you, Gabby," he quickly assured her. He then held his hands—and the knife—out to his sides.

Slowly, Zade moved closer in the most non-threatening way he could manage. "I could never hurt you. I'm just going to cut you loose."

Gabby stopped struggling but kept an uneasy eye on him as he slid the sharp tip of the blade between the chair's wooden arm and the plastic tie. With a quick twist of his wrist, the plastic snapped, releasing her wrist in the process.

Her breath of relief was like a kick to his fucking gut. She'd actually believed he was capable of hurting her. Of *cutting* her.

Christ, what kind of a prick did she think he was?

You did help knock her out and bring her here. Not to mention you've been holding her against her will.

Ignoring the tiny voice, Zade quickly and carefully cut away the remaining ties. When she was completely free, Gabby took a moment to stretch her stiff legs and arms.

His eyes fell to the cuts on her wrists, his chest tightening when he saw the red, raw skin there. Gabby stood, her movements slow and stiff.

Hesitantly, Zade raised a hand to one of hers. Her flinch ripped a giant hole in his heart.

"I'm not going to hurt you, Gabby," he whispered the promise again. This time when he reached for her, she didn't try to pull away.

Thank you, God.

Taking her hand in his, Zade lifted it in order to get a

better look. Using his thumb, he gently caressed the area next to the reddened skin.

"You're bleeding." He shook his head. Feeling like a complete asshole, he ignored the electric zing from her touch and brought his eyes to hers. "You weren't supposed to get hurt. I'm so sorry."

"It's fine." Gabby looked up at him warily. "I'm fine, Zade. Or at least I would be if you'd let me go."

He shook his head and released her hand. "I can't do that, sweetheart. Not yet."

The endearment made her scowl, and Gabby jerked her hand free. Lifting her chin and straightening her shoulders, the strong woman asked, "Why not? You obviously believe me. Otherwise, you would've left me tied to the chair."

"I cut the ties because we're leaving."

"You're leaving me here?" She looked around. "I don't even know where I am. How am I supposed to get back to—"

"I'm not leaving you, Gabby. You're coming with us."

She frowned. "Where are we going?"

"To our hotel."

Gabby studied him a moment. She glanced away and then brought those gorgeous eyes back to his. "Your team?"

Zade nodded. "There are five of us, and despite evidence to the contrary…we're the good guys."

"Right." She let out a little snort that held no humor. "I could tell."

"I promise you, we are."

And I'm going to do whatever it takes to prove that to you.

"You said you don't work for Hector Andino," she spoke softly.

"We don't."

"So who do you work for?"

Bravo was very careful when it came to sharing information about their professional lives. With Gabby, Zade knew the more he divulged about himself and his team, the better chance he had at regaining her trust.

"I work for a company called R.I.S.C. I'm on one of the company's two black ops security teams. We work in both the private sector and also take on jobs for Homeland."

Her brows rose at that. "Homeland? As in Homeland Security?"

One corner of his mouth rose slightly. "The very same."

"Are you really here to take out Andino?"

Zade nodded. "Yes."

"Good." Relief seemed to pour from her soul. Then she surprised the hell out of Zade when she added, "We can take the bastard down, together."

CHAPTER 6

Gabby wiped the condensation from the bathroom mirror. Droplets of water ran down its length as she studied her reflection.

Her long, towel-dried hair hung over one shoulder. Dark circles from lack of sleep and insurmountable stress were impossible to hide without makeup, but at this point, she was too tired to care.

Running her fingers through her damp hair, the marks on her wrists caught her eye. At first, the shower's hot water had stung when it hit her skin there, but the reddened and bruised area now felt soothed.

The hotel where Zade and his team were staying was a hell of an upgrade from the dump she'd chosen when she first arrived in La Paz. Of course, when money was limited, you stayed where you could afford.

After several weeks of endless searching for the girl she thought of as her sister, Gabby's funds were all but depleted. That left her with few—if any—choices.

Her thoughts turned to the man waiting for her on the

other side of the door, knowing she had *no* choice where he was concerned.

Zade had said he and his friends were here to take Andino out. For now, Gabby had to play along and hope to God they were telling the truth. Up to now, she'd been doing everything on her own.

Gabby had to admit, a team of black ops badasses *would* come in handy right about now. The question was how could she be certain Zade and the others were who they said they were?

Once Zade had cut her free, he'd introduced her to the men on his supposed team. To say their greetings were less than warm would be a massive understatement.

They hadn't exactly been rude, per say. But it was clear those guys trusted her about as much as she trusted them.

Which wasn't much.

Having no other choice but to go with them, Gabby had gotten into their SUV. When they pulled up to the place where she'd been staying since coming here, Zade had muttered a low curse before asking for her room key.

He then threw her off guard by ordering her to stay in the vehicle while he and the man named Matt went inside to get her clothes.

Normally, she would have bristled at the order. But she was a little more than outnumbered and decided it was best to pick her battles.

For some reason, Zade seemed even angrier by the time he got back. In fact, he didn't say more than a few clipped words to her for the remainder of the ride.

Now Gabby was here, in a posh hotel. She was clean and about to share room service with the man who'd held her captive less than an hour ago.

Probably nothing compared to what Sam's going through.

Shaking those thoughts away, Gabby slipped out of the thick robe provided by the hotel and hung it on the door's metal hook. She took her time getting dressed, dreading the conversation that would no doubt bring with it more questions.

Questions Gabby still wasn't quite sure she should answer.

Yes, Zade had *sounded* convincing when he'd told her he and his team were here to take down Andino. But then, when she'd made the comment about the two of them working together for the common cause, he'd all but shut down.

And men say we're confusing.

Knowing she couldn't hide out in the bathroom forever, Gabby filled her lungs, let the air out slowly, and opened the door. A delicious aroma filled her nostrils the second she walked into the spacious suite.

"Thought you might be hungry." Zade's low voice drew her focus to the small kitchen area on her right.

Neatly spread across the granite bar top were several different platters with various types of food.

Gabby felt her eyes widen. "Expecting an army?"

Because he'd definitely ordered enough room service to feed one.

One corner of Zade's savory mouth curved upward. "I wasn't sure what you'd want."

Stepping closer, Gabby took in the different dishes he'd had delivered. One plate had a burger and fries, the one next to it, a large plate of tacos and rice. Beside that was an enormous, grilled chicken Caesar salad with the dressing, chicken, and parmesan cheese each in their own separate container on the side.

The salad was nearly identical to the one she'd ordered during their memorable weekend together.

Gabby always ordered her dressing and other toppings

on the side because, inevitably, restaurants always gave her entirely too much.

Her eyes flew to Zade's. From the way he was looking at her, she knew. He'd remembered and had ordered the salad exactly the way she liked it.

If they were back on the island, she'd have thought it was sweet. Now Gabby hated that all she felt was suspicious.

Was he trying to butter her up? Trying to win her trust by using memories from their time together against her?

Maybe he's just being nice and trying to make up for the shitty night you've had.

Regardless, she was starving. Walking over to the bar, Gabby picked up the salad and a fork and went over to sit at the small, round table.

"Thank you."

She offered him the slightest of smiles before taking her first bite. Closing her eyes, a low moan escaped before she could stop it. The salad was even more delicious than the one she'd had the last time they were together.

Forgetting all about everything else, she took another bite. And another. It wasn't until Zade spoke again that she even realized he'd come over to the table to join her.

"When was the last time you ate?" he nearly growled.

She froze, a fork full of lettuce and goodness almost to her mouth. What was his problem? It wasn't like she'd been scarfing her food or anything.

Gabby glanced down at the salad that was already half gone. *Shit.*

"Um..." She set the fork back into her bowl and licked some dressing from her bottom lip. "I had a granola bar this morning, I think. Why?"

"That's all you've eaten today?" Zade shook his head, his tone—and current scowl—made her feel as though she were a child being scolded. "No wonder you look thinner. Your body needs more nutrients than a damn granola bar."

"I've been a little busy," she said defensively.

Yeah, she'd lost a few pounds over the last month. Who wouldn't?

Not in the mood for a chastisement over her lack of nutrition, Gabby said, "Tell me more about your team's plans to stop Hector Andino."

"Finish the salad, and then we'll talk."

She frowned. "You and your friend, Gabe, took your sweet time asking me all sorts of questions. Now it's my turn."

"Food first." He tipped his head toward her bowl. "Then we talk."

"Seriously? I'm perfectly capable of holding a conversation while I eat." Something he damn well knew.

The man's arrogant damn brow rose as he bit into the cheeseburger, and Gabby knew this wasn't an argument she was going to win. Not that she really wanted to waste time arguing out of spite.

She was too hungry, and the salad *was* amazing.

Refusing to let him think she was actually fine with his conditional agreement, Gabby gritted her teeth, picked up her fork, stabbed even more lettuce and shoved the bite into her mouth.

Zade coughed to cover up a chuckle.

On the island, he'd told her he found her feistiness adorable. *Apparently, he still does.*

When Gabby had finished her meal, she set her fork down, wiped her mouth, and crossed her arms in front of her. "There. Happy?"

He didn't answer right away. Wiping his mouth, Zade set his napkin aside and shook his head. "Not really. Tell me why you were in Grand Isle. And why you took off the way you did."

"No."

Zade blinked, clearly surprised by her defiance. "No?"

"It's my turn to ask the questions, remember? I want to know who you guys really are, who you work for, and what your plan is with Andino."

For the next several seconds, he stared at her from across the table. When Gabby thought he was going to argue, Zade sat back in his seat and said, "Okay."

Well that was a lot easier than I thought it would be.

"The guys and I work for a company called R.I.S.C., or 'Risk'. The acronym stands for rescue, intel, security, and capture. There are currently two teams, Alpha and Bravo. We're Bravo."

Gabby thought for a moment. "Is the company really based out of Dallas?"

Zade nodded. "We have an office downtown and everything. You can even Google it."

She'd be doing that the first chance she got. Still...

"I'd rather hear it from you."

He smirked. "R.I.S.C. is owned by a man named Jake McQueen."

"McQueen." Gabby repeated the name. "Why does that sound familiar?"

"Ever hear of Olivia Bradshaw?"

"Uh, who hasn't?"

Olivia Bradshaw was a nurse from Texas. She had been part of a volunteer medical group who'd gone to Africa to offer relief after a massive hurricane hit the island of Madagascar. Their group was attacked by members of a violent cartel, and everyone except Olivia had been killed.

"She was taken and held captive by the men who killed her co-workers, right?"

The story had made international news, filling every headline for weeks—on the T.V., in magazines and newspapers, and every online news and social media site in existence.

Zade nodded grimly. "She was. Thankfully Jake and the rest of Alpha Team found her and brought her home."

It seemed as if he wanted to say something else, almost like there was more to the story, but he didn't.

"So Jake McQueen owns the company and he's on one of the teams?"

"He's Alpha's team leader. Just like Gabe is Bravo's. Jake is also now Olivia's husband."

"Really?" Gabby found that surprising. And romantic.

The hero saves the girl, they fall in love and get married.

Actually, it sounded like something out of one of those romance novels her foster mom always indulged in when she thought no one was paying attention.

"Here." Zade offered her his phone.

"What's this for?"

"It's open to the phone's search engine. Type in R.I.S.C., and you'll see I'm telling the truth about the company."

Following his instructions—because she was too curious not to—Gabby waited for the information to load. She clicked on the first one and began to read.

The company's site showed no pictures of their team members, however it did mention McQueen and how each of R.I.S.C.'s operatives were highly trained individuals specializing in skills including marksmanship, hand-to-hand, demolitions, and more. It also stated every one of the company's operatives were former military and the best in their fields.

Swipe after swipe, each article about the private security firm was unique, yet they all told the same story. R.I.S.C.

protected people. They'd *helped* people, taking down some very bad men in the process.

When they first met, Zade had told her he used to be a Marine. His physique and mannerisms supported his claim, as did his behavior tonight, along with the other four men's.

It was possible he was telling the truth, but she wasn't one to trust easily.

Gabby handed him back the phone. "This doesn't prove anything. You could've picked any security company out there to claim as your place of employment."

"You're right." He set the phone on the table beside him. "I could have, but I didn't. And short of taking you to the office and personally introducing you to McQueen, or to Homeland to meet our handler, I don't really know how to prove to you that I'm telling the truth. Unfortunately, we don't have time to do either of those things, which means, you're just going to have to trust me."

She bit her bottom lip. God, she wanted to believe him. More than anything, she wanted to know *someone* out there was on her side in this.

"I didn't go into the details of my company or what I do, because honestly, most of what we do is confidential. The guys and I don't really talk about it outside the team, other than the ones who are married. I'm sure they tell their spouses what they can."

"Spouses?"

He tilted his head. "That surprises you?"

"Actually, yeah. The other guys on your team all seem so..."

"Dick-like?" Zade smirked.

Gabby couldn't help but chuckle. "Kind of."

"That's because we're on the job, and it's not a particularly pleasant one. Kole, Nate, and Matt are all married, and every member of Alpha Team is now either married or engaged. Actually, Jake and Liv just had their first kid, and one of the other guys on that team recently announced their first is on the way."

It was hard to imagine men as broody and fierce as those she'd met tonight in any sort of relationship, let alone married with children. Especially Kole.

That man could turn fire into ice, his eyes had been so cold.

"You can trust me, sweetheart," Zade continued on. "You can trust us. I know tonight wasn't exactly the best way to show it, but promise you we're the good guys. Hector Andino, on the other hand, is a terrible person who's done a lot of terrible things. The bastard needs to be stopped, which is why my team is here."

Gabby's first reaction was to remain guarded. To be suspicious until she'd been given unfaltering, tangible proof. A product of her upbringing, no doubt.

Despite her suspicious nature and what Zade and his team had done to her tonight, there was no denying the truth. Not anymore.

It was there, staring back at her. It was in the conviction in Zade's rumbling voice.

When they'd first met, Gabby's gut reaction was that this man was good. Honorable.

Also like that first night on that tiny island, Gabby found herself wanting to tell him everything. The good, the bad. All of it.

You can trust him.

The thought was instant and fierce. A truth she suddenly felt to her core.

Her heart beat forcefully inside her chest as she stared back at him. Praying she wasn't wrong, Gabby took a deep breath and said, "Hector Andino took my sister. I came here to find her and get her back."

CHAPTER 7

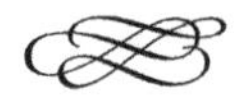

"Are you out of your ever-lovin' mind?" Zade stood and began pacing the length of his overpriced suite. "Do you have any idea how dangerous this man is?"

He couldn't believe the story she'd just told him. Couldn't believe the *danger* she'd purposely put herself in.

For weeks, Gabby had been traipsing around the country trying to track down the head of the largest sex-trafficking ring in the business. *Alone!*

Zade had the sudden urge to put her over his knee.

"Yes." The stubborn woman stood and faced him. "I know exactly how dangerous Hector Andino is. Why do you think I've been working so hard to find him? Sam's life is in danger, Zade. I can't just sit back and let this happen to her. Let him sell her like she's a...a *thing* to possess."

In that moment, she reminded him so much of the other Bravo wives. Something that terrified him.

Gracie and Kat were two of the fiercest and most determined women he'd ever met. They'd both come damn close to losing their lives this past year but had held on. They'd both fought hard and never gave up.

To hear their husbands talk, the two incredible women had even come out of it all even stronger than before.

That familiar twinge of guilt began to seep through, but Zade pushed it back. If he thought about what happened to Kat on his watch, he'd really lose his shit.

Put that shit away, man. Put. It. Away.

If he thought about it now, Zade knew he'd see Gabby in the same sort of dangerous situation, and that shit wasn't going to happen.

Not while I'm still breathing.

With her hands on her hips and that stubborn, daring expression on her face, Gabby met his stare. Goddamn, she was sexy when she was trying to prove her point.

Oh, who was he kidding? Gabriella Stevens was sexy every minute of every day.

If the situation weren't so serious, he'd take her to bed right now and do all the things he'd been dreaming of since he last saw her.

Praying she couldn't see the untimely erection forming behind his zipper, Zade blew out a breath and focused on the conversation.

"You do realize La Paz is at the top of the list of most dangerous cities in Mexico, right?"

"You're here." Gabby crossed her arms and jutted her cute-as-fuck chin even higher.

His dick twitched. *Jesus save me from headstrong women.*

"That's different," he pointed out. "I'm a—"

"Man?" Her challenging brow rose as if she were daring him to say it.

Not that stupid, sweetheart.

Zade's jaw clamped together, his control slipping. "I was going to say I'm a trained operative."

"I have training." Her adorable chin remained steady. "Just

because mine didn't come from the military doesn't mean it isn't useful."

She's talking about what she learned on the streets when she was younger.

It fucking gutted him to imagine Gabby as a child trying to survive with nothing more than a mother who didn't give two shits about her.

"Never said it wasn't, sweetheart. But it's still not the same, and you know it."

He agreed street smarts were invaluable. In *certain* situations. They wouldn't do shit to keep her safe while trying to go up against a man like Hector Andino.

"What I *know* is my sister is still out there somewhere." Gabby refused to back down. "Sam's out there, and she's going through only God knows what. Trust me, I tried doing things the 'right' way. I went to the cops with Sam's parents. We filed a missing persons report. The officer took down the information, but pretty much blew it off. Said because Sam was over eighteen and there was no evidence suggesting foul play, there wasn't a whole lot they could do."

A tear traveled over her soft cheek, and Zade's hand itched to brush it away.

"I tried telling them, Zade. I explained how Sam isn't the type of girl to leave town without telling her family where she was going. But the guy at the station's front desk refused to listen to me. If it were me, with my background, I'd understand. But this is Sam. She's good and sweet. She's not like—"

"You?"

Did she honestly think she wasn't those things and more? Zade had seen evidence of how good and sweet Gabby could be, and it pissed him the hell off that she thought less of herself.

Gabby shook her head. "She's not like me. She's better.

But it's Chicago, and the cops there have a lot bigger things to deal with than one maybe-missing twenty-five year old."

We need to talk about how you see yourself, baby. Soon.

Zade understood what she was saying in regards to the cops. He also understood where the police were coming from.

Samantha was an adult. If she wanted to take off without telling anyone, that was her right, and the cops in Chicago did have a fuck ton of other, provable crimes they had to deal with.

It sucked, but that's how it was.

That still didn't mean what Gabby had been doing was a good idea. Hell it didn't even make the *bad* idea category.

What she was doing—going off on her own to places no person, let alone an American woman should even consider going—was fucking suicidal.

"So you, what?" he continued chiding her. "Took it upon yourself to form a one-man search and rescue team?"

Gabby tossed her hands out to the side. "What was I supposed to do? It's not like I had anywhere else to go, or anyone left to turn to. The only other option would've been to simply let it go. To accept that Sam was gone and go about living our lives as usual. Could you do that, Zade?"

"I'm in a different position. It's not just me by myself, here, Gabby."

"But what if it was?" She walked toward him. "When we were in Grand Isle, you told me you had two sisters. Is that true?"

Shit. He walked right into that one. "Yes."

"What if one of them went missing without a trace?" Zade opened his mouth to say he'd turn to his teammates—because fuck, yeah, that's what he'd do—but she put a hand up to keep him from it. "Pretend for a second you're *not* on a black ops team."

Damn. She knows me better than I thought.

"Pretend one of your sisters was missing, and you have no one you could turn to for help." She stopped walking less than a foot away from him. "Would you forget about your missing sister and move on with your life, or would you do everything in your power to find her? Even if it meant putting your own safety at risk…or worse, your *life*…would you still do whatever you could to track down the son of a bitch who took her and get her back?"

Shit. Fuck. Shit.

She had him dead to rights on this one, and Zade couldn't bring himself to say anything other than the God's honest truth. "I'd walk through fire if it meant saving one of my sisters from a man like Andino."

Gabby's shoulders relaxed slightly, and her pursed lips curved upward. "Guess we're not so different after all."

"Gabby—"

"Samantha may not be my sister by blood, Zade, but we're siblings in every other sense of the word. After I was released from the juvenile detention center, I was put back in the state's custody. They put me in one of the smaller schools in hopes it would 'keep me out of trouble'."

She rolled her eyes and shook her head, and he understood why. *She* hadn't been the problem. The fucker who'd attacked her was.

Don't think I've forgotten about you, asshole.

Unaware of his plans of revenge on her behalf, Gabby kept right on talking.

"I pretty much stayed to myself because by then I knew it was too dangerous to get too close to anyone. The other kids seemed fine with it. No one ever asked me to sit with them at lunch or hang out after school. Why would they? I was the 'bad girl'."

She made air quotes before blowing out a breath and

finishing her story. “Anyway, this one day, a group of girls had cornered me by my locker after school. They were mouthing me, making fun of my clothes, and crap like that. Sam overheard them.” Gabby smiled. “There she was, a year younger and barely five feet tall, but man. She was a spitfire, even back then. Sam let those girls have it. Called each and every one out on their bullshit and told them what she thought of their behavior. After the other girls left, Sam pretty much forced me to go into the music room where her mom taught.”

“Annabelle?”

Gabby nodded. “Mrs. Shoemaker was my favorite teacher there. Between the two of them, I found myself ushered to their house for dinner. I went back the next night and the next. Before long, they were petitioning the court for full custody. I lived with them from the end of my junior year until the end of the next summer, after I graduated high school.”

Remembering what she’d told them when they’d first met, Zade asked, “Are you really a teacher?”

Her smile turned sad. “Not yet. But I hope to become one. The Shoemakers offered to pay my way through college, but I refused to let them. I told them I wanted to do that part of my life on my own. They’d already done so much, and I didn’t want to take money away from what should’ve been for Sam.”

“How did Sam feel about that?”

Gabby chuckled. “She called me a dumbass. I refused to give in, though. Annabelle and Everett didn’t have a lot of extra, but they’d worked hard their whole lives to make sure Sam’s college was paid for after she graduated. I wasn’t going to take a dime of that money.”

See? Fiercely independent.

“So what happened after you graduated high school?”

"I got a job at the neighborhood grocery store and also at one of those big, home improvement places. I found a community college that was close by and signed up for internet classes. I was nearly finished with their associate degree program when the school lost their accreditation status over some stupid clerical error. The school closed down, and just like that, I was back at square one."

"Surely you would've qualified for some sort of state grant or a student loan. Right? Something you could've used at a different school?"

One that wouldn't screw over their students.

"I could have gone that route, and hindsight, it probably would've been the smart choice. But you have to understand, I grew up with a mom who lived off of handouts. All she cared about was where her next fix was coming from, and she didn't give a damn what...or who...she had to do to get it. We used food stamps and when those ran out, she'd mooch off of her so-called friends. That or she'd find some way other than cash to pay for what she wanted."

Son of a bitch.

Zade's heart ached for the little girl this woman used to be. Not only was Gabby's mom a druggie, she'd whored herself out to *get* the drugs.

It was a miracle Gabby hadn't gotten caught up in the life, too.

Thank Christ that didn't happen.

It was no wonder Gabby didn't want a hand-out from the state for her schooling. Zade understood and respected her need to pay for college on her own terms.

"Is that where you work now?" he asked. "The home improvement store?"

"It was."

His gut tightened. "What happened?"

"After we got nowhere with the authorities, Sam's dad

came to me. Everett begged me to try to find her. He was well-aware of my time living on the streets, both before and after my mom went to prison. Between that and my stint in juvie, he assumed I still had connections in what he called the 'seedy' parts of town."

Part of him understood Everett Shoemaker's decision to ask Gabby for help. He was a father desperate to find his only daughter. Except she *wasn't* his only.

The second he and his wife agreed to take Gabby in, she'd become theirs.

Apparently, the man was willing to sacrifice one to save the other. *That* made Zade want to find the man and beat the shit out of him.

"Was he right?" Zade asked her. "Did you know people who could help?" Obviously she did, or she wouldn't have made it this far.

Embarrassed, Gabby nodded, confirming his thoughts. "I made a lot of…contacts in the years before Sam's parents took me in. I learned a lot about a side of life most people don't even realize is there."

Zade understood that. His time in the military and with R.I.S.C. taught him all about the dark, terrifying evils that existed in the world.

"I started spending every spare second I could tracking those people down," she continued. "Soon, it began to interfere with my job. I called in sick a lot in order to walk the city looking for information on Sam. I finally went and talked to my boss. I explained what had happened and asked if I could take a leave of absence so I could keep searching. He told me he understood my need to find Sam and felt really bad about it all. But then he said if I wasn't making my shifts every week, he'd have no choice but to find someone else who could."

"What did you do?"

"I quit." She shrugged. "I knew I wasn't going to stop until I found Sam, but my boss…he was a good guy. I didn't want him to have to make that call."

Damn. Even in the midst of her own, personal hell, Gabby was still taking other people's feelings into consideration.

You're a much better person than you realize, baby. Why can't you see that?

Running a hand over his jaw, Zade took a minute to consider all she'd told him. "With no job, how did you manage to travel the places needed to track down Andino? Louisiana's a hell of a long way from Chicago."

Travel. Food. Lodging. That shit wasn't cheap.

"Everett had a separate savings account," she explained. "One Anna didn't know about. He's been secretly putting money back for years with the plan of surprising Anna with a grand vacation for their fortieth wedding anniversary next year. He said he was going to take her to Paris. Instead, he gave me the money and told me to do whatever it took to find his daughter."

Zade shook his head because he couldn't imagine what those poor parents were going through. Or what it had been like for Gabby to be put in such an impossible position.

"Tell me about Grand Isle." He changed the topic. His voice was steady, but damn if he didn't feel as though he were standing on rocky ground.

A slight blush began crawling up her neck, and Gabby hugged herself again. The reason for the move was obvious.

She was trying to put a barrier between them. Protecting herself.

Yeah, we'll have to work on that, sweetheart.

Because he was the last person she needed to hide from.

Gabby cleared her throat. "What about it?"

"Why were you there? Did you find a lead that took you to the island, or…" He let his voice trail off.

Biting her lip, a nervous habit he'd noticed right away, Gabby hesitated a couple of seconds before answering. "I had a lead that took me to New Orleans. A guy I knew, knew a guy who knew a guy...you know how it goes."

Zade nodded.

"Anyway." She waved it off. "Someone recognized Sam from the photo I had circulating throughout my contacts. Supposedly this person knew of a trafficking ring running girls from New Orleans to Mexico. Word got back to me, so I hopped the first flight I could get and went to the Big Easy to meet the guy."

"And?"

"He never showed." Gabby sighed and looked away. "I asked around. Looked all over the city for him. At first, no one seemed to know anything. I called my contact. He had the same issue finding the source. Said it was like the guy had vanished. Then I found out he'd been arrested on a breaking and entering charge and was being held at the city jail. I went there, but they weren't allowing any visitors other than family. So that ended that."

Zade's gut churned at the thought of Gabby walking the streets of New Orleans alone. At least she was familiar with Chicago. Had grown up there.

New Orleans was a different beast altogether.

"Why go to Grand Isle?"

"To hide out." Her eyes met his again. "I was angry and sad. I felt so *hopeless.*" She shook her head. "My funds were starting to run low, and the only real lead I'd come across had disappeared. The idea of going back to Chicago without Sam..." Gabby swallowed, breaking eye contact again. "I know it was a totally selfish move, but I couldn't bear the thought of facing Everett. Of telling him that, after all he and Anna had done for me, I'd failed them. So I went to Grande Isle because I wanted a few days to think about something other than what Sam was probably going through. I wanted to *feel* something more than the desperation and sadness...the hopelessness that had consumed my soul."

Gabby stared up at him, her emerald eyes swimming with unshed tears. "You did that for me, Zade," she whispered softly. "You gave me exactly what I needed when I needed it, and I have never felt more passion or more joy than when I was in your arms. I'll never forget that."

A tear escaped, but she caught it before it could fall. She looked away from him again.

You need to stop doing that, baby.

"Hey." Zade closed the distance between them. "Look at me." When Gabby refused, he decided to help her along. With his thumb and forefinger at her chin, he gently lifted her head so she would face him once more. "If what you're telling me is true"—she started to pull away at his words, but Zade finished before she got the chance—"and I believe that it *is*...then you have nothing to feel bad about."

"I spent Everett's entire savings, Zade. I chased my tail, following one lead to another and then another. I cashed in favors from people I never wanted to see, let alone talk to again, and for what?" Her voice cracked. "Samantha's still missing, and I'm—"

"We're going to find her, Gabby," he vowed solemnly. "My team and I will stop Hector Andino, and we will do everything in our power to find Sam and bring her home."

Another tear slid from the corner of her eye. This time, Zade was the one who caught it.

"I missed you." He brushed his thumb across her smooth skin. He hadn't meant to say those words out loud, but he didn't regret telling her.

Gabby's pupils widened, the green surrounding them becoming dark with arousal. "I missed you, too."

"I have to ask." Zade swallowed tightly. "Why did you sneak away?"

"Honestly?"

Zade nodded. "Of course." He waited patiently for her answer.

After a moment's hesitation, she said, "The time we spent together was…incredible. The best three days of my life."

If his dick wasn't already hard, those words would've made it stand up and cheer.

"But?"

Gabby sighed. "But when you asked me to come to Texas with you…I don't know. It was like I got slammed with this enormous sense of guilt."

"Guilt?"

Her eyes began to well again. "Sam was missing, and every piece of evidence I could find said she'd been taken by that sadistic prick, Andino. Yet there I was living it up with you on a beautiful island. Dancing and eating. Making love for hours on end." She swiped at another stray tear. "When you asked me to come to Dallas, I wanted to say yes *so* badly. But the second you went into the bathroom to shower, it hit me."

"What hit you?"

"How selfish I was being."

"You weren't being selfish, sweetheart." He cupped her face. "You were being human."

She shook her head. "What kind of person goes off to find their missing sister and decides to make a weekend of it with a handsome stranger?"

"Stop." He stared down at her. "You already explained that. You were upset, and you didn't know how to face Sam's parents. Wanting to escape all that for a little while is perfectly normal, Gabby."

"I know. I'm just explaining what was going through my head at the time."

He wasn't so sure that was the case but decided not to press the issue.

"And now?" Zade brushed some hair from her forehead and tucked it behind her ear. "What's going on in your head, now?"

The green in her eyes darkened. Her luscious lips parted. "I—"

Someone knocked on the door, cutting her off.

As if the sound had broken the spell, Gabby stepped back, just out of his reach.

Damn it. "Stay here."

Pulling his weapon from the back of his waistband, Zade moved silently across the room's soft carpet. Looking through the peephole, he sighed, slipping the gun against this lower back where it had been before.

From over his shoulder he caught her eye and said, "It's Gabe."

All traces of the heat he'd seen mere seconds before had vanished, replaced by a cool, guarded expression.

That's okay, baby. We'll get there again, soon.

Releasing the chain guard and flipping the lock, Zade opened the door to greet his team leader.

"Hey, Dawson. What's up?"

"Just checking in. Wanted to see how things were going with Miss Stevens." The man's eyes slid over Zade's shoulder and back to Zade.

Things were about to go really fucking well until you knocked on the damn door.

"Good." Zade stepped aside. "Come on in. You're gonna want to hear what she has to say."

"Should we call the others?"

"Yes, please," Gabby answered for him.

Both men swung their heads in her direction.

She gave Gabe a pointed look. “It was bad enough going through it all with Zade. I’d prefer to not have to repeat the same story over and over again.” As if she realized how short she sounded, Gabby cleared her throat before offering a softer, “If you don’t mind.”

Gabe looked at Zade, back to Gabby, and then back to Zade. “Okay, then. Send out a group text and get their asses in here. Sooner we figure out our next step, the sooner we stop Andino.”

CHAPTER 8

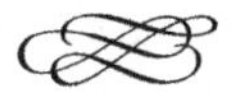

"So that's it." Gabby looked at the intimidating men staring back at her. "That's everything."

The entire Bravo Team was huddled around the suite. They'd all listened quietly as Gabby had repeated what she'd told Zade before they'd joined them.

In an attempt to avoid a bunch of questions afterward, she'd decided to share it all. The lead that had taken her to New Orleans, why she went to Grand Isle. All of it.

She'd even explained that her guilt is what drove her to run out on Zade the way she had. Thought maybe it would make her a little more likeable in their eyes.

If they liked her, they'd be more apt to help her.

"So let me get this straight," Kole addressed Gabby directly. "You're saying you and our boy, here, showing up at the same island at the same time, and then again in La Paz was nothing more than pure coincidence?"

Coincidence or fate. Take your pick.

"Yes."

"And Shoemaker went to you for help. The guy entrusted

you with his entire life's savings, all because you spent some time in juvie and practically grew up on the streets?"

Rather than shrink back or look ashamed, Gabby kept her spine straight and her voice strong when she answered the suspicious operative. "Yes."

"Gabby was his foster daughter, Kole," Zade told his friend. "He had every reason to trust her."

She slid Zade a look. Damn, he was adorable when he was being protective.

Still, he needed to know she could handle herself.

"Everett knew what my life was like before," she spoke up in her own defense. "He studied human culture. The man understands better than most the way people like my mother and I lived."

"People like you?" Kole stared over at her. "You mean homeless?"

"Kole." Zade shot his friend a narrowed gaze. The warning in his tone was impossible to miss.

"It's okay, Zade." Gabby gave him a tight smile before bringing her gaze back to the suspicious man's. "To answer your question, Kole, Yes. My mother and I were without a home for a stretch of time. A few times, actually. But I'm not only referring to the homeless. I'm talking about men and women who grow up with nothing and have to fight for everything. There's a sort of…code, I guess you'd call it."

"She's right, Jameson."

All eyes went to the man Zade had introduced as Nate. The supposed genius of the group explained further.

"The States are filled with hundreds of different cultures, including those who live in low-income areas or on the streets. They all have their own way of doing things. Their own hierarchy of power and control. A way they do business and their own way of *handling* their business."

"Exactly." Gabby nodded. She understood precisely what

Nate was saying. "The two most valuable things to people who live on the street are trust and loyalty. If those two qualities aren't there, a person's out of that group before they ever had the chance to join. In many ways, life in that type of setting is actually a lot like it was when this country was first established."

Matt looked genuinely curious. "Meaning?"

"Your word is your bond," Gabby told him.

"And these people from your past," Gabe joined in. "The ones who helped you find your leads on your sister's whereabouts. They trusted you enough, even after all these years, to help you?"

Gabby looked him square in the eye. "Yes."

"Why?" Kole spoke up again. Clearly, he was the one who would need to most convincing.

"Because when I knew them back in the day, I helped them." Gabby shrugged. "They owed me." When the men in the room shared a look, she quickly added, "It's not what you're thinking. When I was younger, I'd watch their kids while they looked for jobs. Or for those who were lucky enough to find one, I babysat while they worked. I didn't charge them anything more than the occasional meal. I like kids, and it gave me something to do. Plus, my mom wasn't around much."

Babysitting also meant she didn't have to spend her days all alone.

Refusing to look Zade's way for fear she'd see pity in his eyes, she continued on, "As I got older and found myself moving around from this area to that, I had a tendency to gravitate toward the groups that were 'in the know', so to speak. I never got involved in their illegal dealings, though they sometimes asked me to. They never pushed, mainly because I helped them in other ways."

Gabe studied her closely. "Like what?"

"I taught some of them how to read on the side. It helped them appear more intelligent to their…associates. Thankfully learning always came very easily to me." A handy characteristic to have when you went from school to school because your mom couldn't seem to stay in one place for more than a month or two.

The group was quiet as they processed what she was saying.

"My point in all this"—she summed it up for them—"is all the things I did for these people was all stuff that most people would consider simple or beneath them. But to those I helped along the way…those little things meant a lot."

"So when you went to them for help, they were happy to do it," Matt surmised.

"Exactly." Gabby's heart felt heavy. "I thought it was paying off, too. Until tonight. Now I know it was all for nothing."

"Why do you say that?" Zade asked from his place beside her.

She met his gaze. "I was finally going to make contact with Hector Andino tonight. Then you guys showed up and"—she looked around the room—"here we are. I don't know if he went to the club tonight, or if he'll be there tomorrow. Either way, I'm pretty sure I've lost my chances with him."

"Your *chances* with him?" Zade's brows rose in a high arch.

Gabby had a feeling he wasn't going to like this part. But a girl's gotta do what a girl's gotta do, right?

"I…may have heard Andino has a thing for redheads." She bit her lip as that little tidbit sank in.

It took all of two seconds.

"You were hoping to *hook up* with him?" Muttering a low curse, Zade shot up from the couch and swung around. He stared down at her with a look of shock and anger. "I thought you were going there to follow him or something."

Yep. He's pissed.

"I wasn't trying to hook up with the sick bastard, but yes. I was hoping to catch his eye."

"Catch his eye?" Zade looked down at her like she'd lost her damn mind.

At this point, she was beginning to think maybe she had.

Even so, Gabby refused to let him or anyone else make her feel bad for doing the only thing she could to try to save the woman she considered her sister.

Rising to her feet, she faced off with the very pissed off man. "Yes, Zade. I wanted to catch his eye. I thought maybe, if I could get close enough to him, I could find out more about his business. Overhear a conversation or see something that would lead me to where Sam is being held."

"That's actually not a bad idea," Nate commented.

If looks could kill, the one Zade gave his friend in that moment would've been lethal. "Are you out of your fucking mind?"

"Just hear me out." Nate held up a hand. He looked at her then back to Zade. "What if Gabby could get close to Andino?" When Zade started shaking his head before his friend had even finished the question, Nate added, "Not by herself. With you there, too."

Wait, what?

Confused, Gabby looked over at Nate. "I don't understand."

The handsome tech guy explained, "I've done a shit ton of reading on human trafficking, lately. Most of the buyers in this game are wealthy, middle-aged men. But sometimes it's a woman. They're either looking for a girl for themselves or a boyfriend or spouse, or a woman will act on a buyer's behalf."

"Like the middleman?" Matt asked.

"Exactly." Nate nodded. "Oftentimes, those women meet with the seller ahead of the actual sale." He looked over at Zade. "And they're almost always accompanied by at least one bodyguard. If not more."

Gabe was the next to speak. "So you're saying we send Gabby in, posing as a buyer with Zade as her bodyguard?"

"That's what I'm thinking," Nate answered his boss. "We can run the idea by Ghost tonight, see if his team has any objections. If not, I think it's our best shot at getting close to Andino's operation." Nate's eyes found Gabby's. "That is, if you agree to it, of course. You don't have to, by any means. Not gonna lie, it's a dangerous assignment. I'm sure you'll want to take a few minutes to think abou—"

"I'll do it!" Gabby blurted, cutting him off.

"No." Zade scowled at the others and then her. "No way."

With her hands now resting on her narrow hips, Gabby glared up at him. "I don't recall asking for your permission."

Zade put his hands on his *own* hips and leaned in toward her. "This is not happening."

Gabby refused to back down. "*This* is a chance to save Sam. This is also not your decision to make."

A muscle in his jaw twitched as he clenched his teeth together. She expected him to yell or scream. Instead, Zade's voice turned scary low.

Eyes still locked with hers, he said, "Give us the room."

Much to her surprise—and a little to her dismay—the other men started moving toward the door without so much as a peep.

As they began filtering out of the room, Zade slowly made his way closer to her, not stopping until he'd closed the gap between them.

Needing him to understand, Gabby started talking the second they left.

"Look, I get your job is to be the protector and all that, but I'm willing to do whatever I can to help—"

Zade grabbed the back of her neck and slammed his mouth against hers. Electricity jolted where their lips met, and when his tongue pressed its way inside, Gabby forgot everything she'd been about to say.

Though the kiss was sudden and more than a little unexpected, she wasn't about to waste time questioning it or, God forbid, stopping it.

Instead Gabby tilted her head, opening her mouth wider in order to take as much of him in as she could. Her hands fisted the material covering his taut chest as she rose onto her tiptoes and pulled him closer.

By the time Zade broke away, they were both fighting to catch their breaths.

"W-what was that for?" She blinked up at him.

"I've wanted to do that since we saw you in the club." He brushed her bottom lip with his thumb. "Actually, I've thought about little else since the last time we kissed."

"Oh." Gabby blinked some more, still working to slow her breath. "I thought you were mad at me."

"I can't stand the thought of you being in the same room as a man like Hector Andino. You being close enough to talk to him?" Zade shook his head. "That shit terrifies me."

The independent woman in her wanted to tell him where he could shove his controlling ways. Another part, however —the part that knew he'd gone all caveman because he cared about her—that part couldn't help but think it was a little sweet.

Even so, "Sam is still out there, Zade," she reminded him. "I can't stop looking for her. Not when I've come this far."

He cupped her cheek. "We can figure something else out. Something that doesn't involve you going into the lion's den."

Gabby's eyes filled with unshed tears. "Thank you. For helping me. For...caring. After the way I left you—"

He pressed a finger to her lips, cutting her off. "You don't ever have to thank me for helping you. As for Grand Isle, that's all in the past."

She could tell by the way he was looking at her that he meant it. "Okay."

"I do want you to promise me one thing."

Aaand here comes the catch. *There's always a catch.*

"What's that?"

"You won't put yourself in harm's way, again. Not for any reason."

Gabby rested her palm against his chest, directly over his racing heart. "I'm sorry, but I can't promise you that."

Worry crossed over his face. "Gabby, please."

"If there's something I can do to help Sam and those other girls, I can't ignore that, Zade. Not for you or anyone else. I'm sorry."

Zade closed his eyes and leaned his forehead against hers. "What am I going to do with you?"

Whatever you want.

That's what Gabby wanted to say. What she actually said was, "Who's Ghost?"

Zade lifted his head. "He's the leader of a special forces team we're working with to bring down Andino's organization."

"They're here...in La Paz?"

He nodded. "They're close by."

"Then have Ghost set everything up. I'll pose as a buyer, and you can pretend to be my protector."

"No pretending here, baby." Zade's eyes seemed to stare straight into her soul. "I'll always protect you. But I don't want to do it like this. There has to be another way. We just have to find it." His eyes widened as if a lightbulb had suddenly lit up. "We'll bring in another operative. A female who can—"

"There isn't time for that, Zade," Gabby interrupted him. "*Sam* doesn't have time for that. Trust me, I don't want to do this, either. If there was another way, I'd be the first one to jump on board with it, but I'm already here, and as much as I hate to think about it, I'm his type. We can use that. If we go back to the club tomorrow and he's there, I'll make sure Andino notices me."

The skin between his dark brows became furrowed. "That's what scares me."

Gabby raised her hand to his cheek, the stubble there tickling her fingertips. "I can do this, Zade. *We* can do this. Together."

Concern swept over his features. "You're a civilian, Gabby. You're not—"

"Please," she practically begged, interrupting his attempt to talk her out of this. "I swear to you I can pull this off. I just need you to trust me."

It was a pretty tall order, given recent events, but Gabby knew she was right about this.

With a low curse, Zade took her mouth into his, halting the discussion in the most delicious of ways. He took the kiss slow and deep, his tongue dancing with hers as if they had all the time in the world.

When he pulled back, his eyes were dark and hungry, his impressive erection pressing against her lower belly.

"How is it possible?" she whispered.

"What?"

"This. Us. We hardly know each other. I've lied to you about almost everything, and yet..."

"I know." He nibbled her bottom lip again. "Our connection doesn't make sense to me either, but that doesn't make it any less real."

Oh, it's real, all right. Gabby could feel it to the very depths of her soul.

"Stay here," Zade kissed her forehead and headed for the door.

"Where are you going?"

"To talk to Gabe. This whole thing may not even be possible. It's all going to depend on whether or not we find Andino again, whether he buys your cover…there's a fuck load of unknowns with something like this, but…" He turned back around to face her. His eyes locked with hers as his hand curled around the doorknob. "We'll never know unless we try."

She smiled. "Thank you."

He shook his head. "Don't thank me yet, sweetheart. Not sure you understand what you just signed up for."

All of a sudden, Gabby found herself wondering if he was talking about the undercover mission or something else.

It didn't matter, either way.

There was no doubt she was ready and willing to risk herself for Sam. But was she ready to risk her heart for a man like Zade?

Gabby watched him walk out of the room.

He was going to tell his team leader he was on board with Nate's plan. A plan that would put them both in danger.

Not only was he going to help her get Sam back, Zade was also playing a very active role in taking down one of the most abominable human beings on the planet.

So was she willing to risk her heart for a man like that?

Staring at the closed door, she whispered, "You bet your ass, I am."

When he came back twenty minutes later, Gabby *thought* she'd get the chance to tell him that. To finally have the kind of reunion she'd been fantasizing about since the moment he stepped into that shower and she'd snuck away.

While he was busy talking to Gabe, she'd conjured up a new fantasy. One that involved Zade returning to the room and shoving her up against a wall.

That's what she'd *hoped* would happen.

Instead, he'd returned to the room only to rush her out and down into the team's SUV. The only explanation he'd given was that they were meeting with this Ghost character and his team to go over the new plan.

The one she'd insisted they go with.

Me and my big mouth.

So they'd have to wait. After all, anticipation wasn't necessarily a bad thing, right?

Twenty minutes later, they were pulling up to the abandoned house Zade and his team had first taken her to. *Was that only a few hours ago?*

With a quick glance over her shoulder, she noticed Gabe and the rest of Bravo were following closely behind.

A million thoughts ran through her head at once.

Had he changed his mind about her?

Was she wrong about Zade?

Had this all been a trick to try to get her to talk about... whatever it is they thought she was hiding?

Not that she was hiding. Not anymore.

Gabby had told them *everything.* Split herself wide open for Zade and his teammates by sharing the truth about her past in all its ugly truth.

Could that be it? They'd gotten everything they wanted from her, and now they were turning her over to someone else?

"W-why are we back here?"

Gabby hated that her voice sounded so unsteady, but

could he blame her? She and Zade got out of the SUV and started toward the house.

Oh, God.

What if this Ghost person wasn't really someone wanting to help? What if he and his team had been given orders to take her back to the States like Zade had said while she'd still been tied to that chair? What if—

"Relax, baby." Zade threaded his fingers with hers and gave her a little squeeze. "We're meeting Ghost and his team here because this area has already been cleared and secured."

Gabby's eyes flew to his. "How did you…"

"That connection we talked about?" His gaze darkened. "Soul deep."

Warmth spread throughout her chest.

Before she could think of a response, Zade pulled her to a stop and leaned in so only she could hear his next words.

"We've got three magical days and a shit ton of baggage between us, but whatever this is…whatever's happening here, it's stronger and more real than anything I've ever felt before."

No one. *No one* had ever said anything like that to her before.

Gabby licked her lips. "It's crazy and probably the worst timing ever, but I feel the same way about you."

"Good to know." Zade's mouth curled into a boyish grin. "Now come on. Faster we get this plan set up, the faster I can get you back to the hotel room."

With a wink, he stepped back and pushed the structure's rickety door open. He went in first rather than hold the door open for her.

Always protecting me.

Forcing the unspoken promise of what would happen once they were back at the hotel away—which, after that little speech of his had better be a whole lot of sex—Gabby followed Zade into the small house she'd hoped to never see again.

Lit up by a handful of work lamps strategically placed around the room, her eyes landed on a group of very large, very intense-looking men waiting to greet them.

Dressed in jeans and t-shirts, they all had the same sort of casual-yet-stoic thing going on.

Definitely military.

"King." One of the men stepped forward to greet Zade. "Thanks for coming all the way back out here."

"No problem," Zade released her hand to offer it to the other man. He looked at her from over his shoulder. "This is Gabriella Stevens. Gabby, this is Ghost."

"Pleasure to meet you, Miss Stevens." The man's large hand swallowed hers.

"Please, call me Gabby."

"All right, Gabby." He smiled, the move making him appear less scary. "This is my team. That's Truck, Coach, Fletch, and Hollywood."

Ghost pointed to each of the men respectively. All four tipped their heads and greeted her with a kind smile.

It was obvious they all used nicknames. She assumed it was to protect their real identity on jobs like this one.

The origins of Ghost, Truck, and Hollywood were pretty easy to figure out. However, Gabby had no clue where the names Coach and Fletch had come from.

The one called Ghost had short, brown hair and the same stoic, badass look Zade had. Her guess was the guy was probably really good at the whole secret spy stealthy stuff, hence the nickname.

Truck clearly came by his name honestly. The guy was an enormously large dude. Like six and a half feet tall large.

With a scar on his cheek and a nose that had been broken at least once, everything about the man screamed *stay the hell away*. Everything except an innate kindness she could see shining behind his pretty, blue eyes.

The man Zade had introduced as Hollywood was...well, to be honest the dark-haired, brown-eyed god of a man was flat-out, panty-dropping gorgeous.

Not that Gabby would drop her panties for him or any other man who wasn't Zade. Her panties practically incinerated into a pile of ashes whenever he was around.

Stop thinking about your panties!

It was a damn hard thing to do, especially when Zade was near. Especially after the comment he'd made about the hotel room.

Yep, one look at Zade King and Gabby found herself wanting to toss those puppies aside, hop on board, and ride that man like the wind.

Seriously, Gabriella.

Stop. With. The. Panties.

"No Beatle or Fish?" Zade's voice snapped her back to the situation at hand. "And where are...shit. What are the other guys' names?"

Ghost chuckled, his very deep voice rumbling low. "Beatle, Fish, Chase, Blade, and Colt are on loan to another De—" the guy cut himself off, his eyes sliding to hers then back to Zade's—"uh...they're working a separate project."

"Copy that."

Zade gave the other man a look that said he understood perfectly. Gabby did not. From the expressions on the men's faces, she never would, and she was one hundred percent A-Okay with that.

The less I know, the better.

"So, Gabby." Ghost looked down at her. "I hear you have a sister who needs saving."

Gabby nodded. "Yes. And I'm willing to do whatever it takes to make that happen."

The corner of Ghost's lips twitched. "So I hear." To the entire group, he said, "Dawson filled me in on the gist of their plan when he called earlier. I think Bravo's on the right track, but we've got a lot of fine-tuning to do so let's get to it."

CHAPTER 9

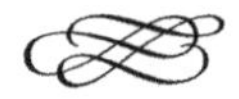

This sucks huge fucking donkey balls.

From the corner of his eye, Zade watched Gabby as he and Kole nursed their drinks. The two operatives talked and laughed, pretending as though they were simply two buddies out for a night of fun.

In reality, Zade was wound tighter than a roll of ones at a Vegas strip club. He hated everything about this plan. Why?

Because Gabby was a part of it.

If it were any other job…any other *woman,* it would be different. No, he wouldn't like the idea of putting a woman—operative or otherwise—within arm's reach of a guy like Andino.

But Gabby wasn't just any woman. She was his.

"Dude."

Zade turned to Kole and frowned. "What?"

"We're supposed to be having fun, remember?"

"And?"

"*And…*you hold that glass any tighter, the damn thing's gonna shatter."

Glancing down at his hand, Zade saw how white his

knuckles were. *Shit.* With a stretch of his hand, he forced himself to relax.

"We shouldn't be here. *She* shouldn't fucking be here."

"We've gone over the plan a million times, man. She's got this."

"She's a civilian, Kole. With absolutely no formal training whatsoever."

"You heard what Gabe said when we were going over all the shit earlier. Guys like Andino would probably spot someone with that kind of training from a mile away. Probably why he's been spooked all those times before."

"We're trained," Zade pointed out.

"For us, it's different. We're *supposed* to be trained because, in this little scenario, she's hired us to protect her. Trust me, Gabby will come off more believable this way."

The guy had a point, but Zade hated that fucking point with every tensed-up fiber of his being.

His eyes slid to where she stood. She looked mouthwatering in her black leather skirt and sheer, white blouse. The matching lace tank beneath it covered up her perfect breasts —barely, and her red heels…

God, they made Zade think of all the things he wanted to do to her while she wore nothing *but* those fuck-me heels. Things he was planning to do to her tonight, after they got her the hell out of this place and back to the hotel.

They just had to make sure she didn't wind up dead before that could happen.

No! He couldn't think like that.

"We're ten feet away, man." Kole's voice interrupted his thoughts. "Nothing's gonna happen to her."

Zade forced his gaze back onto his friend. "Kat was *two* feet away and look what happened to her."

"Jesus, man. You gotta let that shit go."

"Easy for you to say. You weren't the one in charge of

protecting her. You weren't the one who let her slip through your goddamn fingers and into the hands of that asshole, Walker."

Adrian Walker was a former military man who'd served alongside Matt for a while. Then the guy went AWOL and started working for the other side.

He was a lethal thorn in Bravo's side and had taken part in both Gracie's and Kat's abductions. Walker was a gun for hire—the most expensive around—and damn good at his fucked-up job.

"You didn't *let* anything happen to Kat, or to the cop Walker shot. So shut the fuck up with that shit."

Kole never was one to pull any punches.

"You know what I mean," Zade muttered as he pretended to take another sip.

"Yeah." Kole nodded. "I do. I also know you blaming yourself for what happened to Kat would be like me blaming myself for my diagnosis. There wasn't anything we could've done differently to prevent either one of those things. I know that. Hell, the whole team knows that. You've got to get it through that thick fucking skull of yours."

Kole, one of the most talented snipers Zade had ever seen, was diagnosed with relapsing-remitting MS. The news came as one hell of a shock to them all, but especially Kole and his now-wife, Sarah.

Thankfully, RRMS isn't a death sentence like most people think.

The two were engaged to be married, and after a fluke injury on the job, Kole's doctors discovered the disease. The news put Kole into a major funk for a stretch, worrying the hell out of all of them.

During that same time, Sarah became victim of a stalker. As bad as that situation was for both her and Kole, it turned out to be a blessing in disguise of sorts.

Knowing Sarah needed him had snapped Kole out of his depression. He saved her from the asshole watching her, and they'd been happy ever since.

Having gone into remission shortly after his diagnosis, the badass was able to continue his full duties as Bravo's lead sniper. So far—thank fuck—Kole hadn't had any further issues.

"You being diagnosed with a disease is a little different than my being shot."

"Is it?" The man's brow arched high. "Both were completely out of our control. The only difference is mine was internal and what happened to you was because you were pinned in a fucking car."

Zade started to shake his head, but Kole persisted. "If you could've reached your gun, would you have shot Walker?"

"What the hell kind of question is that?"

The other man repeated the question, enunciating every word as he spoke. "Would you have shot and killed Adrian Walker?"

"Hell yes, I would've killed him."

Kole smiled. "There ya go."

"There I *go*?"

"You know as well as I do, you would've put a bullet between that fucker's eyes if you'd been able to. But you couldn't. *That's* what you're pissed off about." Kole's brown eyes stared back at him knowingly. "You didn't let it happen, Zade. It happened. Period. If it were me sitting in that driver's seat when that car wrecked, I'm the one who would've been trapped. I'm the one who would've been shot."

"But it wasn't you."

"No. It wasn't. If it had been, would you be sitting there judging me like you're judging yourself?"

"Kole—"

"If I had been the one driving Kat that day, would you blame me for what happened to her?"

"I know what you're doing." Zade shook his head.

"I'm asking a fucking question, and I want a goddamn answer. Would you—"

"No, okay! I wouldn't fucking blame you!" Zade yelled loudly enough the bartender and those in the immediate area —including Gabby—turned and looked at them.

With an almost indiscernible tip of his chin, he let her know all was well and gave Kole a forced smile. "You trying to blow our cover?"

"Nope." Kole pretended to take a swig of his beer. "Just trying to pull your head out of your ass for you."

Zade stared at his friend and teammate. He thought about what the other man had been through, and how worried they'd all been for Kole during his ordeal.

They're worried about you, too.

He knew that. But he'd been too caught up in his own pity party to accept what they'd all told him as truth.

What happened in the car that day could've happened to anyone.

The problem was it hadn't happened to just anyone. It had happened to *him*, and he didn't know how to get past that.

You need to, dipshit. Gabby's counting on you.

The voice in his head was right. So was Kole. It was high time he got his head out of his ass and focused on the now, rather than the past.

But damn, he really hated having to admit that.

"Thanks, man. Guess I needed to hear that."

"So did I, once upon a time."

Zade studied his friend for a moment. "Nate?"

Kole snorted. "That bastard tore me a new one when he found me hiding away in my cabin."

"He come down hard on you, too?" He took a small drink.

"You could say that." The other man grinned. "Nate came to the cabin and called me out on my shit. Told me to stop being such a douche canoe and get my ass back home to Sarah, where I belonged."

Nearly choking on his beer, Zade wiped his mouth with the back of his hand. "Douche canoe?"

Shrugging, Kole grinned. "Not one of my finest moments, I'll admit. But that's pretty much how I was acting, and Nate wasn't afraid to let me know it. As hard as it was to listen to, it was what I needed to hear."

Understanding slapped him in the face, and Zade realized what had just happened.

Kole had tossed down a hefty dose of tough love to help him out, the same way Nate had helped Kole.

The fucker was paying it forward.

"Well played, asshole." Zade's words held no bite.

Looking cocky as fuck, Kole smirked. "You'll thank me later."

"I will?"

The other man set his beer down and turned to him. "Your girl standing down there?" He tipped his head toward where Gabby was standing. "She's a tough one. You think she'd ever go for a guy who spends his days drowning in self-pity?"

With a quick glance Gabby's way, Zade looked back at his friend. "And here I thought you didn't like her."

"I didn't *trust* her." Kole shrugged unapologetically. "There's a difference."

"What changed your mind?"

"She did. Last night, when she was telling us about her sister, I could see the pain behind her eyes."

"Good thing, too, since I was about two seconds away

from knocking your ass to the ground for grilling her like you were."

"You're my teammate, Zade." Kole got serious for a moment. "My friend."

"So you were, what…pushing her into proving herself?"

Another shrug. "I've got your back, brother. We all do, whether you want it or not. Although, I'll admit, I may have come down on Gabby a little harder than necessary." He looked chagrined. "Sorry, about that."

"I'm not the one you need to apologize to." Zade looked Gabby's way again. It was nearly impossible to keep his eyes off her and not because he was supposed to be protecting her.

The woman was the whole package, all neatly wrapped in leather and lace. A gift Zade couldn't wait to get home and unwrap.

He'd hoped to delve into that particular bit of heaven last night, but after their meeting with the Delta guys, Gabby had been completely spent.

With her head resting on his shoulder, she'd fallen asleep on the way back to the hotel. Didn't even stir when Zade slid her out of the SUV and carried her up to their room.

As much as he'd wanted to slide into her warm heat—and God, had he wanted to—Zade had decided not to wake her. Instead, he'd slid up next to her and pulled her close.

It was the best night's sleep he'd had in weeks.

They'd woken this morning to a phone call from Gabe telling them he and Gabby had fifteen minutes to get dress and be in the hotel lobby. Ghost and his team wanted to meet and discuss some new intel they could use for tonight's operation.

The two teams went over the plan again and again…and *again* to make sure Gabby was comfortable with how it was going to work. Afterward, Zade and Kole took her on an impromptu hair, nail, and spa treatment at one of the local resorts—a suggestion of Ghost's so Gabby could look the part she needed to play.

Not that she wasn't already stunning. The woman had a natural beauty unlike anyone Zade had ever laid eyes on. But with the tweaks in their plan, she needed to come off wealthy and refined, but also have a bit of a party girl inside.

That last part was thrown in there because Andino had already spotted her once. If he remembered Gabby from the club the other night, and chances were he would, she'd need to be ready to explain the slight change in her appearance.

After the spa and a quick shopping spree—courtesy of Zade's company credit card—the three of them grabbed a quick bite to eat before returning to the hotel to get ready for tonight.

In short, he and Gabby had little to no alone time. Something Zade planned to rectify the second they got back to the hotel.

His phone buzzed with a text from Nate.

Turn on coms. Target is pulling up.

Parked down the street from the club's entrance, Nate, Ghost, and Ghost's teammate, Truck, were hanging out in a van Delta had somehow managed to procure. Before coming here tonight, Nate and Truck set up all the electronic equipment.

Showing Kole the message, both men discretely pressed the tiny receivers in their ears. With a loud cough, Zade caught Gabby's eye. Giving her a single nod, he told her to do the same.

The devices worked both ways so they could all listen and communicate when necessary.

Acting as if he were talking to Kole, Zade asked Gabby, "Can you hear me okay, sweetheart?"

"Hear you loud and clear, sugarplum," Nate teased.

Fucking Carter. "I was talking to Gabby, assmunch."

A low, whispering chuckle reached his ear, followed by an angelic voice.

"I can hear you, Zade."

When he turned, he saw that she'd brought a wine glass up to her mouth to hide the movement of her lips. Exactly as they'd practiced.

"Good girl." He offered her a smile before looking away.

"Gabby, I don't want you to react, but Hector Andino is walking into the club as we speak," Nate informed her. "Let him come to you. Just like we planned."

"What if he doesn't?"

"He will," Zade assure her. "Trust me." There was no way Andino wouldn't notice her.

Asshole had better keep his hands to himself.

"You've got that look again," Kole nudged him.

"What look?" Gabby asked.

"Not you, sweetheart," Zade told her. "He's talking to me."

"Oh. Okay."

"Andino's in," Gabe informed them all. "Black dress pants, Gray button up. Two very large goons right behind him."

"Guess it's showtime," Gabby whispered.

Thanks to R.I.S.C.'s state-of-the-art electronics, Zade heard her words perfectly over the loud music. He also heard the tremor in her voice.

"Take a breath, Gabby. Stick to the plan, and you'll be fine. You've got this."

Her eyes slid his way briefly, so he offered her a comforting smile. Even from all the way over here, he could see some of the tension leave her shoulders.

That's my girl.

Zade saw Hector Andino the second he approached the bar. It was kind of hard not to, given the crowd of women who immediately began gravitating toward him.

Asshole that he was, Andino dismissed them all with a wave of his hand. At the gesture, they all walked away looking like someone had stolen their kittens or some shit.

"Seriously?" Zade shook his head. "Do these women not now what kind of animal this guy is?"

"They know." Gabe's voice came through. "They just don't care."

Andino slid up to the bar and ordered a drink. Of course, the bartender ignored the other orders she'd already been given and immediately went about making his.

Handing it to him with what Zade would consider a nervous smile, the young woman waited for Andino to take his first sip. When he gave her a nod and what Zade could only assume to be a large tip, the bartender's smile widened into one that was genuine.

Going about her business, the young woman walked away, leaving Andino at the bar with his two guards. As planned, Gabby got into character. Her hips began swaying to the sensual music, her eyes closing now and again as she pretended to be completely enthralled by the song's lyrics.

Dipping a finger into her glass, Gabby then pulled it back out, slipping the digit between her succulent lips.

Fuck. Me.

Hard as it was—literally—Zade refrained from verbally reacting. Not only was his team listening in, but Ghost and the others were, as well. The last thing he needed was two teams razzing him for getting a fucking hard-on in the middle of a mission.

Baseball. Your sisters. Your mother in the shower.

Zade thought of everything he could to tamper down his growing erection. It helped some, but not completely. He always seemed to be hard whenever Gabby was around.

The hairs on the back of Zade's neck stood on end, and he glanced in Gabby's direction right as a look of heat spread across Andino's face. The man was staring directly at her.

Making his way across the few feet that separated them, Andino approached Gabby.

"I'd offer to buy you a drink, but it seems you already have one." The man's Hispanic accent was thick and deep.

"Yes, I do."

Gabby's voice was smooth as silk, all traces of the tremble Zade had heard seconds earlier gone. She'd put on her game face and had gotten into character.

"Forgive me for being so forward, but you are a very beautiful woman. One might say…unforgettable."

Bastard remembers her.

"Thank you," Gabby smiled at the bastard. "That's very kind of you to say."

"You're welcome. I say it, because it is true. You were here two nights ago, yes?"

"I was."

"As was I."

"I know. I saw you."

Andino's perfect, dark brows rose. "So you remember me. I'm flattered."

"Don't be." Gabby set her drink down and faced the other man. "I know who you are, Hector. I also know where all of that money of yours comes from. That's why I came here two nights ago. It's why I'm here, now."

"You are here for business and not pleasure?"

Gabby's voice lowered and became raspy with feigned desire. "I'm hoping for a little of both."

Zade ground his teeth together.

"What is your name?" Hector asked. "Why are you in my club?"

"My name is Gabriella Smith." Gabby held out her hand. "I'm what you'd call a…broker, of sorts."

"A broker?"

"Yes. And I have a client who is very, very interested in the…product…you're planning to sell tomorrow night."

That little tidbit had been given to Ghost by his asset that morning. The guy had somehow managed to learn the scheduled date for Andino's skin auction. The fucker was planning to sell the girls he had in his possession *tomorrow*.

Which meant they needed to work damn fast.

"I'm afraid you are mistaken, Miss Smith. I am a business owner." Andino looked around the club's interior. "This place, plus over a dozen other properties in La Paz and the surrounding area, is mine. I am not planning to sell them anytime soon. Definitely not in the next twenty-four hours. I'm sorry you came all this way for nothing. If you'll excuse me…"

Andino turned to leave, but Gabby kept her cool. Using the name Ghost had given them earlier, Gabby said, "I'm sorry to hear that, too. Mr. Webb will be very disappointed."

"Webb?" Andino stopped and turned back toward her.

"Geoffrey Alan Webb the Third, to be exact. He said he and you had done business together in the recent past. Claimed to be a valuable customer of yours. I really hope I haven't been played a fool."

Good 'ole Geoff had been a customer of Andino's…until he got picked up two days ago during an FBI sting for possession and distribution of kiddie porn. Sick bastard started singing like a fucking canary before the cuffs were on him, throwing everyone he could think of under the bus in an attempt to make a deal. Including Hector Andino.

Word traveled fast through the various agencies, and once Jason Ryker—R.I.S.C.'s Homeland handler—got wind of it, he immediately contacted Ghost.

When Bravo Team and Gabby met with Delta this morning, they were informed of the recent break in the case against Andino. Rather than risk the lives of the girls Andino was currently holding by rushing in and grabbing the fucker right then, they decided to use it in their operation to not only take Andino down but also find Samantha Shoemaker.

As part of Geoffrey Webb's plea deal, he'd agreed to play along. One wrong move on his part, the man would spend the rest of his life behind bars.

"You work for Geoffrey Webb?" Andino's thick voice was laced with suspicion.

"Yes."

"It's unlike Geoffrey to hire someone else to come here. Especially someone so tempting."

Andino moved in closer to her. When he did, Zade instinctively started to stand. Kole stopped him by grabbing his arm.

"Easy, man. They're just talking."

"He lays a finger on her, I swear to God..."

As if she were talking to Zade rather than Hector—probably both—Gabby spoke again. "I'm good."

"I bet you are," Andino all but purred.

Zade held back a growl.

"It's very loud in here," Andino noted. "Let's go upstairs, into my private office. I don't like doing business out in the open like this. Too many prying eyes."

You mean too many witnesses.

"Don't do it," Zade ordered Gabby. But it was too late.

At the same time he was talking, she was already telling Andino, "Lead the way."

Goddamnit.

"We're coming with you, Gabby. When you walk by, Kole and I will stand and follow. Don't react or look our way. Tell me you understand."

"I understand."

Andino frowned. "I'm sorry?"

Without blinking an eye, Gabby looked up at him. "I understand your need for privacy, Mr. Andino. I would assume it's a must for a man in your position."

Zade let out a slow breath.

"Damn." Kole looked at him. "She's good."

Yes, she was. And Zade hated it.

He didn't want her anywhere near the bastard, let alone agreeing to go to the man's private office.

I can do this. I just need you to trust me.

Her words from last night rang through his head as Gabby and Andino—along with the two walls of muscle—walked past them toward the darkened staircase to the left of the bar.

He and Kole waited until they started up those stairs before standing and following in their path.

Gabby was right. He needed to trust her. After all, he was here. His *team* was here.

What could go wrong?

The answer to that question came less than a minute later when Zade and Kole turned the corner at the top of the stairs and found themselves staring down the barrels of two very large guns.

CHAPTER 10

Maybe this wasn't such a good idea, after all.

Gabby's heart felt like it was trying to fight its way out of her chest as she followed Hector Andino up the dark, enclosed staircase to the office space above the bar.

She felt more than could see Zade and Kole's presence behind them and prayed they didn't get hurt because of her decision. She'd heard Zade's order to not come up here loud and clear, but there was no way she was risking scaring off Andino by refusing.

Not when they were this close.

At the top of the stairs, they came to a small, open hallway. A single, black door was at the end of it, no doubt leading to Andino's office.

Of course the man would have a private room above his club. One where he could keep an eye on everything happening below.

Gabby had only taken a few steps toward that office when she heard an angry voice behind her, ordering her to stop.

"Not another step."

She swung around, fully expecting to see one of Andino's

men homing in on her. She knew they'd somehow figured out she was up to no good and planned to stop her.

Instead, Gabby found Andino's men standing with their *backs* to her, their guns pointed directly at Zade and Kole's heads.

Ohmygod.

"Don't!" she blurted before she could stop herself. Zade's eyes lifted to hers, the almost indiscernible shake of his head telling her to stand down.

"You know them?" Andino stepped up behind her. He stood close enough she could feel the heat from his body.

Recovering quickly, Gabby relaxed her shoulders and lifted her chin. Sliding her mask back into place, she put her hands on her hips and gave Zade and Kole a chastising look.

"I thought I told you two not to act unless I ordered you to."

"These are your men?"

"Two of my best." Gabby turned to face him. "Surely you don't think a woman such as myself would travel to a place like this without protection. After all, La Paz is one of Mexico's most dangerous cities. It would be foolish of any woman to come here alone."

It was a good thing she wasn't looking at Zade right then, because inside Gabby was grinning from ear to ear. She'd used his own words to help get him and Kole out of a jam.

You're saving your own ass, too, don't forget.

She could tell Andino was still on the fence, so Gabby added, "You'll have to forgive them. While they can be a little overzealous, they are paid very well to ensure my safety."

"Boss?" The man holding the gun on Zade looked to Andino for direction.

"Take them back downstairs."

"No." The growled, one-word response came from Zade.

Gabby locked eyes with him, praying he could see what her eyes were trying to convey.

I've got this.

His cool eyes sent their own message.

I'm not leaving you.

"Gentlemen, please." She smiled, acting as cool as a cucumber. "Are the weapons really necessary?" Gabby glanced at Andino. "As long as I remain safe, there will be no issue. Surely they can at least wait up here, in the hallway, while you and I discuss our possible...arrangement."

She purposely lowered her voice to a come-hither tone in an attempt to take Andino's focus off of Zade and Kole and back onto her. The guy's attraction to her was blatantly obvious, and at the moment, it was all Gabby had to work with.

"Fine. They may wait out here with my men." To his goons, Andino ordered, "Search them."

"They have weapons, of course." Gabby looked at Hector as if he were crazy. "How else do you expect them to protect me?"

"My men will hold on to their weapons until we are finished. They will get them back when you leave."

"Like hell," Zade spoke up again.

What was he trying to do, get them all killed?

"You'll do as Mr. Andino requests," Gabby ordered him. "Give him your weapons, or you're fired."

Zade's gaze slid to hers. To anyone else, he'd come off as calm and in control. Indifferent, even. But what he'd said about their connection last night was right.

Soul deep.

Right now, that connection let her know he was ready to strangle her. Oh, yeah...she'd definitely be paying for that one later.

As long as there is a later, I'll take whatever he wants to throw at me.

With a bulging jaw and gritted teeth, Zade reached behind his back and pulled his gun free. He handed it to Goon Number One. Kole shot him a look but thankfully did the same, giving his gun to Goon Number Two.

"Shall we?" Andino opened the door to his office and waited.

With a smile and a barely-there glance at Zade, she turned and walked past Andino. "Thank you."

From behind her, Andino told his men, "They try to come in here, shoot them."

Gabby's eyes met Zade's a second before Andino shut the door.

"Was that necessary?" She turned to him.

"You pay your men to protect you, I do the same. Now, would you like a drink? I have whiskey, tequila…"

"I'm good, thank you. I like to keep a level head when conducting business on behalf of my clients."

"Yes, please tell me more about what it is you do."

"Like I said downstairs, I'm a broker. My clients wish to purchase a product you own, they tell me, and I contact you. We make the arrangements, I pay you using their money, I deliver the product to my client. They pay me for my trouble, and everyone walks away with something they want."

"And what is it you want, Miss Smith?"

"Money."

"Interesting. However, until tonight, I have not heard of you, nor have I heard of any of my clients using you before now."

"Because they only recently hired me."

"And why is that? Why pay someone else to do a job they are perfectly capable of doing themselves?"

"Oh, come now, Hector. You know as well as I do, some jobs are worth paying for. Especially the dirty ones."

"Are you saying my business is dirty?"

"You buy and sell women and young girls to be used as sex toys. Don't get me wrong, I'm not judging. But even you have to admit there's a certain level of immorality in what you do."

"Yet here you are, trying to insert yourself into the middle of that immorality."

"Because it pays very, very well." Gabby shrugged. "Like I said, I'm not judging. Merely explaining why more and more of your customers are turning to people like me."

He studied her for several seconds. "It doesn't bother you, as a woman? To know what will happen to those your clients purchase?"

Keep it together. This is for Sam. Keep. It. Together.

"Would I be standing here if it did?"

Andino's lips curled into a slow, evil grin. "Beautiful and ruthless. I knew the minute I saw you, there was something special about you."

Someone coughed and Gabby damn near reacted before realizing the sound had come from her ear and not Andino, himself.

Zade.

Zade had coughed. An angry, purposeful move on his part.

Gabby glanced at her wrist. "Not that I don't enjoy talking with you, because I do, but it's getting late, and I'd like to get to why I'm here tonight."

"Why are you here?"

"The auction you have scheduled for tomorrow night. I would like an invitation to participate."

The quick blink of the man's dark eyes told Gabby that little bomb had come as quite a shock to him.

"What auction would that be?"

"Come on, Hector. Like I said, it's late and I like my sleep. Henry Webb is willing to pay top dollar for the right purchase. Mr. Webb informed me it's been a while since his last transaction with you. It's my understanding he's more than a little anxious to acquire something new. Preferably something young and blonde. He'll pay extra if she has blue eyes."

"My…sales…are kept private until a few hours before." Andino set his glass down and walked toward her. No, *stalked* toward her, was more like it. "So tell me, Miss Smith. How is it you know so much about my business when we've only just met?"

He stopped directly in front of her, inches from where she stood. Andino was so close, Gabby had to tilt her head back to look him in the eye.

Her heart raced, her pulse spiking with fear, but she refused to give in to it. Refused to come this close after all this time, only to screw it up now.

She told Zade she could do this, and she could. She would.

For Sam.

"I honestly have no idea where Mr. Webb learned of the planned event. All I know is, he called me two days ago and told me his jet was ready to fly me here. He also said if I was on board within the hour of that phone call, I'd receive a sizeable bonus. As I've already stated, I really like money, Mr. Andino. So my ass was on that plane in time to ensure that bonus."

He stared down at her, his expression unreadable. Not wanting to sound too desperate, but needing to close the deal, Gabby said a prayer and tried one more tactic.

"It sounds to me as if you have a leaky faucet in your kitchen, Hector. Might want to call a plumber to take care of that problem. However, that is not my concern." She reached up, her finger tracing a button on his shirt. "My concern is making sure my client is happy when I return. If he's happy, then I'm happy." Gabby swallowed back a rush of bile and flattened her hand against the man's taut chest. "Can you make me happy, Hector?"

Another strong, *loud* cough hit her ear, but Gabby ignored it. As much as it pained her to do so, she kept her eyes glued to Andino's, pouring every ounce of feigned arousal she could muster his way.

"I think I can make us both happy, carina." He wrapped a hand around her waist and pulled her to him.

The man's rock-hard erection pressed against her lower belly making Gabby want to puke all over his thousand-dollar shoes. But she smiled up at him as if he was the best thing she'd ever felt in her life.

Not. Even. Close.

Wanting to gag, Gabby said, "I'm glad to hear that. Here." She slipped a piece of paper into his palm. "These are other customers of yours I've done business with recently. Feel free to…check me out."

"Why would a woman like you put herself in such a dangerous and risky position?"

"Why does anyone do anything these days, Hector?" Gabby chuckled as she continued to let him hold her close. "I mean, look at me. Do I look like the kind of woman who'd be happy with a nine-to-five job making thirty grand a year?"

"No." Andino's eyes slinked down to her exposed cleavage. "You do not."

"Because I'm not that kind of woman. I like money, I like danger, and…" She let her own eyes wander. "I like men like you."

This time, Zade cleared his throat. Loudly.

"Men like me?"

"Strong and fearless." She traced his chest with her fingertip. "Powerful."

A sickening heat began to shine brightly behind his eyes.

Andino raised his hand, as if he were going to brush some hair away from her face. On reflex, Gabby quickly reached up and grabbed his wrist to stop him.

If he moves my hair, he might see the com in my ear.

Anger began to replace the heat, and she knew she had to act fast.

Working hard to school her expression—because being here, like this, with a man like Andino made her physically ill —Gabby reached up with her free hand and gently ran her thumb across his bottom lip.

"Business before pleasure, Hector."

That heat flared to life as he stared back at her. "Most women know better than to keep me from taking what I want."

Don't react...don't react...do not react!

"I'm not like most women." She let go of his wrist and stepped back, out of his reach. Thankfully, he let her. "Call the men whose names I gave you. They'll vouch for me, I assure you. If you decide you want to do business together, let me know. I have a suite at the Rancho Las Cruces Resort. You can leave a message at the front desk with the details."

Praying she wasn't pushing *too* hard, Gabby turned her back on the dangerous man and walked toward the door.

"I do hope to hear from you, Hector." She grabbed the doorknob and looked over her shoulder. "I believe you and I could make a fortune working together."

His eyes were still darkened with arousal, his nauseating erection obvious behind his expensive silk dress pants. "What if I want there to be more than work, Gabriella?"

"Like I said before." She let her eyes become heavy-lidded, her expression turning hot and sultry. "Business first."

"And then pleasure?" He stared back at her hungrily.

Gabby smiled, because she knew she had him exactly

where she wanted him. "Oh, yes." She licked her bottom lip for added effect. "Lots and lots of pleasure."

Needing to leave while still having the upper hand, Gabby opened the door and walked out. Pushing themselves off the wall facing her, Zade and Kole immediately snapped to attention.

From the look on Zade's face, he was ready to pummel someone. Probably her.

"Everything okay, Miss Smith?" he asked, sounding like the dutiful employee he was portraying.

"I'm fine." She released an exaggerated sigh. "Just as I told you I would be."

Gabby hoped like mad he understood her snippy response was all part of the act. She knew he was probably going out of his mind with worry and hated that she couldn't wrap her arms around him right that second.

"Glad your meeting went well, Boss." Kole offered her a grin. He looked at the man who'd been watching over him. "Thanks for holding my gun for me. Kind of nice getting rid of that extra weight for a while." He held out his hand and looked at the man expectantly.

The two guards looked at Andino, who gave them a nod. They handed Zade and Kole back their weapons.

"I look forward to hearing from you, Hector." Gabby smiled at the cartel leader. "I do hope you won't keep me waiting long."

With that, Gabby turned and walked toward the stairs, putting an extra sway in her hips for one, final shot at securing the man in her deceitful web.

It wasn't until they were back in the SUV and on their way back to the resort that either man spoke a single word to her.

"Holy shit!" Kole leaned up from the back seat when they

were a safe distance from the club. "You were freaking amazing in there. Like, Oscar-winning performance."

Gabby let out a breath and smiled. She kept her hands twisted together on her lap to keep Zade from noticing how badly she was shaking.

"Really? You don't think I came off too strong?"

"Hell, no. Did you see Andino's face? That man was ready to fall at your feet and give you whatever the hell you wanted. Ghost's asset was right. The guy has a serious weakness when it comes to good-looking redheads."

Some of her shaking subsided. "Let's hope it was enough to get an invite to that auction." She also prayed the men Andino would almost assuredly call would back her up like they'd agreed to.

If not, she and the rest of Bravo would have to haul ass and get the hell out of Mexico before Andino and his crew could hunt them down.

Because a man like Hector Andino would not be made a fool without someone paying the price.

Gabby glanced over at Zade who was staring straight ahead at the road in front of them. His knuckles were white as they gripped the steering wheel tightly. He didn't say a word to her the entire ride.

I went too far. He sees, now, who I really am. Who I can make myself be when it's for my benefit.

She'd tried to tell him. Tried to make Zade understand how it had been for her growing up. Gabby thought she could use those learned skills to help catch the bad guy. It seemed as if the plan was working but at what cost?

For the rest of the trip, as Gabby rode next to a silent, unreadable Zade, she couldn't help but wonder if she'd also lost the good guy in the process.

CHAPTER 11

Zade secured the chain and locked the deadbolt but didn't turn around. Didn't look at the woman standing behind him, waiting for him to say something.

I need to get myself under control, first.

Control, then talk. It had to be in that order, because if it wasn't...if Zade blurted out what he really *wanted* to say, it would scare Gabby off faster than a whore in church on a Sunday.

He hadn't uttered a single word to her since before she'd threatened to 'fire' him and Kole. Jesus, he still couldn't believe how that shit had gone down.

"Zade?" The same voice that, less than an hour ago, had sounded so strong and confident was now soft and unsure.

She thought he was mad. He wasn't mad.

He was...shit, Zade didn't know *what* he was. Whatever he was feeling, 'mad' wasn't it.

Say something, dickhead.

That damn voice in his head was right...again. He needed to quit staring at that fucking door and explain what he was feeling. Find a way to make her understand, but how?

Say. Something.

"I don't give up my gun." The statement was more of a growl than a blurt. Not exactly the smoothest line, but it was a start.

Zade turned around slowly. Maintaining his control was imperative, but damn. In this moment, feeling what he was feeling, he was about two seconds from losing it completely.

"I'm sorry." Gabby stared back at him. Her eyes weren't as guarded as before. They were dark and warm. Soft and…scared?

She should never be scared of him. Ever. Except…

"I don't give up my gun," he repeated. "Not for anyone. Ever."

"Zade—" She took a step forward, stopping abruptly when he began speaking again.

"I did that tonight. For you."

Gabby's brows turned inward in a confused and apologetic manner. "I'm sorry." She began walking toward him hesitantly. "I didn't know what else to do. Andino was—"

"Too fucking close to you," Zade cut her off a second time.

She stopped walking again. "What?"

"Andino was right next to you. He could've reached over and taken your hand in his, if he'd wanted."

Fucker's damn lucky he hadn't.

"I-I don't…I don't understand."

"Andino was close to you. If I'd continued to argue with him about giving up my weapon, he could've grabbed you. Put a gun to your head and forced Kole and I to disarm."

That particular scenario ran through Zade's mind when he'd refused to hand over his gun.

He'd wanted to tell the bastard to go to hell and order Gabby to leave the club with him and Kole, but then thought about the possible consequences.

"So I gave up my gun. For you."

Because letting something like that happen to this woman wasn't an option. Fucking ever.

Gabby blinked and started toward him again. "I was so scared," she admitted quietly. "I saw the way Andino was looking at you. His men were so close to you, and I knew on Andino's order they wouldn't have hesitated to hurt you and Kole. Or worse." She licked her lips, sending another rush of blood to his already hard-as-steel shaft. "I couldn't let that happen."

She stopped walking, mostly because she now stood less than two inches away from him.

Without blinking an eye, the damn fool woman had put on that little act of power for Hector in order to protect him and his teammate.

Jesus, she's incredible.

Of course, Zade already knew that. Tonight's performance only solidified the thought.

"There's not a lot that scares me." His voice deepened. "Seeing you walk through that door with Andino tonight, knowing I was unarmed and it would be hell getting to you if you needed me…that shit terrified me."

Zade's hands became two, tightened fists at his sides to keep from reaching for her. His control was too volatile. Too close to imploding.

If he touched her now, Zade knew he'd lose it completely. Gabby deserved the gentle lover he'd been on that island. One that took his time, savoring every inch of her delectable body.

She didn't need a lover who was seconds away from pouncing on her like an animal making its claim.

"Zade." Her eyes softened. "I was okay. Knowing you were right outside and could hear everything being said made me feel safe and protected. It was like you were standing right next to me the whole time."

He shook his head. "I was out of my mind with worry, waiting for you to finish making your little deal with that asshole." Zade stretched his fingers before curling them back into a pair of white-knuckle fists. "I could tell when he was close enough to touch you. I wanted to break down that damn door when he tried to—"

"But he didn't." Gabby raised her hand to his chest and touched *him*. Right over his racing heart.

Her eyes widened when she felt how powerful her touch affected him. How *much* she affected him.

Doesn't she know?

"It always feels like that when you're around," he admitted. "I see you, and my heart beats faster. It pounds against my ribs as if it's fighting to get out…to get closer to you."

"Zade." His name fell from her luscious lips like a whispered prayer.

"Every part of me wants to be closer to you. Always." Zade brushed some hair from her forehead so he could see every inch of her gorgeous face. "I see you, and I want." He leaned in, his lips whispering over hers. "I feel the warmth from your touch, and I crave."

"Zade?" That time she said it as a question.

You need to tell her. Make her understand what you're trying to say.

"I'm a greedy bastard, baby." Zade stared into her emerald eyes. "No matter how many times we're together, it's never going to be enough. I'm always going to want more."

"I want you, too," Gabby whispered the greatest words he'd ever heard. "I'll always want you, Zade. Only you."

Before he even knew he was moving, Zade spun them around. He pushed her up against the door, his hand cupping the back of her head to keep from hurting her as his mouth slammed against hers in a rush of need.

Go easy, damn it!

He'd rather cut off his own arm than ever hurt this woman.

He pulled back. "Sorry." His chest heaved. "I'll slow down. Be more gentle."

"I don't want slow, Zade." Heated eyes stared up into his. "And I don't want gentle."

Zade swallowed hard, the sound filling the otherwise silent room. "What do you want, baby?"

She needed to tread lightly. Should tell him to make slow, sweet love to her like a gentleman should. Either that or to get the hell off of her.

Because if she said—

"I want you to fuck me."

His control snapped.

Zade's mouth began to devour hers. The kiss was exactly like him—demanding and selfish—and his hands weren't any better.

In a fury of passion and need, he shoved her skirt up to her waist and ripped her panties off. Somewhere in the back of his mind, he made a mental note to buy her another pair, later.

Much, *much* later.

Going straight for the gold, Zade slid his hand between her thighs and pushed two fingers into her slick, wet heat. Gabby cried out as he speared her body, pumping his digits in and out, over and over again.

She tilted her head back, allowing him access to kiss and nip at the skin along her jawline and neck. She moaned loudly, her freshly manicured nails digging into his shoulders as Zade gently pressed his teeth against her thundering pulse point.

"Now, Zade." Gabby's rough breathing matched his own. "Please. I need you inside me."

She'd never have to beg him for that.

Moving lightning fast, Zade pulled his hand from her body and reached for his belt. He unclasped it, pulled it free, and had his pants unbuttoned and unzipped in record time.

Later he'd go slow. *Later* he'd take his time reminding her how good they could be together. Right now his only goal was to get his dick inside her and make her come.

After they finished this first round, he'd carry her to the huge ass bed behind him and spend the rest of the night making her forget every other man she'd ever been with.

He thought he was going too fast, but apparently, he wasn't moving fast enough. Because in the next second, Gabby was reaching between them to pull his pounding cock free.

Zade hissed in a sharp breath when he felt her fingers wrap around him. She began stroking him with determined vigor, her rhythm matching his hand as he slid his fingers back into her body, thrusting them in and out of her tight sex.

A familiar tingling ran the length of his spine, and shit, he was even closer to losing it than he thought.

Gabby first, asshole.

She would always come first. In every possible way.

Continuing to lick and nip against her delicate skin, Zade pulled his fingers free for a second time. Gabby let out a sound of protest but stopped when he wrapped his hands around her hips and picked her up.

On reflex, she wrapped her legs around his waist and locked her hands behind his neck. Bodies perfectly aligned, Zade started to push forward but froze.

"Shit." He'd been so wrapped up in her he'd forgotten to grab a condom.

As if reading his mind, Gabby said, "It's fine. I'm on birth control. Have been since…for a long time."

Since her foster brother. "I'm clean," Zade blurted. He wanted to ask her more about what happened back then, but not while his dick was one slip away from the one place it had been craving. "We get tested regularly, and I've never had unprotected sex."

Not that he had a lot. In fact, Zade got razzed on the regular about how few women he'd been with. But for him, sex should mean something.

With Gabby, it meant so much more.

"So what are you waiting for?" Gabby gently bit his bottom lip. When she tilted her pelvis toward him, her wet, *bare* slit brushed against his sensitive tip.

Zade surged forward, not stopping until he was seated balls-deep inside her welcoming core.

He and Gabby moaned in unison. God, she felt good. *Better* than good.

Zade started to move. He pulled himself out, almost to the point of breaking contact before pounding back into her. She cried out, so he did it again.

And again.

And again.

Best…Thing…Ever!

"Oh, God!" Gabby moaned loudly.

Her eyes closed, and she leaned her head back on the door. He continued pumping himself in and out, hard and fast, until the tingling in his spine returned.

He felt his balls tighten and wanted nothing more than to let go, but…

"You first."

Zade wrapped an arm behind her back, supporting her that way while squeezing a hand between them. He slid it down to where their bodies were connected, his fingers finding her swollen clit with ease.

Gabby jolted in his arms, her inner muscles clamping down on his aching dick. Though her body had just given him the answer, Zade rasped, "That feel good, baby?"

"God, yes!" Gabby's nails dug into the skin on the back of his neck. "So good!"

Twirling and swirling, he gave her body the attention he knew it needed. He needed to get her there. Now.

"Mine," Zade rasped the declaration.

"Oh, God, Zade...I'm going to—"

"Say it." He pushed into her again. "I want to hear you say it."

"I'm yours!"

Gabby practically screamed it as she erupted in an explosive release. A low, keening sound escaped the back of her throat, her orgasm sending a rush of hot liquid over his cock.

Her channel tightened, its quivering muscles sending Zade straight into his own earthshattering climax. Zade pumped once...twice...three more times before finally letting himself go.

Growling her name, he held on tight, riding out each electrifying wave of pleasure that rolled through him.

Rough, ragged breaths and the smell of sex and desire filled the air around them. Aftershocks of the best, most intense orgasm Zade had ever experienced left his body trembling and his knees weak.

A set of heavy-lidded, sated eyes met his, and in that moment, Zade knew those were the eyes he wanted to stare into for the rest of his life. He wouldn't tell her that yet. It was too soon, and their situation was anything but ideal.

After the mission, however...after they took Andino down and Gabby and her sister were home and safe...all bets were fucking off.

"That was…I can't even…" Gabby licked her lips as she searched for words to describe what had just happened.

There are no words, baby.

For now, he'd go with, "Incredible."

Her smile lit up her entire face. "It really was."

Leaning down, Zade pressed his lips to hers. The slow, languid kiss was meant to show her what he couldn't say with words. *Yet.*

Knowing he couldn't keep her shoved up against the door all damn night, Zade ended the kiss and pulled himself free of her body. Their sharp intakes of breaths matched as he set her back down on her feet.

Looking down, he realized his pants and boxer briefs were gathered around his ankles. He still had his shoes on, for crying out loud.

Smooth, King. Real fucking smooth.

"Sorry." He offered her a chagrined smile.

"For what?" Gabby pushed her skirt down over her hips.

Zade hated to lose the view of her magnificent body. If he had anything to say about it, he'd be seeing it again, soon. And often.

"I just fucked you up against a door." He pulled his boxers and pants up and began buttoning them. "Hard."

Was he too hard? Too rough? She'd said she didn't want gentle, but shit.

Now that Zade thought back to the last few minutes, he realized how *not* gentle he'd been.

"Do you hear me complaining?" Gabby cupped his face with her hands. "I wanted it hard." She rose to her tiptoes and kissed him. "I wanted *you* hard."

His cock twitched behind his open zipper. The damn thing *was* getting hard again. A common condition when Gabby was around.

"Right now, I want a shower." She looked up at him with an ornery smile. "Feel like joining me?"

Zade stared back at her, deadpan. "Just so you know, I will never say no to that question. Ever."

She laughed softly. "I'll get the water started.

"I'll be there in a second."

"Okay." Gabby stepped past him and headed across the tiled floor. When she reached the bathroom doorway, she looked back over her shoulder and grinned. "Don't take too long, or I'll be forced to start without you." Then she disappeared.

The image of Gabby in the shower, naked and wet...*touching* herself...

Jesus!

Zade started stripping off his shirt, leaving a trail of clothes as he covered the distance to that bathroom. Already hard and ready for more, his dick bobbed with his movements.

And when he took her again in the shower, Zade did take his time. He tasted and laved. Treasured every ounce of pleasure she was willing to give. And Gabby did the same.

Later, after that amazing round of shower sex, he carried her to bed and cuddled in close. He knew it probably wasn't the best time, but he felt himself compelled to broach the topic.

"Tell me about what happened when you were sixteen."

She turned her head to look back at him. "You know what happened."

"I know what the court record shows." When she didn't respond right away, he shook his head and let her off the hook. "Never mind. I shouldn't have brought it up."

"No, it's okay." Gabby shifted so she was lying flat on her back, the movement causing a swishing sound against the expensive sheets. "I mean, it's the total cliché story, right?

Older foster brother forces himself on the damaged and vulnerable foster sister. Girl fights back, parents blame the girl to protect their precious reputations. The end."

But that wasn't the end. Gabby had been sent to juvie because of what that asshole had done to her.

"I want to kill him."

The boy was now well over eighteen. That made him fair game for the major ass kicking Zade would most definitely be dishing out.

"Zade, no." Gabby turned even further so her entire body was facing his. "It's done and over with. Besides, I'm pretty sure I got my message across to him loud and clear."

"What did you do to him?" He hadn't read the details of the assault.

"He was big into baseball. Always leaving his bat lying around the house. After he...finished, he got off of me and started talking about the next time. Next time would be better, he said. Next time he'd go slower, take his time with me. I would rather have died than go through that again, so I found his bat and hid it in my room. The next time he came after me, I was ready. Pretended to be asleep and when he started to climb onto my bed, I slammed it right into his crotch."

He couldn't hold back his cringe. "I'm so sorry you had to go through that, baby."

"Thanks." She offered him a half-smile. "But I dealt with it a long time ago. I'm past it, now."

She hadn't merely dealt with it. Gabby had *used* what happened as fuel for her own personal fire.

The strength and tenacity with which she handled what life threw at her was amazing. While it terrified him to no end, the bravery and courage she possessed was also proof of a past she'd overcome.

Proof of the incredible woman she'd chosen to be. One he was damn lucky to have found.

She looked up at him and bit her bottom lip. "I didn't make a direct hit with that first swing, but when he came at me again, I tried a second time. He threw his hand up to block the blow. It broke in three places."

"Good."

Her eyes widened as if his immediate response surprised her. It shouldn't have.

She should know...

"Anyone ever tries to hurt you again, I'll end them."

Those eyes grew even wider. "I don't want you hurting someone because of me."

"Ah, baby." He ran his knuckles down her cheek. "Someone dares to come after you, I'll do a hell of a lot worse than hurt them.

Her brows turned inward with confusion. "Why?"

"Why?" Zade parroted her question as he propped himself up on one elbow in order to see her better. He needed to look her in the eyes for this next part. "I meant it when I said you were mine, Gabriella. With that, you get all of me. My heart, my soul...and my protection. Mine and the team's. Anyone lays a finger on you, it'll be the last thing they do."

He could hear her trembling breath. "Why me? I'm...a criminal. A nobody."

"You're not a fucking criminal." Zade threw the covers off and got out of the bed. "Some judge may have been too fucking blind to see what really happened that night, but I'm not."

"W-where are you going?"

Uncaring of their nudity, he walked around the foot of the bed to her side and reached for her hand. When she gave it to him, he gently pulled Gabby to her feet as well.

Again, Zade remained silent as he led her into the bathroom. Flipping on the lights, he stopped in front of the vanity. Positioning Gabby in front of him, they locked eyes in the large, ornate mirror.

"Tell me what you see."

"What?" She tried turning around, but he held her in place.

"Look at yourself in the mirror and tell me what you see."

"Zade," Gabby looked away with embarrassment.

"Fine, I'll start. I see a strong, intelligent woman. She's funny and unpredictable. She's also stubborn as hell. Though she's come a long way in a short period of time, she's still somewhat guarded. But got these eyes that I find myself getting lost in and the most beautiful, caring soul I've ever met."

Her eyes rose hesitantly to meet his reflection. "W-what else do you see?" she whispered almost shyly.

The woman truly didn't see how amazing she was. Had no one in her life ever told her?

Zade thought about her childhood and the way she'd grown up. His heart broke when he realized they probably hadn't. Or if they had, it had been too damn long since she'd heard it.

"I see a woman whose beauty nearly knocks me on my ass every time I lay eyes on her. One who isn't afraid to defend herself and is willing to risk her own life to save someone she loves."

Gabby's gaze seemed burrowed deep inside his. "You said you'd kill to keep me safe. That means you'd risk your life for mine, too. Right?"

"Damn straight I would."

She frowned, but he could see the wheels turning. His gut was telling him she understood exactly what that meant. Still, he needed to make sure of it.

"I know it's too early for the words, but you need to know where I stand on this, baby."

"This?"

He nodded. "Us."

Zade swallowed hard. He was moving fast, but despite his earlier thoughts about waiting to talk about their future, he couldn't help it. He'd never felt this way about anyone before and was filled with a sudden need for her to know it.

"I'll admit, our relationship has been anything but normal or conventional up to this point, but I'm falling hard and fast here, Gabby." He heard her suck in a breath. Hoping like hell he wasn't about to send her running in the opposite direction, Zade pushed on with what he felt compelled to say. "Once this mess with Andino is over and your sister's safe, I'd really like to see where this thing between us can go." Feeling vulnerable himself, he added, "Please tell me I'm not alone in that thought."

"You're not alone, Zade." This time, when Gabby turned to face him, he let her. Resting a hand on his bare chest, she blinked quickly, sending a silver trail down her cheek. "I'm falling for you, too. Pretty sure I started to that first night we met. But..."

"But?" he asked, holding his breath while she finished the thought.

"But I don't want you killing anyone for me. Ever. And I sure as hell don't want you dying for me. If you did that, if you risked your own life for mine, I'd be so pissed off at you."

His lips twitched. "Yeah?"

"I'm serious. Like, worse than baseball bat pissed."

Zade threw his head back and laughed. God, he loved this woman. "Well I definitely don't want you coming at me swinging, so how about this? I promise I will do my best not to get killed while protecting you."

It was the best promise he could make. The *only* promise. Because hell yeah, he'd lay his life down for hers.

In a fucking heartbeat.

"Make sure you do." She poked him in the chest. "Because my swing has only gotten better with time and trust me…I hit what I aim for."

Laughing again, Zade pulled her close, his erection pressing against her bare, lower belly. You'd think the damn thing would be satisfied after two rounds of the best sex he'd ever had. But that was the thing about Gabby.

The more he had her, the more he wanted her.

With his hands framing her face, he asked, "How did I get so lucky?"

Gabby smiled the most genuine smile and answered, "You've got it all wrong, Zade. I'm the lucky one."

"Do you have to argue about everything?" he teased.

"We could argue." She shrugged. "Or you could kiss me."

There was no question which one he was going to pick.

CHAPTER 12

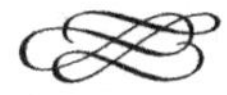

The aroma of bacon and coffee filled the entire suite, pulling Gabby out of a restful night's sleep. She stretched, her muscles deliciously sore after three—*Three!*—rounds of amazing, mind-blowing sex.

Most of her recent nights had been spent tossing and turning. Worrying about Sam or fighting her way out of memory-filled nightmares. Lying in the safety and comfort of Zade's arms, she'd slept like a baby.

Thoughts of Sam and where *she'd* been sleeping chipped away at Gabby's euphoric state. Guilt began to seep in as it had when she and Zade were together in Grand Isle.

Sam was out there, somewhere, and Gabby was here, having the best sex of her life. But this time it was different. They were together, yes, but they were also working to get Sam back.

There'd be no running this time. Not only because Gabby needed Zade and his team's help—and Ghost's—but because she needed Zade. Period.

I'm falling hard and fast, here, Gabby.

Her heart flipped inside her chest every time she remembered Zade's confession. How it happened, she didn't know, but Gabby had fallen for him, too.

As in completely and totally in love with him.

It was crazy, right? And *way* too soon. At the same time, it felt as if she'd known the man forever. As if she'd loved him her entire life.

He was everything she'd ever dreamed about, but thought she'd never have.

"Sure hope that look on your face has something to do with me."

Gabby swung her gaze to the doorway where Zade stood. In his hands were two steaming cups of coffee.

"It might." She smiled.

His eyes glittered with humor and a bit of primal, male pride. Walking toward her side of the bed, his lips curled into a cocky grin.

"Gotta tell you, baby. A man wakes up to see his woman smiling like that after a night like the one we just had…that's a damn good stroke to the old male ego."

"Oh, I don't think your ego needs any more stroking."

"Maybe not my ego." He handed her one of the mugs. "But there's another part of me that will take all the stroking you're willing to offer."

Giggling, Gabby took a sip of the hot brew and moaned. "Keep bringing me coffee in bed, and we'll talk."

Zade placed his mug on the nightstand before sitting on the mattress beside her. The bed dipped and Gabby scooted over a smidge to give him more room.

"Morning, baby." He leaned down and kissed her forehead. That was followed by a kiss to the tip of her nose and one on her lips. "How'd you sleep?"

"Like the dead." She took another sip, careful not to burn her tongue. "Any word from Andino, yet?"

Zade rested his hand on her thigh, caressing her through the sheet. "Not yet."

"Damn. I was hoping he would've made contact by now."

"He will. We just have to be patient."

"The auction's tonight, Zade. There's not a whole lot of time to be patient."

"He'll make contact," he assured her again.

"How can you be so sure?"

"I saw the way he was looking at you last night. Bastard was practically salivating."

Gabby tilted her head and smirked. "Careful, soldier. You almost sound jealous."

"Of course I'm fucking jealous." He frowned. Taking the mug from her hand, he set it down next to his. Leaning in, he brushed the tip of his nose against hers before giving her a soft, sweet kiss. "Told you last night, you're mine. I'm a selfish bastard, baby. I don't like to share."

Her mouth grew into a wide grin. "That's good because I don't share either."

"No?"

"No." She shook her head. "I blame it on growing up with next to nothing. On the rare occasions I got something special, I held on tightly and never let it go."

"You trying to say I'm special?" He nipped her bottom lip.

"Not *trying* to say anything."

Heat flared to life behind his brown eyes. Eyes that were staring back at her with an emotion she was terrified to assume.

Not because the *emotion* scared her, but because she didn't want to be wrong.

Zade lifted a hand, pressed the palm of that hand to her cheek. "Gabby, I—"

The phone next to the bed rang, the sound piercing through the air…and Zade's words.

Don't answer it. Ignore it and finish saying whatever it was you were going to say.

Muttering a low curse, he reached for the phone. Picking up the receiver, Zade answered with a frustrated, "King."

His eyes shot to hers. "Thank you. I'll be right down." He hung up the phone and blew out a breath. "Someone left an envelope for you at the front desk."

Her heartrate spiked. "Andino?"

"That's my guess."

Gabby practically pushed him off the bed. "I'll get dressed."

"Whoa." Zade nearly stumbled as he stood to get out of her way. "Where's the fire?"

"Sorry." She didn't bother looking back at him. Rushing to the bathroom, she said, "I need to get myself presentable before going downstairs. If he has someone watching, they'll be expecting the *me* from last night."

"The what?"

"You know." She peeked back out of the bathroom doorway. "The woman who was all poised and professional. And sexy."

That woman would definitely not go out in public with hair that screamed all-night-sex-fest.

Gabby smiled as she started the water, thoughts of said sex-fest entering her mind. She was also smiling because Hector Andino had taken the bait.

As she rushed through washing her hair and body, Gabby couldn't help but feel hopeful. She was going to see Sam at that auction tonight.

She'd 'buy' her, and once she and Sam were a safe distance away, Bravo Team and Ghost's men would take Andino down. Sam would finally be safe, and Gabby's life would go back to normal.

Do you really want normal?

No. She wanted a different life than before. One that included Zade.

She was almost certain he'd been about to tell her he loved her. It had been right there, staring back at her. The words ready to fall off the tip of his tongue.

At least she was pretty sure that's what he was going to say.

Whatever it was, there'd be time for it later. Time for that and, with any luck, a whole lot more.

Twenty minutes later, a put-together Gabby was walking to the hotel's front desk. Her trusted bodyguards—a.k.a., Zade and Kole—followed a few steps behind. She'd tried to tell them it wasn't necessary, but Zade had insisted a woman like Gabriella Smith would always have her protective guards in tow.

"Thank you." She smiled at the kind clerk who handed her the envelope. It was black with her name stamped in gold on the front. "Andino goes all out, doesn't he?" Gabby mumbled to Zade as they got onto the elevator.

She started to rip it open, but he stopped her.

"Not here."

Feeling as anxious as a kid on Christmas morning, she looked over a him quizzically. "Why wait?" She needed to see what the envelope held.

"He could have someone watching," Kole mumbled. His eyes slid to the camera in on corner of the ceiling.

"Oh." Gabby smiled. "Right."

Doing her best to appear indifferent and not at all ready to tear into that damn envelope, Gabby forced herself to wait until they'd returned to the room. The second she stepped foot inside, however, she *was* tearing into it.

She stared at the mostly white slip of paper. "It's an address and a time." Her eyes rose to meet Zade's. "That's it."

He took the paper from her and studied it. "This is all we need."

"Oh." Gabby frowned. "I was expecting some sort of formal invite."

"That *is* your invite, darlin'," Kole grinned and gave her a wink.

He'd been much nicer to her since they'd left the club last night. Not that Gabby had held his standoffish behavior against him.

Kole was Zade's friend and teammate and had only been looking out for Zade. How could she be mad at someone for wanting to protect the man she loves?

However, it *did* make things a lot easier when Kole wasn't acting all burly and suspicious of her.

"Eight-thirty," Zade read the time aloud. "That gives us"—he glanced at his watch—"Less than twelve hours to find out what we can about that location and get things ready to go." He glanced at Gabby. "I need to show this to Gabe. I'm sure he's going to want to meet back up with Ghost and those guys to go over everything in detail."

"Okay."

To Kole, he said, "Stay with her while I take this to Gabe?"

"Didn't even have to ask, brother."

Zade tipped his head to his teammate. He took her hand in his and pulled her close. "I'll be right back. A few minutes tops."

"Kole doesn't have to stay here, Zade." Gabby stared up at him. "I'm not going anywhere."

One corner of his mouth rose into that sexy, half-smile of his. "Kole's not staying to keep you from running off, baby. He's staying to keep you safe."

Her heart flipped again. "Not necessary, but I won't argue."

"Thank you." He leaned down, kissed her softly, and left.

Surprised by the blatant show of affection in front of his teammate, Gabby felt herself becoming a bit flushed.

"I owe you an apology."

She blinked and then frowned. "You do?"

"I was an asshole to you. I'm sorry."

"You were looking out for Zade." Gabby smiled. "He's lucky to have a friend like you."

The man nodded but didn't respond. A stretch of awkward silence had her looking away while she tried to think of something else to say.

"He's in love with you, you know."

Kole's shocking words had Gabby's eyes flying back up to meet his. "What?"

"You don't see it?" He shook his head. "Maybe you don't, because you haven't known him as long as I have. Trust me, Gabby. That man is head over ass for you."

Her heart didn't just flip inside her chest. It stood up and cheered. Except…

"Why are *you* telling me this?" And why did it sound like more of a warning than a declaration?

"Like you said, Zade's my friend. He's been through a lot recently, and I don't want to see him get hurt."

Her heart stopped cheering. "You think I'll hurt him?"

"You already did. The second you walked out on him."

"I explained that to him. And to you and the others."

"I know. And this isn't me shoving it in your face or trying to make you feel bad. You did what you thought you had to do to help your sister, and I respect that. Doesn't mean there weren't consequences to that decision, though."

"He was upset."

Kole chuckled. "He was a hell of a lot more than upset, darlin'. That man was devastated. I've never seen him like that. He spent every spare minute he had trying to track you down."

She thought of the scarring near his collar bone and felt like an ass because she hadn't asked him about it yet.

"What happened?" When Kole remained quiet, she said, "I've seen the scars, Kole. I know he was hurt.

"You didn't ask him about it?"

"We haven't had a lot of time to sit and talk." They'd had time for other things…other, deliciously amazing things… but she wasn't about to tell Kole that.

With an almost knowing smirk, he said, "The short of it is, Zade was hurt trying to protect Matt's wife, although she wasn't his wife at the time."

"But he's okay, and I'm assuming Matt's wife is okay, too?"

"She is, now. Almost wasn't." A shadow fell over the man's face. "She was taken by some very bad men. Zade was pinned inside a wrecked car and couldn't do anything to stop it. He was shot, and we damn near lost him."

Oh god. "That's awful."

"It was. We were able to get Katherine back, but Zade…he wasn't quite the same after that."

She thought of how overprotective he'd been with her and what he'd said last night about being terrified when she'd gone into that room with Andino.

"He blames himself, doesn't he?" Gabby looked up at Kole. "For what happened to Matt's wife."

"He did. I think he's finally starting to get past it. Something happens to you, though…" Kole shook his head. "That shit will stay with him for the rest of his life."

Gabby's chest tightened. "I don't have a death wish, Kole. I plan to go into that auction tonight, get my sister out, and walk away from this whole mess."

"What about Zade? You gonna walk away from him, too?"

"No." Her answer was instant and certain.

A slow smile began to spread across Kole's handsome face. "Good."

"Okay, so Gabe got ahold of Ghost and—"

Both Gabby and Kole swung their heads around toward Zade, who'd just walked back into the room. He looked like he was watching a ping-pong tournament, his eyes bouncing back and forth between the two.

"Everything okay, here?" Zade asked slowly.

"Everything's great." Kole grinned. "You were saying?

Eyeing her suspiciously, Zade continued only after Gabby gave him a reassuring smile. "Uh...I was saying, Gabe got ahold of Ghost, and those guys want to meet up in an hour."

"Sounds good. Gives me time to call Sarah before she has to go into the office."

Gabby assumed Sarah was the reason for the thin, pewter-colored band on Kole's left hand. "Thanks, Kole," she offered as an afterthought.

He turned to her and winked. "Any time."

Zade waited until the other man left before turning back to Gabby. "What was that all about"

"What?"

"When I walked in, you two looked like you were in the middle of a pretty serious conversation."

"We were discussing the weather."

"The weather, huh?" Zade strolled toward her, clearly aware of her obvious lie. "You sure there wasn't something more to it? Something you'd like to share with me?"

Gabby smiled as he pulled her into his arms. "Only that I'm glad you have such good friends watching your back."

The skin on his forehead bunched together. "Kole wasn't being a dick to you again, was he? Because I can—"

Gabby cut him off with a quick, hard kiss. "No, Kole wasn't being an asshole. Actually, he apologized for being one before."

"He did?"

"He did. I told him that wasn't necessary."

"Uh…yeah. It was."

"No, it wasn't." She kissed him again. "He was only looking out for you."

"And that's all it was? An apology? Because it sure looked like a lot more than that."

"Are you always this suspicious?"

Zade shrugged. "Occupational hazard."

Gabby's smile fell as she thought about what that occupation was. "Kole told me what happened. About the wreck and you getting shot while protecting Matt's wife."

A shadow similar to Kole's darkened Zade's expression. "He shouldn't have told you that. You don't need to worry about—"

She put a finger to his lips. "I'm glad he told me. It helps me to understand your need to protect me even more." When he shook his head, Gabby let her hand drop back to her side.

"What happened to Kat has no bearing on my need to keep you safe, Gabby. That need would be there whether Kat had been taken or not."

"But you blame yourself for what happened to her."

"I did." He shrugged. "I don't know, maybe I still do." He put a hand to her cheek. "But God, baby. If something happened to you—"

"It won't."

"You can't know that."

He had a point. "Maybe not, but I've come too far to back out, now."

"I know." He tucked some hair behind her ear. "I understand your need to do this. Don't like it. Fucking hate it, actually. But I understand it."

Gabby pressed a palm over his beating heart. It was one of her favorite places to touch him. "I promise I'll be careful,

Zade. Like I told Kole, I don't have a death wish. I want to get out of this thing alive so I can continue having a life after this."

Suddenly nervous, Zade asked, "You think that life could include someone like me?"

Her heart began cheering again. "No." She shook her head and did her best not to smile.

"Oh." His adorable face fell.

Unable to keep him on the hook for too long, Gabby leaned up and framed his face with both hands. "I don't want someone *like* you in my life, Zade. I want *you*." She pressed her lips to his. "Only you."

Zade took what was meant to be a quick, loving gesture and deepened into something so much more. Forty-five minutes later, they were scrambling to find the clothes they'd strewn all over the suite, getting re-dressed, and making themselves appear presentable once more.

Gabby forced herself to put her teenage-esque hormones on pause until later. Once the auction was over and Sam was safe, she'd return to the land of Zade.

Until then, she needed to keep a clear head and focus on the task at hand. Her sister's life depended on it, as did hers.

For the first time in her life, Gabby had found someone to share her life with. Someone who, for reasons she still didn't quite understand, wanted to share his life with her, too.

Zade King had managed to worm his way into her shielded heart, and if all went well, Gabby had no intentions of ever letting him go.

CHAPTER 13

"You don't have to do this." Zade glanced at Gabby from his place behind the wheel. Despite her efforts to hide it, he could tell she was nervous as hell.

She should be scared. After all, she was getting ready to crawl into a snake pit with the deadliest viper in existence.

"Yes," she told him with a straightened spine. "I do."

The gnawing feeling in his gut had him shaking his head before she'd even finished speaking. "No, you don't. Say the word and we turn around and head back to the hotel. Bravo and the others will deal with Andino. We'll find Sam and get you both out of Mexico. In fact, I'd love nothing more than to put you on the next flight out of here."

"You know I can't do that, Zade." Gabby drew in a long breath before letting it out slowly. "I'm good. Just ready for this to be over."

His jaw clenched, his knuckles turning white as he squeezed the steering wheel to the point he thought it would snap.

Something touched his thigh, making him jump. He realized it was only Gabby's hand.

"Relax, Zade." She smiled over at him. "We went through the plan about a billion times. We go in, I buy my sister, we leave."

Goddamn, she was beautiful. Gabby was always beautiful, but she was dressed for the part tonight.

"Have I told you how beautiful you look in that dress?"

Her eyes lit up. "Yes, but I still like hearing it." Gabby glanced down at the long, black, sequined dress. "Although, I'm still not sure where Ghost and his men managed to find an evening gown that fits me perfectly."

"Never underestimate the men of…" Kole cut himself off from his seat in the back.

Shit. Zade had almost forgotten the man was there.

"They're Delta Force, aren't they? Don't worry, I'm not going to say anything."

Zade's head spun toward Gabby's. From the corner of his eye, he saw Kole sit up straight, as well. "Why would you say that?"

She waved them both off. "I know you can't confirm or deny, but it's so blatantly obvious."

"You're right. We can't divulge what team they're on."

A smug expression crossed over her face. "It's okay. That pretty much does confirm my suspicions. Not that it really matters. I don't care what team they're on. As long as they can keep you guys safe and help me get my sister out of there, that's all I care about."

"And keep you safe," Zade reminded her.

Her smile softened. "Of course."

It drove him nuts the way she put everyone above herself. Gabby had promised him she didn't have a death wish, and he didn't think that was the case. He did, however, know if things went sideways, she wouldn't hesitate to sacrifice herself for her sister. Or him and Kole.

Yeah, that shit's not happening, sweetheart. Not on my watch.

Another woman's face flashed through his mind, but Zade pushed it away. Now was not the time to think of Kat and that whole fucked-up situation. Besides, he'd thought a lot about what Kole had said to him in the bar—was that just last night?

He wouldn't even think about blaming his teammates if they'd been in the same position he'd been in when she was taken. So maybe it was time he gave himself a break, too.

Zade looked over at Gabby again. Her hair was swept up into a pile of curls on top of her head. Several loose tendrils fell in a messy-yet-perfect way, framing her gorgeous face.

Diamond studded earrings adorned her delicate earlobes. Attached to those were thin, studded chains that ran to a clasp positioned at the middle of her outer ears. She also wore a matching necklace, ring, and bracelet as well.

They'd found the costume jewelry at a shop inside the resort. It was very pretty, but it also served a purpose.

Microscopic cameras had been embedded in the center jewel on her necklace, and the clasps on her earrings were actually receivers that worked the same way their ear coms did. Nate had even added a tiny mic in her ring.

It was all merely a precaution, but no fucking way was he going to take any chances tonight. Not with her.

Zade's one main goal tonight was to keep Gabby safe. With Delta having their backs, it *shouldn't* be a problem.

Speaking of Delta…

"What made you say that about Ghost and his team?"

She shrugged one of her bare shoulders, and Zade had to swallow down his desire to lean over and plant a kiss on her there.

Not now, dickhead. Jesus, you'd think he was a damn teenager again.

"When we first went to meet them, Matt almost slipped

up and said it. Plus, you guys mentioned Ghost and his team, but have never said *what* team they're actually on. If they were SEALs, you would've said it. They're obviously very well-trained in all this covert stuff, and as careful as everyone's been to not mention what they are, that makes me think Delta."

"But why Delta?" Kole leaned up between their seat. "I mean, how do you even know about that sort of stuff?"

"Uh...I read?" Gabby looked back at him from over her shoulder.

"You read about Delta Force?" Zade felt his brows arch high.

"Sure. I read about all sorts of things. Plus, a lot of my romance novels are about special forces teams like that."

"Romance novels, huh?" Kole's voice turned all smooth and sexy. "So like, mommy porn?"

Zade couldn't help but laugh right along with Kole.

Gabby's jaw dropped. "It is *not* mommy porn. For your information, the stories I read are deep and meaningful. They're beautiful love stories about couples overcoming insurmountable odds in order to find their happily ever after."

"Yep." Kole smirked. "And men read those nudie magazines for the articles."

Gabby laughed, the sound sending a strong dose of something wonderful straight into Zade's heart.

"They do have good articles," Zade chimed in.

"I know, right?" Kole slapped him on his shoulder. "That's what I tried telling Sarah when she found an old stash of mine in the cabin once."

"Did she toss them out?"

"Worse. She burned them."

Zade and Gabby both laughed while Kole feigned devastation over losing his treasured magazines. Zade knew the truth, though.

After meeting Sarah, Kole lost interest in any other woman—in person or on paper.

Feeling a bit more relaxed than before, Zade turned onto the gravel road leading to the address Andino had given Gabby. The road was tree-lined, and seemed to be leading them into the middle of nowhere.

No huge surprise given the type of business they were about to conduct.

The road ended at a large, iron gate. It was closed and was currently being guarded by two heavily armed men.

Zade looked around but couldn't see anyone else. Of course, it was getting dark, and they were dealing with Hector Andino. There was no doubt in his mind Andino had other men scattered about.

So do we, asshole.

Still..."I don't like this."

"Of course you don't," Kole said flippantly. "But we're here, and your girl's all dressed up and ready to party." To Gabby, Kole asked, "You ready?"

Zade watched her reaction carefully. If she hesitated or appeared unsure in *any* way, he was turning the car around and saying *fuck it* to the plan.

Of course, she didn't hesitate because his Gabby was one of the strongest, bravest women he'd ever known. She was going to fit right in with the other Bravo wives.

Whoa. He was skipping about a thousand steps with that thought. Oddly, it didn't scare him to imagine him and Gabby married. Not even a little bit.

Truth be told, the idea excited the hell out of him. But it was an idea that would have to wait, because right now, they had a job to do. His?

To protect the woman he loved.

That same woman took a deep breath and let it out slowly. Gabby locked her beautiful eyes on his and said, "Let's go get my sister."

Zade reached over and linked his fingers with hers. "You've got this."

With Gabby's nod of agreement, he pressed his foot on the gas pedal and eased the SUV forward, stopping at the gate. As expected, the two guards came forward.

Rolling down his and Gabby's windows, Zade waited while a man came to each one.

"Good evening, gentlemen. I believe Mr. Andino is expecting me." Gabby handed the slip of paper she'd received to the man on her side of the vehicle.

"Name?" The guy's eyes wandered down to her very visible cleavage.

Gabby cleared her throat. "Excuse me."

The man's gaze snapped back to her face.

"Hi." She smiled. "Welcome back." Her sarcastic tone making Kole snicker from his spot in the back. "The name's Gabriella Smith."

Looking embarrassed at being called out for his ogling, the man got on his phone and waited for someone—either Andino himself or one of his lackeys—to pick up.

After announcing Gabby's arrival, he also told the person on the other end she had two men escorting her. With a quick nod, he ended the call and motioned for the other guard to open the gate.

Zade rolled the windows up and drove forward.

"Well that was easier than I thought." Gabby sounded relieved.

She was more nervous than she wanted to let on. Not that he blamed her.

"You did great, baby." He gave her a smile and a wink. "This will all be over before you know it."

"I hope you're right."

"I'll be right by your side the entire time."

Kole cleared his throat loudly. "Ahem."

"Correction, we'll be right by your side the entire time."

Gabby chuckled softly. "Well I, for one, can't wait until this night is over."

That makes two of us.

Eventually the trees gave way to a clearing and one of Andino's many mansions came into view. It was enormous, beautiful, and creepy, all at the same time.

A low whistle came from the back seat. "Dude, this place is huge," Kole commented, clearly impressed.

"It's like a Spanish revival home had a baby with that hotel from *The Shining*."

Zade burst out laughing at Gabby's unique description. As he pulled around the large, circle drive he had to admit… "You're right. It is."

The home's beige stone walls, arched windows, and ceramic tiled roof definitely fit with the Spanish-style feel. But it's intimidating size and layout, along with the yellow sconces near the arched entryway sent its creep-factor to the top end of Zade's scale.

Following directions from yet another set of armed guards, Zade pulled the SUV into a parking spot near a few early arrivals.

"It's not quite eight-fifteen yet," Kole noted. "Guess some people couldn't wait for the fun to begin."

Suddenly quiet, Gabby reached for the door, but Zade kept his tight grip on her other hand. "Wait for Kole to open the door for you."

"We work for you, tonight. Remember?" Kole smirked as he slid over to his door and got out of the vehicle.

"Right." Gabby shook her head. "That was stupid."

"Not stupid, baby." He waited for her to look back over at

him. "I know you're anxious to get in there and find Samantha, but we've all got a part to play. And like last night, I need you to be that same, take-no-prisoners woman we all met in the club last night. Don't forget...you're in charge. Okay?"

"Okay." Gabby licked her lips and blew out a breath. With a lift of her chin and spine, she added, "You're right. I can do this."

Because he could—and because the windows were tinted enough no one could see in from the sides or back—Zade pulled her to him and pressed his lips to hers. "Yes, you can."

He started for his door, but this time, Gabby stopped him. "Wait."

Zade looked back at her thinking maybe she'd changed her mind. "Yeah?"

"If push comes to shove, you get Sam out of here."

Understanding made his heart ache. "We're all getting out of here. Together. Got it?"

"I know that's what we want to happen, but I'm saying if things don't go as planned, Sam's the priority." Her eyes began to well. "Promise me, Zade. Promise you'll get my sister out."

He lifted her hand and kissed her smooth knuckles. "I promise if Sam is in there, we will get her out."

You too, baby.

There was no way in hell Zade was going to leave Gabby behind. No matter what the cost.

As they got out of the car, Kole went over the intel they had on the house.

"If Nate's schematics of this place are correct, and I'm sure they are, I'm guessing the auction will take place in the common area, over there." Kole tipped his chin toward the more elaborate entrance of the three they could see.

Each one was guarded by at least one man, but that

particular door had two. They began walking in that direction.

"Pretty sure those guys will tell us if we're headed for the wrong door," Gabby spoke low so only they could hear.

Falling in place behind her, Zade and Kole got into their roles as bodyguards. Not hard to do since his main goal in this whole operation was to keep Gabby safe.

After tonight, it'll be my main goal in life, if she'll have me.

And damn if he wasn't praying like hell she would.

"Five guards where you are, one on the east and west ends of the house, and three more covering the north," Ghost informed them all through their coms.

Using one of Nate's many, patent-pending software and hardware designs he'd dubbed the Stealth Drone, they had an undetectable, UAV—or unmanned aerial vehicle—flying high in the night sky above the property.

It could reach altitudes matching that of any military-grade drone in existence, as well as detecting human heat signals at levels surpassing the government's devices, but with near silent movement.

Hence the nickname, Stealth Drone.

"You get that okay, baby?" Zade whispered to Gabby who was two steps ahead of them.

She coughed into her hand. "Yep."

Like before, they'd tested the system multiple times before arriving, but Zade couldn't help but check it again. This was Gabby they were talking about. She was his to protect and keep safe.

"Good girl."

"As expected, SD can't see through the ceramic roof, but at least there won't be any surprises outside," Nate informed them.

"Speaking of outside"—Gabe's deep voice came through —"we're in position and ready. We'll wait until you give the signal, Zade, and then we will go after the guards. Once we take care of them, we'll all make our way inside to you."

The 'we' his team leader was referring to was Gabe, Matt, Ghost, Truck, Fletch, and Hollywood. According to their plan, Gabe and Matt were in charge of taking out the two guards by the gate while Ghost and his team members took care of any others waiting in the wings.

"We've each got one tango in our sights," Ghost informed them.

"There are a handful of others scattered between your positions and the house," Nate made sure they knew.

Using the van they'd set up for the club scene the night before, Nate was tucked safely away in the trees at the end of the turnoff.

"Damn," Kole shook his head as he listened to Nate spout off where Andino's men were stationed. "You'd think the guy was paranoid or something."

"Or something," Zade growled.

They were almost to the entry's double doors when the two men guarding it opened it for them. "Thank you, gentlemen," Gabby nodded and smiled.

Like a pro.

Once inside, Kole gave another, low whistle. Zade couldn't blame him. The place was ridiculously large and over-the-top elaborate.

Black and white marble tiles gave the entryway floor a checkerboard pattern. In the middle beneath an enormous crystal chandelier was what Zade could only guess to be an expensive as fuck elaborate rug.

The wide, wooden staircase that greeted them split off into two directions at the top and was edged in a traditional-style Spanish wrought iron railing.

Large floor-to-ceiling windows lined the lower and

upper walls, and vintage furniture had been strategically placed throughout the space.

"So this is how the other half live," Gabby said softly.

Nate scoffed. "If by other half, you mean sadistic cartel leader and skin trade expert, then yeah."

"Gabriella!"

Their heads turned toward the familiar voice. Speaking of sadistic assholes...

Hector Andino made his way through the encased entryway on their left and walked toward them. "You look absolutely breathtaking."

Probably the only thing he and Zade would ever agree on.

"Thank you." Transitioning into character flawlessly, Gabby let her eyes trail down the bastard's lean frame and back up again. "You're looking quite handsome yourself."

"That's quite the compliment coming from such a stunning beauty. I'm so glad you could make it."

Even Zade could see the heat pouring from the twisted bastard's dark eyes. The man's blatant flirting made Zade want to punch Andino in the throat.

"I almost didn't." Gabby lied. "I had hoped to hear from you sooner and thought maybe you'd decided not to do business with me, after all. I was on the phone with Webb's pilot instructing him to get the jet ready when the front desk rang my room about your note."

In reality, they hadn't expected to hear from him as early as they had. However, thanks to a phone call from Gabe to Ryker, Zade had known late last night that Andino had already looked into Gabby's claims about the man she supposedly worked for.

Each one she'd mentioned to Andino had backed her up, as per their individual deals with the Feds. Fuckers were lucky they had.

If even one of them had tried to go back on their word

and had thrown Gabby under the bus with Andino, there wouldn't have been a prison in existence that could've kept them safe from Zade.

"My apologies, Gabriella." Andino reached for her hand and brought it to his lips. The asshole let them linger on her knuckles, the same ones Zade had kissed minutes earlier in the SUV. "As you can imagine, it took some time for me to, how do you Americans say…vet you."

Zade slid his gaze to Kole who looked like he wanted to roll his eyes at the prick's dramatic demeanor.

"Given that I'm here, I trust my references were adequate?"

"More than adequate. You were given rave reviews by them all. Especially Señor Webb."

"Glad to hear it, although I can't say I'm surprised. Like I told you last night, I'm very good at what I do."

"So they told me." Andino's thin lips curled into smile that matched his lust-filled gaze.

You can't kill him. Yet.

First chance he got…

"Please, come." The man held out his arm for Gabby to take. "The auction is about to begin."

Sliding her hand along Andino's elbow, Gabby looked up at him and said, "I hope there is something available that will be to Mr. Webb's liking."

Meaning she hoped there was a certain blonde-haired, blue-eyed girl amongst the others.

"Trust me, Gabriella. I have something that will fit Señor Webb's needs perfectly."

"I'm sure you do. Otherwise, this entire evening will be a huge waste for the both of us."

Damn, she wasn't just good at this. *She's fucking phenomenal.*

"I would never waste such a beautiful woman's time.

Especially when I know so much pleasure awaits me after we've completed our business."

Gabby arched a confident brow. "The business will only be complete once I've gotten what I came for."

"Don't worry, Gabriella. I am sure we'll both get exactly what we want before the night is over."

CHAPTER 14

Gabby's heart felt like it was going to fly right out of her chest as she allowed Hector Andino to lead her into what appeared to be a grand ballroom. The only thing keeping her grounded was knowing Zade and Kole were following closely behind.

When they crossed over into the large, open space, Gabby couldn't help but be in awe of its beauty. The room's high ceiling was adorned with multiple intersecting beams, and six matching chandeliers hung from the opposite walls.

They provided the perfect amount of lighting for an intimate dinner party or dance. Too bad this was neither.

As they made their way further into the room, Andino was greeted by several of his guests. In order to keep herself in check and not react to the vile reason behind their presence, Gabby took in as many details as she could about the room.

Never know when you might need an impromptu escape plan.

Along the wall to her right were several large, arched windows. Not the best option for an escape, but if worse came to worse, Gabby wasn't above throwing herself out one.

To her left was a balcony that ran the entire length of the wall. She made a mental note of the small staircase that appeared to lead up to it.

Like the entryway, the floors were made of a gorgeous, marble tile. However, instead of a checkerboard pattern, these were all white with gray swirls.

It was the most beautiful room Gabby had ever been in, but the small stage lit up at the far end of the room was a stark reminder of the horrible, ugly event that was about to take place, here.

The two men from the club stood guard, one at each end of the stage. The one on the left—the same one who'd taken Zade's gun after she'd threatened to 'fire' him—was staring over at her with a cold intensity that made her spine shiver.

"Would you care for a drink, Gabriella? Some champagne, perhaps." Andino snapped his finger. A man in a black suit came to them. He moved surprisingly fast for someone balancing a large tray of filled crystal flutes in his hand.

She looked away from the intimidating guard's stare and smiled at Andino. "Champagne? Are we celebrating something, already?"

Hector laughed. "Think of it as a pre-celebration drink."

"I like the way you think, Hector."

She probably shouldn't drink tonight but refusing Andino didn't seem like a very good idea.

Carefully, he lifted two champagne glasses from the tray and handed her one. "To a successful night for us both."

Gabby touched the rim of her glass to his. "I'll drink to that."

Though she wanted to chug the whole damn thing down to help calm her nerves, she refrained and took an acceptable sip. Gabby opened her mouth to try and ask about the auction's *inventory* when a shorter, older man approached Andino.

With a tap on his shoulder, Andino turned and leaned toward the other man. Whispering something Gabby wished she could hear, the guy said whatever he came to say and was gone as quickly as he'd appeared.

Gabby thought maybe she'd seen a harshness flash behind Andino's eyes, but when the man left and he looked back at her, it was gone. If it was even there to begin with.

Quit being so paranoid.

Kind of hard to do when you're sharing a drink with a monster.

"Is everything okay?" she couldn't help but ask.

"Of course." Hector smiled. "The auction is slated to begin in five minutes. My assistant merely wanted to remind me of the time and give me this." He handed her a bidding card like she'd seen in the movies. "This is your bidding number. I must go to the stage to begin the evening, but once the auction begins, I will come find you."

"Oh, you don't have to—"

"It would be my honor to stand next to you this evening. Besides"—he leaned in *way* too closely—"having the host next to you during the bidding can only help your chances, si?"

"I don't suppose it would hurt." Gabby kept her smile steady. "Although I have to say, I can usually handle myself quite well."

Arousal ignited behind the brown of his eyes, making her want to claw them out with a rusty, jagged spoon.

"I bet you do, mi amor," Andino purred, turning her comment into something it wasn't. "This won't take long. I promise to return shortly."

Forcing her own heated gaze, Gabby licked her lips and told him, "I'll be waiting."

If the man were any more turned on, he'd probably jump

her bones right there on ballroom floor. The thought nearly made her gag.

Zade stepped up beside her. "You did great, baby."

"Thanks," Gabby blew out a breath and swallowed the rest of her champagne in one gulp.

"Easy, there, Gabs." Kole stood on her other side. "Don't want you going crazy and spending all of Homeland's money. On second thought." He took a cue from Andino and snapped to get a waiter's attention.

Smiling—at both the ultra-short version of her name and the man's obvious attempt to lighten the mood—Gabby looked over at Kole.

"No, you're right. The last thing I need is to get drunk while in the middle of a mission. I'm usually a lightweight, so it wouldn't take much."

Before the waiter Kole had called over could get to them, another man brought over a tray with a single glass. He handed it to Gabby. "For the lady, courtesy of tonight's host."

"Oh." Gabby took the glass. "Thank you."

The younger man nodded and walked away.

"Cheap date." Kole slid Zade a knowing smirk. "You're a lucky man, King."

Still looking like he was about to punch his friend in the nose, Zade instructed her sharply, "Don't drink that."

She put a hand to Zade's solid bicep. "Kole's only teasing, Zade. I'm not *that* much of a lightweight."

His intense gaze slid to hers. "It has nothing to do with your low tolerance. But if this dickhead calls you a cheap date one more time, we'll see who ends up laughing."

"Down boy." Kole grinned. "Your girl's right. I was merely trying to lighten the mood."

"Mood's fine, thanks."

Clearly not, but Gabby wasn't about to point out the obvious. "Hector sent this specifically for me. What if he's watching? Won't he suspect something if I don't at least have a sip?"

"Exactly. The fucker sent that drink over specifically for you."

She glanced down at the drink in her hand. Understanding began to sink in. "You think it's drugged?"

"Don't want to take any chances."

Gabby thought he was simply being overprotective. "It would be pretty stupid of him to do that, wouldn't it? I mean, you two are right here and I'm in the middle of a large crowd."

"Don't worry, Gabs," Kole grinned. "Zade's just pissed because Andino has his sights on you."

Yes, Kole. Because that helps.

"Better be the only fucking thing he puts on her," Zade grumbled. "Asshole could barely keep his eyes above her neckline the entire time he was here."

"Kind of the point of the dress, wasn't it? To entice Andino and keep him close?"

"Not that close."

"It's all part of an act, Zade." She quickly tried to assure him. "Trust me."

"Oh, I trust *you* plenty. It's Andino I don't trust."

"None of us do. But until I can get to Sam, we all have to put our disgust for the man aside."

"She's right." Gabe's voice hit their ears. "Lock it down, King, or I'll send Turner in to take your place."

Zade blinked, but then smirked as he responded to his team leader. "Matt's not wearing a tux, Dawson. He wouldn't get past the front gate."

But Zade was wearing a tuxedo, and damn. Talk about panty-dropping *gorgeous*.

Gabby thought about how surprisingly prepared they'd been. They'd thought to bring tuxes and all that other stuff with them on the off chance they *might* end up attending one of Andino's skin auctions...

Who thinks that far ahead?

They must've been Boy Scouts when they were younger. *Had* to be. Maybe it was some sort of R.I.S.C. prerequisite or something. That and all the other qualities she'd noticed the Bravo men had in common.

Boy Scout? *Check.*

Military badass? *Check.*

Look gorgeous all the freaking time, know how to use a gun, and be strong enough to have wild monkey sex while holding your woman up against a door?

Check, check, and...definitely check.

While she had no first-hand knowledge of the other men's abilities in regard to that last item on the list, Gabby would bet what little money she had that they'd have no problem performing with the same...vigor and tenacity... Zade had last night.

Without thinking, Gabby absentmindedly took a sip of the beverage in her hand before pulling it away.

Crap. She swallowed what was already in her mouth. She wasn't supposed to do that, but...

Damn, that's good.

This second glass was much sweeter than the first. Though she didn't drink alcohol often—like hardly ever—a sweet Moscato and champagne were two of her favorites.

She'd have to find out where she could order a case to be sent back to Chicago.

Right, because you could afford that.

"I could borrow yours." Matt's comment about Zade's tux tore her from her scattered thoughts.

She slid both men a quick glance, relieved to find neither of them had seen her slip-up.

Pretending to be talking to Kole, Zade looked at him with

a smirked response for Matt. "You could, but it wouldn't look nearly as good on you as it does on me."

Kole snickered along with the other men listening from afar.

Gabby would have to agree. Not that Matt wasn't good-looking. Of course, he was. The guy was on Bravo, wasn't he?

Except he wasn't...

"Zade." Kole tipped his chin toward the stage.

Both she and Zade turned to see what Kole was seeing.

"All right, boys and girl. Get your game faces on and your guns ready. The show's about to start."

Gabby didn't have a gun, although she wished she did. A really big one with a bullet specifically made to take out Hector Andino.

She imagined that bullet going into the man's head, right between his evil eyes and smiled.

Blinking, Gabby shook the awful thought away. She'd never even held a gun, let alone fired one.

What's wrong with you?

Her thoughts were all over the place, which was not a good thing. Not now when she was *this* close to getting Samantha back.

Clearing her throat, Gabby lifted her chin and returned her focus to the stage, where Hector Andino was about to speak.

He was about to open the bidding...on human beings. They were someone's daughter. Someone's sister.

Gabby's heart broke as she thought about Sam and how terrified she must be.

She looked around the room at the vile men and women here. The room was filled with them, all smiles and laughter.

These were horrible, awful people, and suddenly, she wanted to be anywhere in the world but in this room.

"You okay?" Zade whispered beside her.

The concern in his voice brought her back into focus. “I'm fine.”

She had to be. *For Sam.*

With her full drink in her right hand, Gabby's left one hung loosely by her side. Keeping her eyes forward, she felt the slightest of touches as Zade whispered his fingertips along the back of her hand.

“We're almost there, baby. Just a little longer.”

“I said I'm good.” She pulled her hand away.

Gabby instantly felt bad. She didn't mean to sound so snippy, but she couldn't think straight when he touched her on a *good* day.

And this…this was about as far from being a good day as she could get.

Though she wasn't looking straight at him, Gabby could feel Zade stiffen beside her. Damn it, she hadn't meant to hurt his feelings.

“Zade, I'm sorry. I—”

“Welcome, ladies and gentlemen.”

Gabby looked around, realizing only then how many other women were present. They were most definitely outnumbered, but at least she didn't stand out completely.

So now you're relieved that you're not the only woman here to buy other women?

She closed her eyes, the room swaying slightly. Or had it?

That's it. Definitely no more champagne for you.

She reopened them and looked to where Andino was standing. After finishing his welcome speech, he began to go over the nauseating rules.

Once the auctioneer announces ‘sold’, that bidder must immediately go to the purchase table located at the south end of the stage to make the payment.

After that, the purchaser will be escorted out the side door with their purchase.

They must immediately leave the property.

As far as their plan went, those rules worked out perfectly for theirs. She'd bid on Sam, pay for her—Ghost had assured her the account number Ryker had provided had more than enough money in it—and they'd be *required* to leave.

"Let's start the bidding, shall we?"

The room filled with excited applause.

"Oh, God." The champagne churned in her stomach.

"You can do this, baby," Zade reassured her. "I'm right here."

"He's right, Gabby," Kole cheered her on. "You've been a freaking rock star during this whole thing. This is the easy part."

"Waiting for your signal, King," Gabe reminded him.

Gabby had heard the men talking this morning about what would happen once they got Sam a safe distance away. Zade would give them the green light and Gabe, Matt, and Ghost's team would storm the property and take Andino into custody. From there, Ghost and his team would transport him across the border where a federal chopper would be waiting.

After that, Gabby wasn't sure where they'd take Andino, and she didn't care. All she cared about was getting Sam out safely, along with the two teams helping her.

As for Andino's customers, Nate was positioned in a spot with a vantage point that allowed him to see the road clearly. He'd record and report the plates and vehicle descriptions to another team of black-ops operatives Ryker had sent in that morning.

Those operatives were positioned in various places along the only road leading out of the property. They'd move fast, gather the men and women who'd participated in one of the worst crimes imaginable, and get the girls to a safe place until they could be taken back to the States.

Please let the girls who'd already crossed over the stage be safe, already.

On paper, the plan was flawless.

Gabby tried to tune out the first several biddings. If she paid attention to the terrified young girls on that stage or to the disgusting individuals buying them, she'd vomit all over her borrowed, designer shoes.

So she did what she'd done the night her foster brother attacked her. She let her mind travel to someplace else. Someplace far, far away.

Gabby thought of the day she'd first met Sam. How the little spitfire of a girl had come to her defense. Kole had called her a rock star, but Sam…she was the real rock star. Actually Sam had simply been her *rock*.

Most days, Gabby still couldn't believe how welcoming the Shoemakers had been to her.

They knew the story her other foster family had strewn about the city. They knew she'd purposely intended to cause her foster brother pain. They knew she came from a fatherless family with a crack whore for a mom.

And they didn't care.

For the first time in her life, she'd been placed with a family who saw her. Really saw her. And it was all thanks to Sam.

Please, God. Please let me save her.

A wave of dizziness hit, but Gabby shook it away. She had to focus, now. Sam had to be on that stage soon.

"There you are." Andino's voice traveled over the auctioneer's ramblings.

Gabby turned to her left and saw him coming toward her. *Great.* She'd rather hoped he'd forgotten his promise to come find her, again.

"I thought you'd forgotten me." She forced a smile.

"Impossible." He grabbed her free hand and kissed it like before. "I see you got the drink I sent over."

"I did. Thank you."

"You've barely touched it. Was it not to your liking?"

She so badly wanted to give Zade an I-told-you-so glance. "Oh, no. It's quite delicious."

"Well, drink up." He smiled. "The night is young, and there is much to celebrate."

Shit. She needed an excuse to explain why she didn't want to drink anymore.

"My men and I got caught up in a discussion about business." She smiled wider. "I'm afraid it's gotten a bit warm. I don't do warm champagne."

"I see. Well, we must rectify the situation." Andino started to motion to the waiter.

"No!" Gabby grabbed his arm to stop him.

The move had been reflexive. She hadn't thought about what she was doing, she'd simply acted.

Oh, crap. "I need to pace myself, Hector. Like you said, the night is young. I need a clear head to ensure I don't spend too much of Mr. Webb's money this evening."

Gabby held her smile—and her breath—and waited nervously for his response. Reaching down, he gently lifted her hand from his arm and kissed it again.

"My apologies, Gabriella. I seem to have momentarily forgotten your rule."

"My rule?"

What rule?

"Business before pleasure. Yes?"

"Oh, yes. Of course." Gabby chuckled nervously. "That rule. As a matter of fact, that is my number *one* rule."

You're rambling.

Seemingly amused, Andino looked back toward the stage where yet another woman had been put on display.

"Are you enjoying yourself?"

"Honestly? No." She gently pulled her hand from his grasp. With more control she told him, "I'd hoped to see what I came for by now. Several girls have come and gone, but none like the one I described to you in your office. I assure you, Mr. Webb is willing to pay top dollar *if* you have the right product on site. If not, tell me. I'll say my goodbye, now, and save us both some time."

"Impatient, I see." Rather than appear ruffled by her insistence, Andino's smile grew even wider. "We are about to take a brief intermission before continuing with the second half of the auction. I believe the young woman you are interested in will be appearing near the end of tonight's event. You know"—he raised his hand toward her face and began toying with one of her loose curls—"I always thought feisty redheads were a myth. I'm pleased to see I was mistaken."

Don't break his hand. Don't break his hand.

Not that she could. Zade, on the other hand...

"You're going to want to stop touching her."

Her eyes rose to meet his. She'd never heard his voice sound so deadly.

Should that be such a turn-on?

Seemingly unfazed—although he *did* stop touching her as Zade suggested—Andino turned and faced him. "It was my understanding you were here as protection for Miss Smith."

"I am."

Kole joined in. "We both are."

"Well, gentlemen." Andino chuckled. "I can assure you, I am of no threat to your boss. I'm simply enamored by her natural beauty and strong will. A perfect combination in a woman, wouldn't you agree?"

Other than to clench his jaw shut, Zade didn't respond.

"Pay no attention to them, Hector." Gabby slid her hand along the other man's arm. "They're upset because I won't buy them each a girl, too. That's what we were discussing when you walked up."

"Ah." Andino chuckled some more. "Maybe next time you'll get yours, yes?"

Zade's mouth slid into a cold smile. "You're right, Mr. Andino. Tonight is all about you getting what you deserve."

"Easy, King," Gabe's warning whispered from Gabby's earrings to her ear. "You're supposed to be her bodyguard, not her lover."

Doing her best to tamper the blush she felt crawling up her neck, Gabby heard herself blurt out, "I changed my mind." All three men turned to look at her. "Like you said"—she smiled, recovering quickly—"the night is young, and this champagne is magnificent. I suppose I could allow myself to indulge in one more drink while we wait for the intermission to end."

What the hell are you doing?

Her gaze slid back to Zade's. His expression mimicked her thoughts, but it was his fault, anyway. If he hadn't gone all caveman on Andino, she wouldn't have felt the need to rescue him—*them*—from the situation.

"I'd love to, Gabriella. There's a bar right over there. Shall we?"

With a stubborn tilt of her chin she focused solely on Andino. "Actually, could I meet you there? There's something I need to discuss with my men. It won't take but a minute."

"Of course. I'll be waiting."

"Thank you, Hector."

Gabby waited until he was far enough away before turning to Zade.

"What are you doing?"

"Me?" His dark brows shot up before turning into a deep scowl. "What are *you* doing? We just had this conversation. This isn't the time to—"

"You know what?" She interrupted his rant. "When I become an official member of Bravo Team, you can order me around. Until then, I suggest you chill the hell out and let me do what I came here to do. I'm playing a part, Zade. That's why you brought me along, right?"

"To help us get close to Andino. Not live it up like we're at a goddamn beach party."

"Beach party? Really?" Fuming, Gabby slid a glance to Hector, who was talking with someone else at the bar and not watching them. She turned back and arched a brow at the man currently acting like an overprotective Neanderthal. "I know my limits, Zade. I can handle two glasses of champagne. I also plan to watch the champagne as it's poured into my glass by the bartender before he hands it straight to me. Now, if you'll excuse me, Andino is waiting."

Not waiting for a response, Gabby turned and walked away. She could practically feel the heat from Zade's stare on her back as she made her way across the room.

Yes, Zade's team and the others were in charge tonight, but she'd been doing a pretty damn good job at keeping it together so far. And sure, maybe she shouldn't have jumped in between him and Andino, but this whole clandestine business was new to her.

Wearing a mask and putting on a show to get by on the streets was one thing. Getting up close and personal with a cartel leader who would probably slit her throat without blinking an eye if he found out who they really were...that was a whole new level of crazy.

She'd gotten nervous, worried Andino would do something to Zade if he'd kept pushing the man, so she'd blurted the first thing that had come to mind.

The bar was within their line of sight, so she was perfectly safe. As safe as she could be in this place, anyway.

"What would you like to drink, mi amor? We have many options available."

God, she hated it when Andino called her that. "I'd love more of this." Gabby set the glass he'd sent over earlier onto the bar. "I promise not to let this one get warm."

Yes, she'd already cut herself off from having any more alcohol but getting another drink had been her brilliant idea. If she told him she'd changed her mind again, he'd most likely get suspicious.

"Champagne it is." Andino gave the bartender a nod. "Two glasses of champagne, please." Andino gave the man a look and added, "Make sure to give the lady the good stuff."

"Yes, sir." The man nodded. "Coming right up."

"So, Gabriella." Andino faced her once more. "How is it you came to be in this business?"

"I sort of fell into it, really."

"Do tell."

"Oh, it's not at all exciting, Hector." The bartender returned. She watched carefully as he filled her glass straight from the bottle and handed it to her. Feeling secure, she looked back up at Andino as his drink was being poured. "I'd much rather talk about you and your success. I mean, look at this place." She let her eyes wander around the room and damn near did a double take when she caught Zade staring straight back at her.

The man was *not* happy.

"Are you all right, my dear?"

Gabby tore her eyes from Zade and brought her focus back to the man at her side.

"I'm fine." She smiled. "Please, continue." She put a hand on his arm for good measure. "I want to hear all about how you became the amazing, powerful man you are today."

Knowing she needed to loosen up or run the risk of

blowing her cover, Gabby decided to use the situation to pay Zade back for his little alpha male moment.

Though she was no longer looking at him, she knew Zade was still watching her closely. *Very* closely.

With purposeful movements, she used her finger to trace the rim of her glass as she pretended to listen to Andino go on and on about his life accomplishments. Making it seem like an absentminded movement while she listened to Andino, who was still talking about himself, she slid her fingers lower.

Gabby began running them up and down the crystal stem slowly, almost as if she were stroking a lover's body.

Andino's eyes followed her movements, his speech almost stuttering as his focus became split between what he was saying and what she was doing. But it was the low, almost indiscernible groan reaching her ear that damn near made her smile.

It was ridiculous, and completely inappropriate given the situation, but knowing Zade was watching—and *liking*—what she was doing was one hell of a turn on.

Like long-distance foreplay.

We should really book that beach house again after this. For a solid month, at least.

Gabby's sex began to swell and ache with need. She could actually feel her panties becoming damp with arousal from thinking about all the things she wanted to do with Zade.

Things they had done to each other last night.

Continuing on with the dangerously erotic game, she lifted the drink to her lips. When a drop of champagne started to drip off of her bottom lip, Gabby used her fingertip to catch it. Then, deliberately making the motion as seductive as she could, she stuck the digit between her lips and sucked until every drop of the cool beverage was gone.

A low, whispered curse hit her ear before she heard, "You're gonna pay for that later, sweetheart."

At the same time, Andino coughed and began ordering another drink.

With his attention elsewhere, Gabby looked across the room at Zade. Using the glass to conceal her mouth, she whispered, "Promises, promises."

"Can we please keep the show g-rated for the kids at home?" Nate groaned from somewhere outside.

Gabby put her hand to her mouth and coughed to cover her laugh. "Sorry, Nate," she whispered into her ring. The entire scene felt like something out of a James Bond flick.

Of course, this wasn't a movie, and she was definitely no Bond Girl.

This was real life, and the game they were all playing was a very dangerous one.

When their drinks were empty, Andino escorted her back to where Zade and Kole were still standing. From the way he was looking at her, Gabby knew she most definitely would be paying for her little performance later.

Whatever punishment he decided to dish out would be totally worth it, because the distraction had worked. She felt more relaxed than she had since coming here.

Relaxed and ready to kick some Andino ass.

A few minutes after rejoining Zade and Kole, however, Gabby began to feel a little *too* relaxed. Her head felt full and heavy, kind of like when she got a cold. The room would sway back and forth whenever she turned her head, and there was an odd tingling sensation in her fingertips and toes.

Shit. Two glasses and she was already feeling this buzzed? That didn't seem right.

Sonofabitch.

He *had* drugged her. But how? She'd seen the other man

pour the drink.

The bottle.

The drugs must've already been in the bottle. Except Andino had drank from it, too. Hadn't he?

Through the growing haze, Gabby remembered she hadn't actually watched Andino's drink being poured. They'd been talking, and she'd only assumed his was from the same bottle.

Oh, God.

Gabby swung her gaze to Zade who was standing a foot away from her and looking straight ahead at the stage. She needed to get his attention, but how? Andino was standing right next to him.

The com. Whisper into the com.

Acting as if she were scratching her face, Gabby whispered his name. Zade immediately turned his head toward her. After what seemed like forever, his brows scrunched together with a questioning frown.

With a quick glance to make sure Andino wasn't watching them, he mouthed the words, "You okay?"

Gabby opened her mouth. She tried to answer him. Thought maybe she'd shaken her head no, but had she, really, or was she imagining it.

Something was wrong. Something was very, *very* wrong.

Black dots filled her vision and Zade's image became blurred. She blinked several times, but it didn't help.

Zade said her name loudly, or at least she thought he had. It was hard to tell because his voice was suddenly muffled and distorted, its pitch much lower than it should've been.

The people standing around them started to stare, but Gabby continued trying to focus on Zade. She opened her mouth again, this time to tell him she was going to pass out. But it was too late.

She already had.

CHAPTER 15

Two minutes earlier...

Zade stared straight ahead. To anyone looking, he would appear to be enthralled by the next young woman to be escorted onto the stage. In truth, he was fighting the urge to grab Gabby by the hand and haul her pretty little ass out of this hell hole.

He'd never wanted to turn her over his knee more than he did in that moment. Naturally, the second he thought that, he pictured a scene where he *did* have her over his knee flashed through his mind, and...*fuck*.

That was *not* what he needed to be thinking about.

The auction had resumed, and Hector Andino was standing less than three feet away. The last thing Zade needed was for the bastard—or Kole—to notice the raging hard-on threatening to burst through his damn zipper.

Lucky for him, his jacket was long enough to cover that particular area.

He gritted his teeth together and kept staring straight ahead. *Damn stubborn woman.*

If he were being honest with himself—which he wasn't, because he was still too pissed—Gabby had done the exact right thing by stepping away with Andino when she had. Seeing him touch her had sent a rush of fury through Zade's veins. One he damn near couldn't control.

So yeah, he was pissed. At himself for letting his emotions almost get the best of him during a fucking op. That didn't happen to Zade. Not ever.

That's because you've never been on an op with Gabriella Stevens before.

As usual, the tiny voice was right. That little show she'd put on had been solely for his benefit, and Zade damn well knew it.

"Zade."

He was so busy mentally kicking his own ass, he almost missed her whispering his name.

Zade turned his head and looked at her. Gabby was staring up at him, her eyes glassy and unfocused. She almost looked...Jesus, was she drunk?

Are you fucking kidding me?

He started to say something to that affect when he noticed something odd about the way she was staring back at him. Like she couldn't focus on him...or anything else.

With a quick, mental run-through, he catalogued the drinks she'd had. Two drinks over the span of nearly an hour. Zade knew she'd said she was a lightweight, but this was taking it to a whole other level.

His eyes locked with hers again, and this time, he zeroed in on her pupils. Frowning—because yeah, they were way too fucking big—Zade shot a quick glance at Andino to make sure he wasn't paying attention before whispering, "You okay?"

Gabby shook her head. She opened her mouth as if to say something, but nothing came out.

"Gabby!" Zade said her name loudly, not giving a shit about the stares they were now getting.

"Is something wrong?" Andino asked, as if he gave two shits about her.

Kole snapped to attention, as well. "What is it? What's the matter?"

Zade didn't have time to answer his teammate because at the exact same time, Gabby's eyes rolled back into her head, and her legs crumpled beneath her.

"Gabby!" He sprang into action, barely catching her in time to keep her head from hitting the hard marble tile.

Ignoring the gasps from the surrounding crowd, Zade tapped her cheek to try and get her to wake up. "Gabby? Gabriella, wake up!"

Shit!

"She's out cold, man." Kole squatted down beside him.

Thank you, Captain Fucking Obvious.

Gabe spoke into the coms. "SITREP."

"She's been drugged."

"I do not know how this could have happened." Andino appeared as worried as they were. "My office is off of the ballroom, right over there. There is a couch. You can lay her down and make her comfortable. Come." He started in that direction. "I'll show you."

Don't know, my ass.

Zade looked at Kole. Besides putting a bullet through that fucker Andino's brain, he wanted nothing more than to get Gabby the hell out of there. But…

The auction wasn't over yet, and they still hadn't seen hide nor hair of Samantha Shoemaker.

Promise you'll get my sister out.

Gabby's words rang through his head reminding him of

the promise he'd made. It was one he damn well intended to keep.

"Fine. We'll take her to your office," Zade told Andino, only so the others would hear and know where they'd be.

Scooping her up, Zade cradled Gabby in his arms and held her against his chest as he followed Andino. He didn't trust the fucker any farther than he could throw him, but right now he didn't have a choice but to play along.

Not if he wanted to maintain their cover and try to figure out where Sam was.

The auction came to a halt and the crowd parted to give them room to walk. As they moved, Matt's voice came through the coms.

"She needs fluids to help dilute and flush the drugs out of her system. There's an IV set-up in the med bag. I made sure there was one in the back of the SUV you guys came in. I can walk one of you through it."

Zade's glance slid to Kole's, his expression clear. He was not leaving Gabby's side.

"I'll get the first-aid kit from the car," Kole offered.

"Use that door there." Andino pointed to an exit near his office door. "My men will let you back in." He gave the guy guarding the door a look and a nod.

"Hurry," Zade growled the order.

Kole split off in that direction, a definite haste in his step.

"In here," Andino entered a four-digit code on a security keypad before opening the door. He turned and motioned for another one of his men to keep an eye on the door.

The whole scene screamed set-up, but with no other option, Zade followed the man into the room.

As described, it was an office. Traditional wood paneling covered the walls, and matching wood trim and a large, wooden desk added to the room's masculine feel. Also as

Andino had claimed, a black, leather couch was positioned against the north wall.

Zade went straight for it, carefully laying down his precious cargo.

"Stay here. I'll go get a glass of water and a pillow for her head."

Gabby didn't need a goddamn pillow. She needed to get as far the fuck away from here as possible. But he didn't argue, because Andino's absence would give him a chance to talk to Gabe freely.

"Appreciate it," he gritted out. Sitting next to her limp form, Zade waited until Andino left the office through yet another door at the back of the room to talk to Gabe.

"Okay, Dawson, I'm clear to talk. Not sure how long he'll be gone."

Gabe wasted no time in responding. "What the fuck happened, King?"

"Andino gave Gabby some champagne that was laced. With what, I don't know, but she's out cold and her pupils are huge and...*Goddamnit!*" He ran his fingers through his hair, ready to tear it out from its roots.

"Take a breath, King. How's her pulse?"

Zade pressed a trembling hand to Gabby's neck. "Too damn fast."

"That's it. We'll bypass the extra guards and hit the ones we need to in order to come in."

"No!" Zade shook his head even though his team leader couldn't see him. Or maybe he could, since Gabby's necklace had that camera in it.

That doesn't fucking matter now!

"What the hell do you mean, no?"

"You come in hot now, gunfire will light this place up like the Fourth of July. Gabby could get hurt, not to mention we

still have no idea where Samantha Shoemaker's being held."
If she was even there, at all.

Zade shook his head again He couldn't think like that. Sam *had* to be here. For Gabby's sake, he wouldn't consider anything else.

"King's right," Ghost cut in. "We need to go one-on-one, silent elimination. Otherwise Andino gets spooked and runs."

"Or worse," a deep voice Zade recognized as Truck's agreed.

"Shit, you're both right. *Goddamnit!*" Gabe took a breath deep enough for Zade to hear then blew it out. "On my order. In the meantime, King…you're gonna have to do whatever you can to stall. Play along with whatever fucked up game Andino's trying to play. We'll clear the perimeter then breach. That time comes, you use the distraction to get your asses out of there. Let us worry about Hector Andino and finding the Shoemaker girl."

"Copy that."

Gabe and Ghost began a new conversation. The two team leaders worked with Nate and his bird's eye view to decide the best way to approach Andino's men.

Zade tuned them out, his entire focus returning to Gabby, who was *still* unconscious.

"Baby?" He checked her pulse again. It was still too fast, but at least it was there. "Gabriella, you need to wake up. Come on, baby. I *really* need you to open your eyes."

She moaned. That was a good sign, right?

"Zade?" His name was barely a whisper.

"I'm here. I'm right here." By her side, where he belonged.

Gabby's eyes fluttered open. "W-what…" She tried to sit up.

"Easy, baby. You've been drugged."

Those fluttering eyes shot open. "Drugged?" Gabby sat up

quickly. Groaning, she laid back down. "Okay, not such a good idea." She took a few slow breaths before asking, "Andino?"

"He went to get you a pillow and some water."

Frowning, she looked around the room...slowly. "Where's...Kole?"

"Getting the med bag. He wants to hook you up to an IV to help flush your system."

"Sam?" Her voice was still quiet and slurred.

"We'll find her. Gabe and the others are making their way to the house as we speak. Once they get inside, I'll get you out and to safety while they find your sister."

"No." She shook her head and pushed herself up again. This time, she took her time, not stopping until she was sitting up straight. "Need to go, now. Have to...f-find her...now.

Keeping her steady with his hands, Zade leaned down in order to look her in the eye. Her pupils were still larger than normal, but not as bad as before. The drugs were clearly still affecting her system, but at least she was conscious and somewhat alert.

Hopefully alert enough to understand what he was trying to tell her.

"Gabby, we can't. I saw Andino motion for a guard to stand right outside that door after we came in. He's armed to the teeth. We try to rush out of here now, Andino and his men will stop us. We have to play along, for now."

"Play along?" She looked at him as if he was the one under the influence of drugs. "*He's* the one who drugged me! Or... had me drugged. Either way...we need to get...out of...here."

"Baby, listen to yourself. You can barely finish a full sentence, let alone fight off a bunch of cartel goons."

Christ, he didn't even want to picture her having to do that. Ever.

"Kole's on his way back with the IV bag. He'll get you hooked up and—"

"Actually, I'm not." Kole spoke in his com again.

"What the fuck do you mean, you're not? Get your ass in here, Jameson. Gabby needs you."

"I would, but Andino's bouncer is refusing to let me back inside."

Damn.

Zade had been so focused on Gabby, his brain had apparently decided to tune everything else out, causing him to miss that particular conversation.

"Kick his ass…K-Kole." Gabby cleared her throat. "Know you…can."

"Appreciate the vote of confidence, Gabs, but if I take one guy down, the rest of them will fill me full of a bunch of new holes I'd prefer not to have."

"Where are you now?"

"Sitting in the damn SUV pretending to wait patiently for you two."

Zade muttered a curse…or three.

This op had gone from relatively simple to totally fucked in a matter of minutes. And if they didn't figure something out soon, Gabby was going to be caught in the middle of one hell of a shit storm.

"Hold tight for now," he told the other man. "You see Gabe and the others approaching, feel free to join in the fun."

"Copy that. You two behave yourselves in there. I'm sure that couch looks tempting, but remember who it belongs to. Probably all kinds of nasty shit growing on that thing."

"Gross," Gabby cringed. Though she'd mumbled the word, her voice was starting to sound a bit stronger.

"Funny, asshole."

"I'll be here all night," Kole joked. "Literally. Or at least until y'all figure a way out."

Any other time, Zade would appreciate Kole's attempt to lighten the mood. This wasn't one of those times.

"You think you can stand?" He stood and held out a hand.

Taking it, Gabby rose to her feet slowly. Cautiously.

"You good?"

"Yeah." She nodded.

He wasn't so sure, but at least she was upright and in a less vulnerable position than before. Zade looked at the door Andino had gone out of and wondered what was taking so damn long.

Not that he wanted the man anywhere near Gabby, but the only way the guard on the other side of the door they'd come through was going to budge would be on his boss's order. The only way that was going to happen was if Zade was somehow able to convince Andino to let them out.

You shouldn't have come in here in the first place. You knew it was a trap, yet you brought her here, anyway.

He wanted to punch the tiny voice square in the throat. Yes, he'd assumed it was a trap—a way to lock him and Gabby away from everyone else. But again, if he'd gone off on the man like he'd wanted to, both their covers would've already been blown, and they'd most likely be dead.

At least by doing it this way—playing along with the fuckhead's twisted game—he'd bought both them and the teams some time.

How much time and to what end, Zade had no idea. What he did know was he felt like a sitting fucking duck waiting to be cooked for Christmas dinner.

"What's wrong?" Gabby shook her head and winced. "I mean, besides the obvious."

Her voice was definitely stronger now. *Thank God.*

"We need to find a way out of here." Preferably one that didn't involve them getting shot at.

"I'm not leaving without Sam."

"I'm not talking about leaving her here, sweetheart. I'll find Sam." Either he would or one of the other guys on the teams coming to save their asses. "Until then, I need to get you out of here."

If he could get her outside and into the SUV, she'd have Kole and two tons of bullet-resistant glass and armor to protect her.

"Forget it." She crossed her arms at her chest and jutted her chin. "I'm not leaving without you, either, Zade."

"Goddamn it, Gabriella!" He leaned in closely. "This is not the time for you to dig your stubborn-assed heels into the ground. We're in serious trouble, here. Andino's been gone way too fucking long, and if we don't figure something out soon, I have a feeling neither one of us will be going anywhere. Which means *Sam* will be screwed, too."

A level of fear washed over her, making him feel like the biggest asshat on the planet. Cupping her face between his hands, he softened his voice and prayed for the words to make her understand.

"I'm sorry, baby. I didn't mean to yell. I'm just...scared." Shit, had he really admitted that for God and everyone to hear?

We make it out alive, I'm going to catch so much flack for that.

Zade didn't care. The only thing he cared about, the only thing that mattered was getting this strong, stubborn, drives-him-crazy woman out of this godforsaken house and into that SUV with Kole.

"You're a badass super-soldier," she whispered up at him. "You don't get scared."

"Ah, baby. Don't you know?" Keeping her face framed between his palms, Zade rested his forehead against hers. "The thought of something happening to you is the one thing that terrifies me."

She opened her mouth, looked like she wanted to say

more, but her eyes shifted to the side. "What about those?" Gabby nodded toward the large windows.

Zade had considered them, but with the guard by the door outside...

Kole's out there, too.

The tiny voice redeemed itself. Kole was out there, something Zade hadn't planned on when they'd first come into the office.

"We'll use the windows."

Hurrying, Zade pulled his phone from his pants pocket and typed out a quick text instructing Kole to momentarily disable his coms.

After hitting send, Zade pressed against the nearly invisible device in his own ear before taking Gabby's hand and covering her ring with his fingers. Not wanting the others to hear this next part, he did his best to muffle whatever the mic may pick up.

As soon as he received the 'done' text from Kole, Zade used his free hand to call the man.

"You know you're killin' my jam," the guy answered casually. "While you're in there playing nursemaid to your girl, I've been jammin' to some tunes. You know, sittin' back and relaxing. Waiting for the Calvary to arrive."

Zade rolled his eyes and shook his head. He knew the former pararescueman and sniper was full of shit. The man hadn't let his guard down for a second.

"I need you to go to the door you came out of."

There was a pause before, "I already told you, that asshole won't let me through."

"I don't need you to go through it. I need you go there and wait for Gabby."

"Gabby? I thought you two were—"

"I need her out of here, Kole," Zade's voice boomed inside

the small room. "I need her out of this house and into that SUV with you."

There was only a slight pause before Kole asked, "What about you? Gabe said to—"

"I know what Gabe said, but my situation's changed. I'll deal with Andino and then go find Sam, but I need Gabby to be with you while I do that. Got it?"

"Roger that. I'll...think of something."

Zade blew out a breath. "Thanks. I owe ya."

"Don't think I won't collect."

Despite the situation, Zade found himself smiling. Damn, he loved his team.

"Heading to the door, now. The guard does not look happy to see me again, but he hasn't shot me yet, so that's something, right?"

Jesus. "You need to distract him long enough for Gabby to get out the window and to you. And Kole?" Zade locked his eyes with hers while he spoke. "With your life, man."

He felt like a selfish prick asking that of his friend, but Kole—and the rest of Bravo—knew he'd do the same for any one of them or their women. He almost *did* die trying to keep Kat safe.

That shit can't happen again.

"You know I will, brother."

"If it was Sarah, I'd—"

"I know, man," Kole assured him. "Trust me, I know."

Zade ended the call and shoved his phone back into his pocket. Gabby's pupils were already almost back to normal, but it didn't matter. He needed to know she was safe.

I can't lose her.

"I know I said I'd go, but...Zade, please. Come with me. You said Gabe and the others were headed this way, right? They can deal with Andino, and"—she swallowed hard—"I trust them to find Sam and keep her safe. But you…I need you to be safe, too."

"And I will be," he promised. "I'll be even safer if I'm not worried about you getting caught in the crossfire. So, please." Zade rested a palm against one side of her face and let his thumb brush across her smooth skin. "Do this, for me."

Gabby brought one of her hands to his wrist, her fingers wrapping as far around it as she could. "I'd do anything for you, Zade. I…" She paused. Looking away, Gabby bit her bottom lip nervously before meeting his gaze once more. "I love you."

He sucked in a breath and was about to respond, but then the crazy, amazing woman started rambling.

"I'm sorry to drop this on you now, and I *swear* it isn't the drugs talking. I wanted to say it last night, but I was afraid it was too soon, and I didn't want you to—"

Zade kissed her. Hard and fast. Deep and full of emotion.

The timing couldn't be worse, but in that moment, he couldn't keep himself from taking everything he could. In return, he gave her every ounce of love he felt. Still, it wasn't enough…

I need to tell her.

Pulling back, Zade framed her face and stared into her gorgeous green eyes. "I love you, too, baby."

Her eyes widened, the greens in them magnified by a well of unshed tears. "Y-you do?"

"More than anything, which is why I need you to go. Now."

Bringing her mouth up to his, Gabby kissed him once more before breaking away quickly. "Okay." She blew out a breath. "I'm ready."

Jesus, she was amazing.

"Stay with Kole. Right by his side, no matter what."

"No matter what."

Gabby spun around on her heels and they both rushed to the closest window. Zade reached up and flipped the two locks before shoving it open. Not wanting to draw attention to the guard he assumed was still around the corner and, with any luck busy with Kole, he grabbed ahold of the screen's tabs and slid it up silently, rather than pushing it out like he wanted.

Once there was enough clearance for Gabby to pass through, Zade helped her climb through the opening. She swung her legs around and hopped down, facing him for one, final glance.

"Please be careful."

"Cross my heart." He drew an X across his chest. "Now, go."

Tapping his ear, he turned his coms back on as he watched her disappear around the corner. "Gabby's on her way to you, Kole."

"I heard," he sounded amused.

"We all heard," Matt joined in.

For a second, Zade couldn't figure out how the hell they knew. Then he remembered the ring.

Sonofabitch. When she'd told him she loved him, Zade had forgotten all about the mic in her ring. He'd uncovered it when he grabbed her face and kissed her. Which means they also heard…

"I love you, too, by the way," Nate decided to join in the fun. "We all do."

Gabe's comment wasn't quite as sweet or loving.

"What the fuck are you doing, King? I told you to wait there until we breached."

Zade winced. "Sorry, Dawson. But something's way the fuck off, here. Andino still hasn't come back, and the prick guarding the door wouldn't let Kole back in, even though I heard him give the order on our way into this office."

"What do you think he's up to?"

"I don't know, but my gut's screaming somethin' fierce. So I made the call to send Gabby out the window and around the corner to Kole so he could get her into the SUV."

"Smart," Nate commented. "It'd take a lot of fire power to pierce through that thing."

"Exactly." Speaking of… "Jameson, you got eyes on Gabby?"

"She just walked up."

"I'm good, Zade," she told him herself. "Go. Do what you've got to do, but make sure you don't die. You do, I'm going to be seriously pissed off."

He chuckled. "Copy that, sweetheart. Jameson, let me know when you're inside the car."

"What are you going to do?"

Zade turned and looked at the door Andino went through. "I'm going hunting."

CHAPTER 16

"What do we do, now?" Gabby asked Kole as they moved across the expansive home's walkway.

"We get our asses to the SUV and wait for reinforcements."

She worked double-time to try and keep up with Kole as they speed-walked to where the SUV was still parked. Not the easiest thing in the world to do in heels and an evening gown, but she wasn't about to stop for any reason.

Not even for the sake of her screaming feet.

Thankfully the first part of the plan had gone off without a hitch. To the guard who'd been posted at the door where Kole had been waiting, Gabby had made it sound as if she'd gone out the front entrance, where they'd first entered the house, and then walked all the way around to the other side in search of Kole.

Kole had played along perfectly, even cowering down and giving the guard a chagrined shrug when Gabby had admonished him for not being where she'd told him to be. They'd continued arguing until they were out of earshot of the asshole with the gun.

They turned the corner and immediately began to walk slower since there were more guards there, and this was where the SUV was parked.

The only problem? She'd talked to Zade when she and Kole had first met up, but after that…nothing. Kole assured her Zade was fine and probably within earshot of someone he couldn't talk in front of. No big deal, he'd said.

Gabby wasn't so sure.

Several cars were already gone, one man she'd seen carrying a bidder card earlier was walking to his car. A young woman was by his side, the look on her face breaking Gabby's heart in two.

"Kole." She motioned in the young woman's direction.

"The others will stop him," he assured her.

God, please let him be right.

From the looks of the other empty parking spaces, several of the night's previous bidders had already left with their winnings, as well.

Don't think about it.

"What about Zade? And Sam?"

"Zade said he'd handle himself and your sister." Kole pulled his keys from his pocket and unlocked the vehicle they'd arrived in.

"He shouldn't be in there alone."

"Not my call."

"Zade? Can you hear me?"

Complete radio silence.

"Kole, wait." Gabby grabbed Kole's arm and spun him around. "He's not responding. I have a really bad feeling about this. We have to go back for him. Please."

"We can't go back, Gabby." Kole got really serious, really fast. "I fucking *hate* that my friend is in there by himself with no coms and zero backup, but I promised Zade I would keep you safe, so that's what I'm going to do." He took a deep breath and opened the door for her. With a much softer voice, Kole pleaded, "Now will you *please* get in the damn car?"

Seeing the struggle Kole was facing, knowing his teammate was in that house, alone, made Gabby feel like a total jerk. She'd been yelling at him as if he didn't realize the danger Zade was in.

Of course he knew. His whole *team* knew.

Zade had put himself at risk in order to protect her.

They also knew about the not-so-private conversation they'd had right before she'd gone out that window. Gabby didn't care.

Her chest tightened with worry for the man she loved, but she climbed into the vehicle like a good girl. Even put her seatbelt on and everything.

When Kole got behind the wheel, Gabby turned to him and said, "I'm sorry. I know you're as worried about Zade as I am."

"It's okay. I shouldn't have yelled at you. I'm just…"

"Scared for him. I get it."

Kole studied her a moment before asking, "You really love him?"

"Yes." She didn't hesitate.

He looked at her a few second longer. "Dawson, what's your location?"

Gabe answered immediately. "Guards by the gate are down, as are the men Andino had stationed in the trees between the gate and the house. Coming up on the northern tree line now."

"There are five tangos along the east wall," Kole gave his team a heads up.

"Copy. Matt and I will take them out while Ghost and his team spread out and clear the home's remaining perimeter."

"Carter, you still on?" Kole asked Nate.

"Loud and clear, brother. What's up?"

"You see any tangos along the tree line?"

"Negative. All of Andino's manpower was either at the gate, spread out in the immediate area following, or in and around the house."

"That's good, right?" Gabby asked, hating that she couldn't do anything but sit and wait.

"Yeah, honey." Kole offered her a kind smile. "That's good."

"Clearing the tree line, now," Gabe announced.

She could almost hear Matt smiling through the coms when he added, "Get ready to party, boys. This is where the fun really starts."

With her head on a constant swivel, Gabby looked out both her window and the windshield. She searched for Zade's teammates and Ghost and his men.

It was dark and each of the men was dressed in black tactical clothing, so it was no surprise she couldn't see them.

What did surprise Gabby was when the man guarding the door closest to the tree line dropped on the ground and didn't get back up. The other four followed immediately after.

Ohmygod! "Are they..."

"Dead?" Kole nodded. "As a doornail."

"East wall secured." Gabe's deep voice was calm and certain.

Exactly how she'd imagined the military leaders she read about in her romance novels sounding.

Ghost sounded the same. "West side clear."

One of the other men, Gabby thought maybe it was Hollywood, added, "South clear."

Just like that, in a matter of two minutes...probably less... nine men had been killed. Gabby wondered if she was a horrible person, because she didn't feel bad for them.

She wasn't sad or regretful. Those men had chosen to lead a horrible life of crime and devastating violence. Not only with the drugs Andino's cartel spread around the world, but also by aiding in something as unthinkable and horrifying as human trafficking.

They'd helped to bring Sam to this place.

That was a decision *they* made, and that choice—*their* choice—ultimately got them killed.

"Preparing to breach the residence."

"Find our boy, Dawson," Kole told his team leader. "Find him, and then get the hell out of there."

Gabby's heart rate spiked, and her palms began to sweat. Working to keep her breathing steady, she tried not to think about Sam being in that house. Tried not to think about *Zade.*

She'd heard what he'd said to Kole about hunting. He was going after Hector Andino by himself, and *God* that thought made her feel physically ill.

"He's going to be okay, Gabs."

Facing Kole, she asked, "How do you know?"

He raised a cocky brow. "Because he's Bravo."

Gabby chuckled. "Right. And you all are invincible, right?"

"Not invincible." He got serious. "Just damn good at what we do."

"You're right. He's going to be fine." She tried hard to convince herself of that as she looked back at the house. "They all will."

"Of course I'm—"

Several loud pops struck Gabby's ears to the point of pain. She winced, her hands pressing against them on reflex to try and drown out the piercing noise.

Gabe's growling voice came through above the screams and hollers. "Drop your weapon!"

More pops.

Not pops. Gunshots.

Her eyes flew to Kole who was listening intently to the scene unfolding inside Andino's house.

"Don't do it, man!" Matt's warning was answered with more gunfire. He let out a string of curses right before there was another shot.

More yelling by the two Bravo man. Ghost's team joined in on the fight.

More screams.

More gunfire.

Out of the corner of her eye, Gabby saw a crowd of people stampeding through every doorway on this side of the house. Some came running around from the same corner she and Kole had traveled past on their way back to the car.

A few of the men had their own weapons out, but most were moving through the night as if their feet were on fire. Running for their lives, fearful of either being shot or captured and sent to prison.

"Damn, it's like watching a bunch of cockroaches scatter when a light gets flipped on," Nate commented from wherever he was parked.

The guy had been relatively quiet, and Gabby guessed he'd been busy helping the other Homeland team round up Andino's customers and the girls.

"What do we do?" Gabby swung her head back around. She prayed Kole had a plan in mind.

He did, it just wasn't what she wanted to hear.

"We sit tight and wait."

Panic settling in, Gabby shot him an incredulous look. "That's your plan? To sit tight? Kole, they're in there right now fighting Andino and his men! Maybe you can wait until it's all over with to find out if they're okay, but I can't."

She reached for the door and pushed it open.

More gunfire and yelling ensued. Gravel spewed into the

air as cars flew from the large parking area and away from the violence and certain bloodshed inside.

"What are you—" Kole reached for her. "Gabby, shut the fucking door!"

Ignoring him, Gabby hopped down and spun back around. "Maybe you can sit here and wait, but I can't, Kole. Sam's in there, somewhere. I know she is. And *Zade's* in there, but he won't answer me. He could be hurt, or if Andino found him he could be..." Her voice cracked, and Kole jumped at the chance to say his peace.

"And what are you going to do if you do go back in there? You have no gun. Hell, you have no weapon of *any* kind. You think you're gonna go in there, and what...walk right up to Andino in the middle of a goddamn gunfight? You gonna ask him nicely to order his men to stop shooting at Gabe and the others and to let your sister go?"

Okay, so he had a point. A really, *really* good point.

Gabby knew she was acting like one of the heroines in some of the books she'd read. The ones who pull a too-stupid-to-live move that makes her want to throw her damn tablet across the room and scream.

But if Sam died...if she lost Zade...what would be the point? The only life she ever wanted would be gone already, anyway. Plus, waiting had never been her strong suit, so...

"I can't sit around and wait for it all to end, Kole. We have to do *something*. I have to—"

"I'll tell you exactly what you're going to do."

Gabby felt something cold and hard pressing against her temple. At the same time, Kole's door flew open. A man she recognized—the one who'd been staring her down from the stage earlier—was there. His weapon was pointed straight at Kole's head.

She froze mid-sentence, her widened gaze matching Kole's as he stared back at her with shock and dismay. His gun was on the console, but he couldn't reach for it. If he did, if Kole even moved a centimeter, the other man would kill him instantly.

Shit, shit, shit!

This was all her fault. If she'd stayed put like Kole had said, this wouldn't be happening. Instead, they'd both been so focused on each other and trying to prove their opposite points, neither had noticed the two men walking toward them until it was too late.

Hector Andino kept his gun steady. "You're going to get behind the wheel of this car, and you're going to drive us both out of here."

Oh, God!

"Sonofabitch!" Gabe's voice came through the coms. "Jameson tell me that's not who I think it is."

"H-Hector," Gabby's voice trembled with fear as she did her best to relay information back to Gabe and the others. "W-what are doing? And why are you and that other man pointing your guns at us?"

"Andino and one tango. Got it." Gabe responded calmly. "I'm sending Matt your way. Ghost you got a couple guys freed up to assist?"

"Already on it."

"What does it look like I'm doing, mi amor ?" Hector answered her question.

Man, it was confusing having all these voices in her head at one time. Gabby didn't know how Zade and the others did this on a regular basis.

Focus, Gabby. Focus!

With her heart in her throat, her mind raced to try to come up with an explanation. *Something* that would appease the angry man with the gun.

"I-I don't know what you think is going on, but I was just telling Kole how worried I was about you."

"So worried you snuck out of my office window to come out here?" The metal dug into her skin as he pushed it even harder against her head. "Quite a coincidence that you and your boyfriend vanish from my office right before my home is raided by men carrying guns and killing my men."

"I didn't know this was going to happen. I swear, I know nothing about—"

Gabby cried as Andino used his other hand to fist the hair on the back of her head.

"Leave her alone!" Kole shouted.

Gabby could tell he wanted to grab his gun and take both men out, but he couldn't. Not without risking certain death in the process.

"We're coming, Gabby," Matt promised in her ear. "Just hold on a little longer, honey."

She heard him curse under his breath, saying something about the place being too fucking big and being too far out. She could tell those last words hadn't been meant for her, and from the jostling in his voice, he was running hard and fast.

Keeping the gun in place, Andino leaned down to whisper in her ear. "I can tolerate a lot of things, Gabriella. But lying is not one of them."

"Hector, please. If you'll just—"

He pulled harder, making her wince. "Choose your next words very carefully, Gabriella. The next lie to come out of that sinful mouth of yours will be the last thing your friend hears."

Gabby closed her eyes, sending a tear down across her cheek.

"Let her go, man," Kole continued to try and reason with the maniac. "This wasn't her idea. She's a civilian. She's not—"

"I know who and what she is," Andino's voice remained

steady. Deadly. "I have since the moment we shared our first drink together this evening."

Her eyes opened and Gabby thought back to earlier in the night. She remembered Hector snapping for the waiter. Toasting to the evening, and then...

The assistant.

The shorter, older man who'd approached him. He'd whispered something into Andino's ear, and Gabby thought she'd imagined the harsh look on Hector's face. That she was being paranoid.

No point in lying now.

"I just want my sister," Gabby admitted.

"Ah, yes. Samantha. Such a beautiful girl. All that long, flowing blonde hair, and those crystal blue eyes."

Her heart pounded against her ribs. "So she is here."

"She was. Pity, she would've made me a lot of money tonight."

Ignoring the pain from her hair damn near being pulled out by the roots, Gabby shoved against Andino with her shoulder. "You sick son of a bitch!"

"We've wasted enough time." The man let go of her hair and grabbed her upper arm. To his minion, he said, "Take care of him."

Kole started to reach for his gun but the other man was already yanking on the front of Kole's shirt and throwing him to the ground.

"No!" Gabby fought to get free. "Kole!"

"Shit, we're almost there!" Fletch, maybe? "Less than two minutes out!"

"It's okay, Gabby," Zade's teammate tried, and failed, to make her feel better. "It's going to be okay."

Keeping his bruising grip tight, Andino pulled her around the back of the vehicle. When she saw Kole, Gabby knew he was so very wrong.

It wasn't going to be okay. Not by a longshot.

Kole pushed himself up to his feet…to face his executioner.

"Kole?"

"Close your eyes, sweetheart." He stood stoically as he accepted his fate.

Screw that.

"Please," Gabby begged his team to hurry. Praying they'd come out in time, Gabby told Matt and Gabe and whoever else that was listening, "He's going to *shoot* him!"

"Of course he is," Andino uttered smugly, assuming she was speaking to him. "What do you think I pay Eduardo for?"

Hector gave his man the signal.

"No!" Gabby screamed as three shots rang out.

Kole's body jerked as each bullet hit him in the chest and torso.

"Kole!"

Her knees started to give out, but Andino's tight grip kept her from falling. She was pulled toward the driver's open door as the other man casually turned and got into the back seat, shutting the door behind him.

"Motherfucker!" Matt's growl barely sounded over the rush of Gabby's own heartbeat filling her ears.

"Get in." Andino shoved her into the driver's seat. To the man sitting behind her, he said, "She tries to run, shoot her."

Gabby couldn't run. All she could do was sit there and stare at Kole's still form.

He was lying on his back, his arms spread out to his sides. His eyes were closed and there were three new, jagged holes in his pristinely pressed, white tuxedo shirt and vest.

She couldn't help but think of his earlier comment about Andino's men filling him full of holes he preferred not to have.

"I'm so sorry," she whispered, knowing he could no longer hear her.

Andino got into the car and slammed the door. With his gun pointed at her side, he said, "Drive."

Gabby woodenly put the car in reverse. She turned the SUV around and did as she was told.

She drove.

Guns in hand, Matt and Fletch burst through the main entrance doors as she sped past.

CHAPTER 17

Gun out, Zade continued down the concrete steps. Leading to what, he had no fucking clue. Andino hadn't gone down here for a pillow and glass of water, that was for damn sure.

It had taken a lot longer than he'd expected to pick the lock on the well-secured door. However, since the door was located inside Andino's private office, it was a simple key lock and not an electronic entrance like the room's main door.

When he'd first begun working on it, Zade was busy listening to the humorous argument Gabby and Kole were having for the guard's benefit. Hearing his woman rip Kole a new asshole for supposedly going to the wrong door to wait for her was one of the most entertaining moments he'd had in a while.

Afterward, at the same time he'd gotten the lock to click free, she'd spoken to him directly. She'd wanted to make sure he was okay and let him know they were together and headed to the SUV.

He assured her he was fine and reminded her to stick with Kole before heading down the staircase he was on now.

When Zade first opened the door inside Andino's office, he'd expected to walk into another room or some sort of hallway leading to another part of the house.

What he hadn't expected to find was a small entryway and yet *another* door. One leading to a creepy-as-fuck, stairway to Hell.

But that's exactly where he was, now…heading down a dark, narrow staircase taking him someplace God only knows, where he'll find only God knows what.

You know what you're going to find.

Zade's heart thundered at the thought. Yeah, he had a pretty good idea what lie ahead. He could only send up a prayer and hope it wasn't as bad as what his imagination had come up with since walking through that damn door.

He turned the knob and...

Jesus.

Silently closing the door behind him, Zade stepped into the fifth level of Hell. A long, straight hallway went on for what seemed like forever. Sconces, identical to the ones by the main entrance outside, were evenly spaced on each wall, their low light giving off an eerie glow.

That glow allowed him to see what appeared to be several cells lining both sides of the long hallway. Cells with iron bars.

Zade's stomach swirled with an instant and fierce need to puke. This was where Andino kept the girls he planned to sell.

Mounted high on the wall to his right were four monitors. Each of the screens was on, their pictures divided into six equal frames. The monitors showed the other rooms in the house, including very clear pictures of Andino's office and the ballroom.

If the bastard was still down here, he saw everything.

"Jameson, watch your back, brother. Pretty sure Andino knows Gabby's no longer in the house."

Silence.

Zade put a hand to his ear. He double-tapped the com to turn it off and back on again. "Kole, you copy?" His teammate didn't answer. "Gabby? Can you hear me?"

More silence.

Frowning, Zade reached out and felt the smooth, dark walls. Solid concrete. Concrete walls that would require some major steel-beam framing to hold the type of house that lay above him.

Concrete and steel were not the electronic device's friend.

Fanfuckingtastic.

Turning to go back into the stairwell to give them a heads-up, his fingertips barely brushed against the knob when a voice came from somewhere down the hall.

"H-hello? I-Is someone there?"

Heart pounding, Zade spun around. His gun held out in front of him, straight and at the ready.

"Hello?" the quiet voice reached him again.

Holy shit. The bastard had left one of the girls down here.

Cautious, because it would be just like Andino to use one of the women he'd abducted to set his ass up, Zade kept his gun raised and took a few steps forward.

"If you're there, please let me out." The voice sounded so desperate. "I'll do anything. Just unlock the door and walk away. *Please.*"

Fuck. He needed to make contact with his team. Let them know where he was and what he'd found. But Zade had no idea where Andino had gone, nor did he know when or if, the bastard was planning to return.

I can't leave her down here.

Sending up a quick prayer that he wasn't getting played

for a fucking fool, Zade told her who he was so she wouldn't be frightened of him.

"My name is Zade King," his deep voice echoed down the long hallway. "I'm here on behalf of the United States government. Where are you?"

The woman's gasp echoed off the walls. "Down here! Last cell on the right!"

Of course she'd be in the very last cell. Christ, the whole set-up was like something out of one of those lame horror films.

He could practically hear the people watching from home screaming at him to not go down the hall… *Don't do it, man! It's a trap!*

"Please," the voice begged. "*Please*, hurry!"

The woman's overwhelming excitement and relief sounded genuine, making Zade's eyes sting. Even so, he knew he still needed to be careful.

With his head on a slow and steady swivel, Zade checked each of the cells as he passed by. It made him physically ill to see the tiny, barren rooms.

Each one was identical to the next, with a stained mattress for a bed and a toilet and wall-mounted sink in one of the corners.

When he finally got to the last cell on the right, Zade held his gun at the ready and looked inside. His heart broke at what he found.

Standing in the middle of the small, degrading space was a young woman. A tiny, blonde woman with the bluest eyes he'd ever seen.

"Samantha."

She blinked in surprise. "H-how do you know my name?"

He hadn't meant to say it out loud, but… "I'm a friend of Gabby's."

Those blue eyes grew wide with both recognition and

fear. "Is she okay? I-I didn't mean to put her in danger. I saw her on the screen and got so excited, I blurted her name. One of Hector's men heard me. H-he made me tell him who she was. I didn't want to, but he..."

She came closer, out of the shadows and into the dim light. Zade muttered a curse. She was dressed in a short, strapless black dress covered in sequins. Her long, blonde hair fell down over her shoulders in soft waves, and she had makeup on as if she'd been ready for a night out on the town.

But what struck an arrow through Zade's heart were the fresh bruises on her face and the marks from where someone had wrapped their meaty hands around her upper arms.

"For the most part, the men here leave us alone, but there's one." Sam brushed her hand over the bruises on one of her arms. "He likes to hit."

Fucking bastards deserved to die. Every. Single. One.

"Please," Samantha begged him. "Is Gabby okay? I couldn't live with myself if something happened to her because of me."

Join the club, sweetheart. "She's fine. She's with a man on my team. He's keeping her safe."

"Are you sure?"

"Nothing's going to happen to her, honey." Zade studied the lock. "Your sister's safe. Right now we need to focus on getting you out of there."

"You need a key. Hector and his men have them, and they left."

"How long ago was that?"

"I-I...I don't know. Twenty minutes ago, maybe? It's been hard to keep track of time down here."

I bet it has been, sweetheart.

"After I told them about Gabby, they threw me back in here. Then they took the other girls who were still down here out of their cells, and they all left through the intake room."

"The intake room?"

"There."

He followed her gaze to his left. They landed on a door at the end of the hall.

"That's where he took us when we first got here. There are enough tables for four girls at a time."

Zade's gut tightened. "Tables?"

"Big, concrete slabs. They have leather restraints for our ankles and wrists so we can't fight them."

"Jesus." He ran a hand over his jaw.

"I heard Hector call it the intake room to one of his men. Hector puts girls in there and leaves them for a day, sometimes more. If you're good and you do what he says, it's not so bad. They bathe and...shave you." Sam looked down as a humiliated blush began crawling up her pale neck and into her cheeks. "Hector said it was to *prepare* us. But the girls who fought him"—she brought her eyes to his again—"he'd use his knife on them. Never on their faces, but...we could hear them screaming."

Motherfucker had better enjoy those last few breaths of his. Because Hector Andino was running on some serious borrowed time.

Pulling his wallet from his pants, Zade flipped it open and grabbed the small tools he'd used to pick the lock upstairs. Shoving the wallet back into his pocket, he wasted no time getting to work.

"Any idea why Andino didn't take you with the others?"

"No." Her voice got thick as she fought to keep fresh tears at bay. "H-he ordered Eduardo to make me tell them about Gabby. Then told him to put me back in here. Before that, several others had been taken upstairs. They never came back. I'm assuming that's because they'd been…" her voice trailed.

"Sold," Zade finished for her. "Don't worry, we've got more guys waiting in the wings to intercept them and get the girls to safety."

"Oh, thank God." Sam's shoulders relaxed. "Are you military or something?"

He smirked. "Or something." He continued working on the bitch of a lock. "Did Hector say anything about coming back, or did you happen to hear him tell the guards where they were going?"

"No." She shook her head, her long, blonde hair swishing around her bare shoulders with the movement. "Wait, he did say something about the dock."

"The dock?"

Sam nodded. "That's how we got here. First we were taken to New Orleans and put on a boat. When we got here, there was a large van waiting where we'd docked. It brought us here, to this place."

"Do you remember how long it took to get from the dock to this place?"

She thought back. "About an hour, I think. It wasn't much more than that, I know." She sighed. "I'm sorry. I know that's not a lot to go on."

"No, that's great, Sam. Really. That's a lot of good information, and I'll be sure to pass it along to the others as soon as we get back upstairs."

If I can ever get this fucking lock to open.

The thing was acting like it was welded shut.

A stretch of silence passed while he continued to try to free her before Sam spoke up again. "The others…are they like you?"

"Like me?"

"You know, the badass, superhero type."

A loud chuckle burst from his chest. "I mean, they aren't quite as badass as I am, but they can hold their own."

His attempt to make her smile worked, giving Zade a warm feeling in his chest. Sam had a beautiful smile. One he hoped the world got to see a lot more of after this.

But then she looked down at the lock and frowned. "Are you sure you know what you're doing?"

"Most of the time." He gave her a sideways grin.

Sam studied him closely. "How do you know Gabby? Wait"—she shook her head—"why is she even here? And how did she know where to find me?"

He didn't want to say they were boyfriend and girlfriend. That sounded too juvenile, and lovers would've made what they shared sound purely physical.

It's more than that. Much, much more.

"Your sister and I are…together."

"Together." She toyed with the word. *"Oh!"* Her lips curved upward. "Figures she'd end up with a guy like you."

"Why is that?"

"You seem very sure of yourself and strong. I mean, you'd have to be, right? I don't know how long you two have known each other, but Gabby can be a bit—"

"Stubborn?"

Sam chuckled. "I was going to say pigheaded, but yeah. I guess you really do know my sister."

Better than most of the people I've known my whole life.

"To answer your other questions, Gabby hasn't stopped looking for you since you went missing."

"Really?"

"That surprise you?"

"No." Sam shook her head. "I guess it doesn't. I just never thought…when I stepped off that boat, I thought that was it. That I'd never see my family again."

She swiped at a tear. Poor girl's emotions had to be skyrocketing all over the damn place.

His heart hurt for what this young woman had been put through. Not that he had any way of knowing specifically what Andino and his men had done to her.

Not going to ask, either.

Those questions would be left to the medical personnel at the Homeland medical facility in Dallas, which was the first stop they'd make once they landed back in Texas.

One thing Zade did know, one thing he was absolutely certain of—the bastards who'd brought her here hadn't broken her.

Like his Gabby, Samantha Shoemaker was strong. A survivor. And he couldn't wait to see the look on Gabby's face when she saw her sister again.

More than that, Zade was most excited about the future and where this thing between he and Gabby would go from here. If he had anything to say about it, it would go on forever.

As he continued working on the hardest lock on the planet to pick open, Zade prayed like mad that Gabby wanted forever with him, too.

CHAPTER 18

"Where are we going?" Gabby stared straight ahead at the long, gravel drive. She felt numb, almost disconnected from the horrifying reality of what was happening. Of what had happened to Kole.

Oh, God. Kole.

It was a blessing, really. To not have to feel the terror and sadness or the overwhelming devastation from knowing Kole was dead. Knowing she would mostly likely be the next to die.

Gabby was grateful she'd lost the ability to really think about the fact that Sam would forever be a memory, ripped away from her parents and friends. From her life.

A life she'd barely had a chance to even live.

And then there was Zade. Thank *God* she couldn't feel the sorrow and pain from that particular loss. If her mind hadn't mercifully shut down that portion of her brain—most likely from shock—Gabby would feel her heart being ripped to shreds, piece by torturous piece.

"Just drive," Andino kept his gun trained on her from the passenger seat. "I'll tell you when to turn."

"You'll be caught, you know." Even to her, her voice sounded wooden. "Maybe not today or next week. It might be a year from now, but eventually, you will have to pay for every horrible thing you've ever done."

The twisted man laughed. "No one knows every horrible thing I've done, mi amor . There are simply too many to count."

"Why?" She blinked as she continued driving. A tear may have fallen, but she wasn't sure.

"What was it you told me when we first met? Money is everything, Gabriella. That's not to say I don't enjoy my…work."

"You're a monster."

"A monster with more money than God." They passed through the open gate and Hector pointed to an almost undetectable clearing in the trees. "Turn there."

"Gabriella, it's Gabe. We lost com connection when you left, but we've got it back now. Matt and Fletch are coming to find you, but we lost your GPS signal."

She schooled her expression, having forgotten the other men could still hear her.

"Honey, can you try to describe your surroundings? Give us as much detail as you can while you drive."

Gabby tried to get her eyes to focus on what he was pointing to. It was completely dark, now, and all she could see were trees.

"There isn't a road here. Only trees."

Andino smiled. "Trust me."

She snorted. "Never going to happen."

He looked back at his goon and tipped his chin. The man sitting behind her shoved his gun against the back of her head. "He said to turn. Now."

Grimacing, Gabby gritted her teeth and did as she was told. She stopped before entering the wooded area, nearly gasping when the vehicle's headlights made it possible to see what she'd missed before.

There, intertwined with what appeared to be the thick foliage was another gate. It was well-hidden by the natural-looking greenery surrounding. Andino got out and went to a tree near the gate's edge.

"There's a gate in the trees?" She pretended to be talking to the man with the gun on her. "I didn't notice it when we first drove here. Of course, I was sitting on the passenger side, so I wouldn't have seen it. This is the west side of the property line, right?"

"Shut up." He pushed against her head.

"Good girl," Gabe commended her. "Turner, you catch that?"

"Affirmative. Headed that way, now."

Gabby wanted to ask about Zade and Kole, but couldn't without alerting Andino to her ability to communicate with the others.

Pushing some leaves to the side, he revealed an electronic keypad much like the one outside his office door. After entering the code, the gate slowly opened, foliage and all.

When he returned to the car, Andino instructed her to move forward. As she pressed her foot on the gas pedal and headed down another dark, tree-lined road, she gave Gabe and the others another little tidbit of useful information.

"Electronic gate with a hidden keypad. Color me impressed."

"What can I say?" The man's lips curled into a smug smirk. "I'm an impressive man."

And a dense one.

"Got you loud and clear, Gabby," Matt assured her. "Hang in there, you're doing great."

Wanting to help as much as she possibly could, she asked Andino, "Where does this road take us?"

"You'll see soon enough."

Damn. She was hoping he'd tell her where it ended so when they got there, Matt and the others would be waiting for them.

Since she knew better than to keep pushing for too much information at once, Gabby asked another question.

"How did you know?"

"Know what, mi amor ?"

He *really* needed to stop calling her that. "How did you figure out who I was?"

"Your sister told me. She told me everything about you. Like the fact that you aren't actually sisters."

Gabby shot him a narrowed glare. "You're lying. Sam would never give me up."

"Not intentionally, no. It was pure luck on my part, really. My men were bringing her upstairs to take her place on the stage when she caught sight of you on one of my security monitors. The poor girl was so excited to see you, she practically shouted out your name. Of course, I had to find out how she knew you, though she refused to tell me, at first. It didn't take long for Eduardo to make her talk."

Oh, Sam. I'm so, so sorry.

"It wasn't her fault, really." Andino continued on. "Seeing a family member at the very event meant to seal her fate? For a young woman who's already been traumatized, I would imagine it would be nearly impossible to hide her reaction to that. Even harder to resist Eduardo's prompting to share all she knew about you." He looked back at the man behind her and smiled. "You're so good at what you do."

"Gracias."

Angrier than she'd ever been in her life, Gabby practically spit out the words when she told Andino, "You and *Eduardo* can both go straight to Hell."

He laughed. The bastard laughed. "Even Hell isn't big

enough for a man as powerful as me, Gabriella." Andino looked out his window and muttered, "We're almost there."

She had no idea where they were going, but the windy, twisty road made it feel as though they were going in one, big circle. Five minutes later, she realized that was exactly what they'd done.

Though it was hard to see through the night sky, Gabby could make out the shape of Andino's home. The same home they'd *just* escaped from.

"That's your house up ahead. Why are we going back there? Aren't you afraid of getting caught?"

"You'll see why, and no. Those men who came running to your rescue saw us drive away. The last place they'll think to look for me is on the property."

Wanna bet?

"Arrogant son of a bitch," Gabe growled in her ear.

Gabby had to work hard at not smiling.

More than ready for the nightmare be over, she pushed the gas harder and got them to their destination quickly. The road they were on ended in front of what looked to be a tiny shed-like structure that sat several yards back from the house.

"You brought me to a shed?"

"It's more than a simple shed, Gabriella. Like I said before. Trust me."

Not even when Hell freezes over.

Andino got out. On his instructions, Gabby opened her door slowly and stepped outside, Eduardo keeping his gun trained on her as he exited the vehicle.

"Shed on the backside of the property. Copy that, Gabby. Nate picked you up with his drone. We know exactly where you are, and I've got men on their way to you, now."

"Be careful," she responded without thinking.

"That's sweet, Gabriella," Andino smiled over at her. "Are you worried about me?"

Feeling much more confident about the situation, Gabby dropped what was left of her refined act. "I was talking to myself, dumbass. It's dark as hell out here, and I'd hate to break a heel. They are designer, after all."

Eduardo prodded her in the back with the gun, forcing her to walk over to where Andino was waiting by the shed door.

Making a clicking sound with his tongue, Andino said, "Such unattractive language coming from an otherwise flawless beauty."

"Go fuck yourself, Hector." She stared him straight in the eye. "Better yet, why don't you and Eddie, here, go at each other. Or has that already been done?"

Eduardo grabbed the hair on the back of her head and jerked, his lips whispering against her ear. "Shut up."

Gabby cried out because, *shit,* that hurt. But she kept talking. The more she talked, the more flustered Andino became.

In her experience, flustered men were distracted men. And *distracted* men were easier to take down.

"What's the matter, Eddie? Don't want anyone to know your secret?"

This time, the big man growled. "You've got a smart mouth for a woman in your position. I suggest you keep it *shut.*"

"Speaking of positions," she kept talking as if he hadn't said a word, "which one do you prefer with Hector? Of course, you are his right-*hand* man. Or do you use your left?"

Gabby went flying as Eduardo threw her to the ground. She grunted when her knees and palms made contact with the hard dirt.

"Easy, Gabby," Gabe warned. "I get what you're trying to do, and I appreciate it. But don't push these guys too far."

"I'm good," she whispered low enough the other two men couldn't hear. "Just hurry."

"Get up!"

Eduardo yanked on her arm with a slightly painful grip, forcefully bringing her back to her feet.

"In case you hadn't noticed, Eduardo has a bit of a temper."

Gabby ignored the stinging in her knees and palms. "Sorry, Eddie. I didn't realize your relationship with Hector was such a touchy subject. My bad."

Andino grabbed her chin and squeezed, his grip so tight she thought he was going to crush her jawbone. "He told you to keep your mouth shut. I suggest you do as you're told."

Hector pushed her chin away.

"Sorry to disappoint, Hector." She blew out a breath. "But as you've probably gathered, I'm not very good at taking orders."

Just ask Zade.

God, please let him be okay.

Even under the night sky, she could see the anger darkening the browns of his eyes. "You *will* learn to follow my orders, Gabriella. One way or another."

With a tip of his chin, Andino gave Eduardo a signal and stepped aside. She heard a low sigh expelling from the man behind her right before a sharp, explosive pain struck the back of her head.

And then…total darkness.

* * *

"Fuck it."

Giving up on the lock—because yeah, they needed to get the hell out of there and find his team—Zade pulled his gun from his waistband and told Gabby's sister, "Get back."

Eyes wide, she pressed herself against the far wall as best she could.

"You might want to cover your ears."

With his hand on the trigger, Zade aimed before squeezing his eyes shut and turning his head away for protection against possible ricochet. He pulled the trigger.

Sparks flew as the deafening bullet destroyed the mechanism keeping the door in place. Sam immediately uncovered her ears and ran to the bars. Zade was already opening them for her.

"Ohmygod!" Her excited words rushed together. "It worked! Thank you!"

Before Zade could react, Sam leapt into his arms, her tight grip nearly choking him.

"You're welcome," Zade breathed out.

"Oh, sorry." She dropped her arms.

"Nothing to be sorry for, honey. I'm happy as hell you're out of there."

"Not as happy as I am."

"Won't argue with you there. Come on." He put a hand on the small of her back. "Let's get you upstairs and to your sister."

"I can't believe I'm really going to see her!"

"Believe it." He looked down at her and winked. Zade couldn't wait to see Gabby, either. He needed to see with his own eyes that she was okay. "Hopefully that shot didn't draw the wrong kind of attention to us."

"It won't," Sam told him with utter certainty. "This place is soundproof. From the intake room all the way to that door at the end by the stairs. No noise created down hear will reach the outside or the rest of the house."

He didn't even want to think of why she knew that. He also figured she was right. If the place was secure enough to knock out his state-of-the-art coms, it pretty much had to be soundproof to the rest of the house.

They'd taken two steps toward the other end of the hall when Zade heard something coming from behind the other door. The one leading to what Sam referred to as the intake room.

Another door slammed shut and Sam's eyes flew to his. Sound may not travel upward from inside here, but they'd sure as hell heard *that*.

"Oh, God." She paled with fear. "He's back."

Zade didn't think it was Andino. More likely, someone from his team had found the second entrance. Still he wasn't taking any chances. "Samantha, I hate to ask this." He glanced at the open cell behind her. "But I don't suppose you'd—"

"The only way I'm going back into that cage is if I'm dead. And since you're with my sister, I'm pretty sure you aren't going to risk pissing her off by killing me."

He couldn't help but smirk. "You sure you and Gabby aren't blood related?"

"Sometimes choice is stronger than blood."

Zade thought of his teammates. He loved each of them as if they were his blood brothers, and their wives were like his sisters.

"Point taken. All right, stay alert. And no matter what happens, stay behind me."

"Trust me, I'm not getting this close to freedom only to screw it up by doing something stupid."

"Good."

Zade gripped his pistol between his tightened fist and began walking toward the ominous door. The closer he got, he realized there were voices coming from the other side of it.

"Thought you said this place was soundproof."

"To the rest of the house, it is. Down here..." Sam shuddered behind him. "Down here, you can hear everything that happens."

They covered several more inches, the voices becoming more and more clear.

"Make sure those are secured before she comes to. This one is quite the fighter."

What the fuck?

Andino had come back, and he'd brought another girl into this hell hole.

"She's a mouthy bitch who needs to learn her place."

"That's Eduardo," Sam whispered softly. "He's never far away when Hector's around."

"She will learn her place," Hector told the other man. "We just need to keep her secure until the property clears."

"That will take days, Hector. And what if authorities find this place?"

"Have you forgotten? I own the authorities."

"Not the Americans. That's who stormed in here tonight. They're the ones who've taken out nearly all of our men."

"Let me worry about that. In the meantime, Gabriella's stay down here will help teach her who is in charge."

Zade's entire system filled with ice, and he could physically feel the color draining from his face.

No. He'd heard the man wrong. He *had* to have heard fucking wrong.

Gabby wasn't in there with that monster. She was with Kole, safe inside the SUV. Right?

"We will do as we've done in the past when things got too close. Leave her here, come back a couple times a day to provide food and water. Once the dust settles, we will move her and her sister to the secondary location where they will join the others and await the next event."

Samantha gasped from behind him. "Oh, God. Did he say he has Gabby in there?"

"If anyone shows at the next one," Eduardo spat pessimistically. "After tonight, our business may be ruined."

"Nonsense," Hector assured him. "Our customers' needs are far too great to let one tiny hiccup keep them from acquiring what they crave."

"I hope you're right, Hector. We've worked much too hard to have it end like this."

"Look." Hector sounded excited. "She is stirring."

Zade was so close to the door, now, he damn near pressed his ear against it. A feminine groan reached his ear and then...

"W-where am I?"

His heart dropped because, yes, that was Gabby's voice. He'd recognize it anywhere, even strained and groggy the way it was now.

God, had the fucker drugged her again?

"Welcome back, mi amor . I apologize for Eduardo's rough behavior toward you. However, I did warn you. You must learn to behave yourself. Otherwise I will have no choice but to let him hurt you again."

Again?

Zade's spine stiffened, as a dark, murderous rage caught flames deep inside his soul. In that instant, the icy fear that had been threatening to take over melted.

All other emotions went into a total lockdown as he became the calculated warrior he'd trained to be. Ready to put an end to the evil force threatening to destroy the best thing that had ever happened to him.

No one takes what's mine.

"Zade?" Sam whispered his name, no doubt sensing the change within him.

Turning to face her, he forced himself to use a gentle touch when he took her elbow and moved them away from the door.

Towering over her, he kept his voice low. "You need to get back in the cell."

"What?" Her light brown brows arched high, the ends of her hair flying out to the side as she shook her head vehemently. "No. I already told you—"

"I know what you said, but those men in there will start shooting the second I open that door."

"I-I don't care. I'd rather be shot than go back in there."

Zade understood her not wanting to go back inside her own personal prison, but damn it...

"Gabby does not have time for us to stand out here and argue. Honey, listen to me." He softened his voice and rested his hands gently onto her bare shoulders. "I'm not going to tell you I understand how you're feeling, because that would be total bullshit. But I do know your sister will be devastated if something happens to you while I'm trying to get her out of there."

Sam's eyes shone with fear, but she was also considering what he'd just said. "She'd blame herself."

"Yes," he answered bluntly. "She would." After a few more seconds—seconds Gabby didn't have—Zade added a persistent, "Please, Sam. Just until I can take Hector and Eduardo out. It's for your safety, as well as Gabby's."

The young woman licked her trembling lips. "Are you going to kill Hector?"

"Yes." Another blunt answer. One that may traumatize the poor girl even more than she already was.

"Promise?"

Or not. He looked her square in the eyes. "I promise."

"O-okay." Sam nodded, straightened her shoulders, and lifted her chin.

He watched as she bravely walked over to where he'd first found her, slid through the open bars, and pulled to make it appear as though the door was still locked.

"Thank you."

"Please…save my sister."

Staring back at her, Zade felt the need to make sure she understood. "Samantha, there are two things you should know about me. The first is I plan to be in your sister's life for the foreseeable future. That means I'm not going to let anything happen to her."

"What's the second thing?"

With a deadly tone in his voice, he told her, "I always keep my promises."

CHAPTER 19

Gabby's head felt like it was going to split wide open. She tried opening her eyes, but even the slightest sliver of light sent a splinter of pain shooting through her throbbing skull. So she kept them closed, for now.

She could feel the warmth of her own blood on the back of her head and neck, which would explain the mind-shattering headache. But for the life of her, she didn't remember how she'd been hurt.

Keeping her eyes closed, she tried to remember where she was and what had happened. When Gabby heard a man's voice, it was as if someone had suddenly pressed the fast-forward button on her memories.

Flashing through the day's events, she pictured waking up in the hotel room with Zade. Seeing him in that mouthwatering tux and fighting the need to rip it from his incredible body.

Gabby remembered arriving at Hector Andino's home, being at the auction, and waking up on the couch inside his office. An image of her climbing out of his window filled her mind's eye right before she saw Kole being brutally gunned down without any chance to defend himself.

Finally, Gabby remembered Andino and his muscle forcing her to drive through the trees. To a tiny shack in the field behind his house.

A flash of pain, and then…she was waking up, here.

She opened her eyes a tiny smidge at a time. Forced herself to push past the pain and adjust to the bright light.

Even though she could see Andino and Eduardo standing nearby, Gabby's first instinct was to try to run. To get as far away from them as she possibly could, and to find Zade and Samantha.

God, please let them be okay.

She tried sitting up, but the leather restraints around her wrists and ankles prevented her from moving more than a couple of inches off the cold concrete surface. The movement was enough for Andino to notice.

"Welcome back, mi amor ."

The certifiable man stepped closer. Staring down at her, his eyes filled with a sympathy she didn't buy for a second.

"I apologize for Eduardo's rough behavior toward you."

He raised a hand toward her face, but Gabby jerked away as best she could. She squeezed her eyes shut when the move sent another shard of pain slicing through her.

Looking displeased, Andino lowered the hand back to his side. "However, I did warn you. You must learn to behave yourself. Otherwise, I will have no choice but to let him hurt you again."

"You're crazy." Gabby looked at Eduardo and back to Hector. "You're both sick, crazy bastards, and I can't wait for the day someone sends the two of you straight to hell."

She should probably play nice. Not poke the bear and all that, but she'd done enough acting around this man to last a lifetime.

At this point, it wasn't like he'd believe her, anyway. So why bother?

"I was hoping maybe Eduardo's earlier reminder would have tampered that ugly temper of yours. I see you may need another one."

"I thought you liked my feistiness, Hector. Wasn't that what you said earlier tonight…right before you drugged me?"

Rather than respond right away, Andino turned and walked over to a shelf attached to the wall a few feet away. Her eyes fell on more tables like the one she was currently strapped to. She hadn't noticed them before, and she really, *really* wished she hadn't seen them now.

Their bases were a crude but sturdy wooden frame. The tops, a two-inch, concrete slab. Each had a few dark, rusty stains that looked a lot like dried blood.

Oh, shit.

"We don't have time for this now, Hector," Eduardo hissed.

This?

Her gaze rose to the shelf where Andino stood. Arranged neatly along its smooth surface were several shiny knives and other lovely things the monster probably used to convince the girls to go along with his nauseating operation.

After what appeared to be much consideration, Andino picked up one of the larger knives and turned back around. He began walking toward her, his steps slow. Intentional.

Gabby's heart began to race wildly, her breathing quickly becoming shallowed.

Don't let him see your fear, Gabby. This is all about power. Men like him get off on that sort of thing.

The words were of her own mind's making, but it was almost as if Zade were right there, talking to her. She could almost feel his presence, though she knew that was simply wishful thinking on her part.

But that's what she did, right? It's how her brain had always coped with being terrified.

Whether it be one of her mom's too-handsy boyfriends, getting caught in a bad part of town, or having to live with the foster brother from hell…anytime she was so scared she could barely speak, Gabby's mind took her someplace else.

Someplace *safe.*

She couldn't imagine a safer place to be than in the warmth and comfort of Zade's strong, protective arms.

With her eyes still on Andino and that damn knife in his hand, Gabby reached deep within herself to find a calm she most definitely did not feel. Almost instantly, her mask fell into place.

Her heart rate slowed, her breathing became close to normal. She could take whatever Andino was about to do to her. She was strong enough.

At least that's what she kept telling herself as he closed the distance between them.

"There she is." He smiled. "See, Eduardo? I told you she was special. My Gabriella is such a strong, brave woman."

"I'm not your anything, you sick freak."

"The bitch isn't worth it, Hector." Eduardo glared down at her from his dutiful post at her feet. "She's already caused us enough trouble as it is. Let's leave her here and move the hell on. I don't have a good feeling about being here with those men still swarming around the house upstairs."

He was talking about Zade's team and Ghost and his men.

They're still here.

Gabby opened her mouth to scream for help, but Hector pressed the blade of his knife to her cheek.

"You can scream, mi amor , but no one will hear you. We

are deep underground and the walls and ceiling are soundproof. No one upstairs even knows we are here."

His words struck a chord with her, creating a nagging feeling almost like she'd forgotten something. Something important.

Nate picked you up with his drone. We know exactly where you are.

Gabe's recent words rang through her pounding head. They *do* know she's here. They're on their way…should be closing in at any moment.

I need to keep him talking.

"How is it no one has found this place before now?" She spoke carefully as to not get cut. "You've been the subject of how many federal investigations? How have you not had this place searched from top to bottom?"

"You forget, my sweet Gabriella." Andino slid the knife down her cheek, lightly tracing her jawline with its tip. "We are not in your country. Without the cooperation of my government, your people have no jurisdiction here. And my government"—he chuckled—"well, I *am* my government. I own them. I provide for them so they can give their families food. Shelter. Those are men who will never turn on me."

She wanted to pull away but didn't for fear the blade would pierce her skin. "So why keep me here? Why not just kill me and get it over with?"

An image flashed behind her eyes. A different house. Different restraints. A very different man.

God, had it only been three days since she'd said those same words to Zade?

A lot can happen in three days.

He slid the knife along her collar bone and over her bare shoulder.

"Don't listen to her, Hector," Eduardo chimed back in. His

angry voice echoing off the walls. "We need to leave the bitch here and be done with this!"

The tip of the blade pricked the skin covering her upper arm. "You forget who is in charge here, Eduardo. I will kill her if and when I am ready to and not a second before."

He continued to cut her, the blade leaving a trail of fire in its wake. Gabby sucked in a breath, pushing back the scream begging to be set free.

She refused to give him the satisfaction,

"Damn it, Hector, stop!" Eduardo's booming demand surprised her. "You're not thinking rationally!"

No, really? You don't say.

"This woman will ruin everything you have worked so hard for." Eduardo's voice raised. "Everything *we've* worked for. Let's leave her and go!"

The blade left her skin as Andino pointed it toward his trusted enforcer. Gabby tried not to look at the fresh blood dripping from its tip.

"She is mine. I will do whatever I want with her, and I will not have you or anyone else telling me what I should or should not do."

Eduardo, who'd moved over to her right side so she was between the two men, continued to face off with his boss. Not a smart move, if you asked her. Although...

The longer they argued amongst themselves, the more time it gave the others to show up.

"You brought me in six months ago because you needed my help, remember? You came to me because you heard I was the best at what I do. I've proven that to you over and over again."

Gabby's self-induced calm went right out the window when she saw Eduardo pull his gun from his waistband. He kept it loose at his side.

"I've nearly died for you," Eduardo continued on with his

rant. "I *killed* a man for you tonight, for fuck's sake! But I will not hang out here and be taken down over the sick infatuation you have for this woman."

Eduardo raised his gun. He pointed that gun…right at her.

"You do not want to do that, my friend," Andino warned him.

"I'd listen to him, Eduardo." Gabby was suddenly more than ready to be on Andino's side. "You know what kind of man your boss is."

His eyes slid down to hers. There was a strange look in them. One Gabby couldn't quite put her finger on.

"Yes, I do. Which is why I have to end this. Now."

It was as though everything began moving in slow motion.

Eduardo curled his finger around the trigger as the door on the wall facing them crashed open. Two gunshots echoed deafeningly, their explosions nearly simultaneous making what sounded like one, loud *boom*.

Gabby squeezed her eyes shut and waited for the pain to strike, but it never came. Something else happened then. Something incredible and miraculous.

She heard Zade's glorious voice.

"Put the weapon down, Andino! Or I swear to God, I will drop you where you stand!"

Her eyes flew open, Gabby's heart nearly bursting from relief when she saw him. Zade was there.

He's really here!

"Zade!" she breathed his name.

Looking like a cross between James Bond and Jason Bourne, he stood in his tuxedo, arms stretched out in front of him. His gun was pointed directly at Andino's head.

Wait. What about...

Gabby turned her head to the side, wincing when a

stinging pain hit her neck. Eduardo was on the floor, his back propped against the wall to her right. Blood oozed from a wound in his right shoulder.

"Sonofabitch," he growled, his voice strained with pain. "You shot me!"

Because you were going to shoot me, you idiot!"

"Make a move toward that gun, and the next one goes in your head."

Gabby spotted Eduardo's gun over in the corner, well out of the man's reach. She assumed it had gone flying when Zade's bullet hit the guy's shoulder.

"I mean it, Hector." He returned his focus to the man behind her. "Drop the fucking knife, or I will drop you. Your choice."

Knife? Zade's first words when he entered the room sank in. But Andino had moved the weapon away from her when he and Eduardo were talking.

Confused, Gabby's gaze returned to Zade's, the movement bringing another quick flash of pain making her wince.

"Baby, you've got to stop moving your head," he spoke to her for the first time since bursting through the door like her own personal action hero. "You're already bleeding too damn much as it is."

Drop the fucking knife, or I will drop you.

Keeping her head still, Gabby slid her eyes to the left. Between the guns firing, her thinking *she* was the one getting shot, and seeing Zade again…she hadn't noticed the knife was now pressed again her neck.

You're already bleeding too damn much as it is.

She felt the blood. Not from her head or arm this time. New, *fresh* blood was dripping down the side of her neck.

Suddenly moving was the very last thing she wanted to do.

"You try to shoot me, she dies," Andino warned.

"Move that blade a fucking millimeter, it'll be the last thing you do."

Gabby held her breath and did her very best not to cause the knife to do anymore damage to her skin. She also tried to ignore the light-headedness that was starting to set in, probably from the blood loss Zade had been worried about.

"Eduardo, don't just sit there!" Andino ordered his man. "Get your gun and shoot this son of a bitch!"

"Don't do it, Eduardo." Zade kept his eyes trained on Hector. "This piece of shit isn't worth it."

"I…know," the wounded man grunted. "That's why…I was about to shoot…his ass." From the corner of her eye, Gabby could tell the man on the floor was shifting to sit up straighter.

Wait. *What?*

Gabby started to shake her head but stopped. "Your gun was pointed at me. Not him."

"I only wanted him to think I was going to shoot you. Needed him to stop…cutting."

Zade scoffed. "Like I'm going to buy that shit. This isn't my first rodeo, dumbass, so don't even fucking try to play me like it is."

"Not…playing. Name's Sawyer. Sawyer…Drake. DEA."

Gabby noticed the man's thick, Hispanic accent had completely vanished.

"You're a cop?" Andino yelled.

He was behind her, so Gabby couldn't see his face. But she imagined the veins in his head were popping out right about now.

"Yeah, I'm a cop." The man spoke between grunts of pain. "And you're under…arrest for distributing illegal substances across state and national borders, human…trafficking, and a fuck ton of other charges I can't think of right now because my shoulder feels like it's…about to burn the fuck…off."

Gabby's mind whirled with all kinds of what-the hell thoughts. First and foremost, was the guy even telling the truth?

He couldn't be. Not after what he'd done to Kole.

"Don't believe him, Zade," she spoke carefully. "He shot Kole. I watched him do it." Her voice cracked at the end. A warm tear ran down her temple and into her hairline.

Anger and disbelief flashed across his hardened face. His eye slid over to Eduardo's. "I will fucking end you!"

"He's not dead!" Eduardo, or whatever his name was, put up a bloody palm. "The guy was wearing a vest. I felt it when I pulled him out of the car. That's why I shot him in the chest and not the head."

Hope bloomed inside her *own* chest. Could Kole really still be alive?

Zade shook his head. "That's a good cover, but it proves nothing."

"I'm telling you the truth! Look, man. I can prove it to you, later, after we take this piece of shit down." When Zade still didn't look convinced, the man said, "I get it. I've been where you are, but it's not like I carry my badge and real I.D. with me while I'm on the job. Shit!" He shifted again, the movement apparently causing the man more pain. "I'm telling you, I'm Special Agent Sawyer Drake with the United States Drug Enforcement Administration."

"You're right." Zade shook his head slowly. "You can't prove shit, and I don't have time to dick with you right now." His focus returned to the man with the knife. "Drop the goddamn knife and step away."

Andino didn't respond right away. Instead, Gabby lay there listening to the man's ragged breaths as he contemplated his next move.

Please put the knife down. Please put the knife down.

"I trusted you," he spat the words at the man on the floor.

It was pretty clear Hector believed the guy's story. "I brought you into my business. Into my home."

"Your *business* is to abduct and sell young girls and women for a fucking profit. You hand them over to people who do unspeakable things to them. Not to mention the drug deals you oversee."

He pushed himself up off the floor, his left hand pressing against the gushing wound on his right shoulder. Gabby expected Zade to shoot him again, or at least warn him. Maybe he was starting to believe the man's story, too.

"The shit you put out on the streets kills thousands of Americans every year," Eduardo/Sawyer continued on. "Most of those under the age of thirty. My sister was one of them."

Okay, now *she* was starting to believe him, too.

"You're a waste of fucking space, Andino, and I hope like *hell* this man does us all a favor and kills you where you stand."

Gabby's eyes shifted to Zade's. His expression was guarded, but she could tell he no longer felt the man next to her was a threat. At least not as much as the man still standing behind her.

"Unbuckle her clasps." Andino finally spoke again. The order was to the man she was starting to think of as Sawyer.

"Fuck you."

The knife pricked her skin again, and a tiny grunt escaped before she could stop it.

"Release her or I slit her throat from ear to ear."

"Do what he says, Drake," Zade barked loudly.

"At least you finally believe me."

Using his good hand, Eduardo, A.K.A. Sawyer Drake, began to unbuckle the restraints on her right side. First her wrist, and then her ankle.

Keeping the knife precariously close to her jugular,

Andino shifted around to her right side as the other man began working on her left ankle.

"What's the plan, Hector?" Zade asked. "There are agents and teams all around you. There's nowhere to go."

"They won't hurt me. Not while I have an American woman as my hostage."

When Drake released the final restraint, Andino ordered her to stand.

Oh so carefully, Gabby kept her eyes locked on Zade, groaning as she sat up and slid from the Table of Horrors. Her left hand shot out when her feet hit the floor as a wave of dizziness washed over her.

From adrenaline, fear, or blood loss, she wasn't sure. Most likely, all three.

"You okay, baby?"

No. "I'm good." She didn't dare nod her head. Not with that damn knife still at her throat.

Leaning down to speak directly in her ear, Andino said, "We're going to go up these steps behind me and back out the way we came in. You're going to drive us out of here, just like before. No stopping for anyone or anything. Do you understand?"

"Yes." Gabby blinked sending twin tears down over her cheeks.

"Don't fucking do this, Andino!" Zade kept his gun pointed at Hector.

She felt herself being pulled back toward the steps.

Zade advanced, his strong legs taking one, huge step forward. "Stop. Fucking. Moving!"

But Andino didn't listen. He kept right on pulling, the knife wobbling a bit as she did her best to move with him.

"Shoot him, Zade," Gabby told the man she loved. "He's going to kill me the first chance he gets, anyway."

"Shut up!" Andino jerked her up the steps.

"Zade, please! Don't let him get away with what he's done to those girls. To Sam." Her voice cracked again. "Shoot him!"

"Easy, baby. I don't want you getting hurt any more than you already are."

"I'm already dead, Zade." Tears fell from her eyes. "Don't let it be for nothing."

"No!" He advanced another step. "You are *not* dying today."

She saw the slight tremble in his gun and knew. He was terrified of hurting her. Terrified *for* her.

"I love you," Gabby blurted. She needed to make sure he knew that. They'd already said the words earlier, but she needed him to *know* it.

Andino jerked her again. Another nick of her skin, but Gabby ignored it. She was too busy listening to Zade say…

"I love you, too, baby. So much."

"Good." She offered him a quivering smile. "That's all I needed to hear."

"I said, shut up!"

Andino was losing it. Gabby knew what she'd said was the truth. This man was going to kill her no matter what.

May as well go down fighting.

Staring deep into Zade's maddeningly intense eyes, she prayed he understood what needed to be done.

Filling her lungs with a steeling breath, she reminded Andino, "And I told you, I'm not very good at taking orders."

In one crazy, hail-Mary move, Gabby raised her left hand and grabbed the hand that held the knife. At the same time, she turned her head to try to prevent her throat from being cut further. Gabby then pushed her body back against Andino's, throwing the man off-balance.

"Gabby, get down!"

Zade didn't need to shout the order. She was already well on her way.

Releasing his wrist, Gabby jumped down, off the few steps they'd managed to climb. As the bullets flew from Zade's gun, her body landed in a less-than-graceful sprawl in the puddle of blood Agent Drake left behind when he'd stood.

It was over within seconds.

"Gabriella!"

Zade sprinted to her. On his way, he bent over and grabbed the gun that was still lying in the corner. Shoving both weapons in his waistband, he knelt down next to her.

"Baby?"

He was there. His *hands* were there. They seemed to be everywhere all at once as they checked over her wounds.

"I-I'm okay."

Maybe *okay* was a bit of a stretch. Her head was still pounding, her arm hurt like a bitch, and she was pretty sure she'd gotten another cut when she'd pushed Andino's knife away from her neck.

But she wasn't dead, so that was a win in her book.

"Fuck, there's so much blood!" Zade's voice shook. This strong, handsome, hero of hers was shaking from head to toe.

She looked back toward the stairs, where a very-much-dead Hector Andino lay. *Rot in hell, asshole.*

Gabby's gaze slid back to the man of her dreams. "It's not all mine."

"What?" He half-listened. His hands were still checking her over.

"Zade, stop!" Gabby grabbed one of those hands and squeezed. "Seriously, I'm all right. Most of this is his." She tipped her chin toward the man walking toward them.

"Christ, I'm glad that's over."

The man whose name Gabby was almost certain was Sawyer sauntered over to them. He was bleeding like a stuck pig, but there was a kindness in his eyes she hadn't seen before, and nothing about the way he moved was threatening in the least.

Still, she had to ask, "Are you really with the DEA?"

Her question had Zade shifting his body to put himself between her and the other man.

Always trying to protect me.

Her heart flipped inside her chest. It seemed to do that a lot when he was around.

"I swear on my mother's grave." He started to hold up a bloody hand but decided against it. "I'm sorry about your head. I didn't want to hurt you, but he gave the order. Had to make it look real. If I hadn't, either my cover would've been blown, or you would've gotten caught in an up-close and personal battle." The guy shrugged his good shoulder. "I figured if you were unconscious, it would buy me some time to—"

He didn't get to finish because Zade had shot up to his feet, his large hand choking off the rest of whatever Agent Drake was trying to say.

"You *hit* her?"

"T-to protect h-her."

"Zade." Gabby stood and put a hand on his back. "It's okay."

He didn't look at her as he spoke through a set of clenched teeth. "He hurt you, baby. That shit sure as fuck is *not* okay."

Maybe not, but… "I'm all right, now. Besides, you can't very well kill a DEA agent."

"Give me one good reason why not."

"You'll go to prison, for starters."

All three heads turned toward the stairs. The door at the top was open and Matt, Fletch, and Hollywood were all staring down at the gruesome scene.

Gabby expected Zade to let go of the other man immediately. He didn't.

"You ever lay a hand on her again, I *will* kill you."

"Understood." Agent Drake's response was barely over a whisper.

"And don't even think about trying to leave until I can verify you are who you say you are."

"Wouldn't dream of it."

With a final glare, Zade finally let him go. He turned back toward the men on the stairs. "Seriously? You couldn't have shown up five minutes earlier?"

"What?" Matt looked down at Andino and over to the man Zade had been choking out. "Looks to me like you had things under control."

Zade opened his mouth to let his teammate know what he thought of that particular assessment when all of the sudden, his expression changed. "Kole?" He nearly shouted the other man's name.

Gabby's heart was in her throat as she waited to hear. Thankfully they didn't have to wait long.

"Kole's fine," Matt assured him. "Truck just checked in with us. Kole was coming to when they got to him. He's bruised as hell and beyond pissed, but he's good."

"Told you," Sawyer muttered.

Zade swung a fierce gaze around and started to say something when they all heard a woman's excited voice.

"Gabby!"

Her focus shot to the door Zade had busted in earlier. Like when he'd first appeared, she could hardly believe her eyes.

"Sam?"

The two women ran to each other, nearly knocking one another down with their joint embrace.

"Oh, my God! You're okay!" Gabby pulled away. Much

like Zade had done to her, she started running her hands along her sister's body. "Are you hurt?" Her eyes landed on Sam's bruised face.

Gabby swung her head around and glared at Sawyer. "Did you do this to her? So help me..." She started for him, ready to put her own hands around the lying bastard's neck, but Sam grabbed her wrist to stop her.

"No, Gabby! It wasn't him." All eyes in the room focused on Sam. "It was one of the other men. Eduardo was sort of... nice to me." Sam's eyes moved from Gabby's to Sawyer's and back. "H-he stepped in a few times when Hector tried to... oh, my God!" 'Eduardo' was momentarily forgotten when she spotted Andino's body. "Is he dead?"

Rather than expect Gabby to answer, Sam looked to Zade for confirmation.

Zade nodded. "He'll never hurt anyone else, ever again."

Everyone in the room watched silently as Sam walked over to the steps. She stared down at Andino for a few long seconds before spitting on the asshole's corpse. Without a word, she came back over to where Gabby and Zade were standing.

Tears welled in Sam's blue eyes as she looked up at Zade. "Thank you for keeping your promise." Wiping at her damp face, she slid a glance to Gabby and smirked. "You'd better hang on to this guy. If not, I might have to steal him."

Gabby laughed even as tears streamed down her own cheeks. She hugged her sister as if she never wanted to let her go.

"Not a chance, Sam," Gabby whispered. "That one's mine."

CHAPTER 20

"You sure you don't want to stay another night, just to be safe?" Zade brushed some hair from Gabby's forehead and tucked it behind her ear.

Jesus, he'd come so damn close to losing her. To losing *everything.*

"It's a few cuts and scrapes, Zade." Gabby shifted on the noisy hospital mattress. "I don't need to stay two nights for that."

He stared down into her emerald eyes. God, she was beautiful. "You were drugged." With what they now knew to be Ketamine, thanks to the traces found by the docs here. "After that, you were knocked unconscious. You could have a concussion."

Thanks to that bastard, Drake.

That shit still made his blood boil.

The first thing Zade had done after his team arrived and Gabby and Sam had their sweet, but brief, reunion, was to have Matt check out Gabby's wounds. The second he confirmed she was, in fact, going to be okay, Matt did a field examination on Sam.

Gabby stayed with Sam, and though he hated to leave Gabby's side for even a second, Zade had but only to check out Drake's story. As it turned out, the bastard was telling the truth.

Sawyer Drake had been a DEA agent for six years. He'd been working the Andino cartel angle for the past eleven months, finally breaking through and joining Hector's crew six months ago.

Exactly as he'd claimed.

According to Drake, he'd been trying to get his boss to use what he'd already gotten on Andino to put the asshole away. Drake's boss, the greedy bastard, had wanted this one last auction as the final nail in Andino's coffin. So Drake had been forced to continue with his cover.

The son of a bitch was damn lucky Zade had been aiming for the shoulder in order to get him to drop the gun.

Much to Zade's dismay, they'd been ordered to give the agent a ride back to Texas, since his cover was no longer needed. Zade couldn't believe the guy's nerve when he found him hovering in the hallway outside Sam's hospital room after he'd been treated for the through-and-through Zade had gladly given him.

Drake claimed he wanted to check on Sam. Make sure she was okay. Zade had promptly threatened to call security and have them toss the ballsy agent out on his ass.

Sawyer Drake made his first good decision of the day and left of his own accord.

"I've been checked out by Matt, Truck, and the doctor here. I don't have a concussion."

Gabby's sweet voice tore him away from his angry thoughts.

No, she wasn't concussed, thank fuck. But she did have one hell of a bump on her head. That and a row of stitches down her upper arm, not to mention a bandage over the cuts Andino's blade had left on her neck.

Zade had no idea what he was going to see when he first kicked that door in. But if there were any doubts to how the scenario would end, they had vanished the second he saw that knife at his woman's throat.

It had been his job to protect her. To keep her safe. Instead, he'd sent her out that damn window and right into the hands of a fucking monster.

"Stop."

The whispered word had his eyes meeting hers. "What?"

"I know what you're doing, and you need to stop. This wasn't your fault."

"The hell it wasn't. I sent you away. If you'd stayed with me, you could've come with me downstairs. We could've gotten Sam out and gone back out the way we came. Andino never would've gotten his hands on you. Kole's chest wouldn't be covered in bruises, and you wouldn't have twenty-four stitches in your arm."

Kole had fallen all over himself apologizing for 'letting' Andino take Gabby from the SUV. Zade had promptly told him to get his head out of his ass and remember the little speech he'd given Zade at the bar.

Tossing Kole's own words back to him struck a chord somewhere deep inside Zade. For the first time since he'd been shot, Zade began to accept that he had no control over the events of that day. He knew he'd probably still have nightmares about that and what had happened to Gabby and her sister. But the healing process had finally begun.

Samantha Shoemaker was in the room right next door. She was checked out properly and had given her statement to the authorities. Other than some dehydration and bruising, the lucky woman was fine.

The doctor had even confirmed she hadn't been sexually assaulted. Another miracle, given who'd taken her.

"I'd be dead if it weren't for you."

"No you wouldn't." He shook his head. "Drake would've killed Andino if I hadn't come into that room."

He could tell she was considering his valid point. "I'd still have twenty-four stitches in my arm," she pointed out.

Also a valid point. Still…

Zade reached over to where her hands were resting in her lap and took one in his. Caressing her soft skin with his thumb, he let go of everything he was feeling.

"The other night we talked about what happened to me a couple of months ago. Do you remember that whole story?"

Gabby nodded. "A man named Adrian Walker shot you and kidnapped Matt's wife.

"That's right." He swallowed a giant lump filling his throat. "When I saw that gun pointed at me, I was *certain* I was going to die. I'd never been more terrified."

She squeezed his hand. "But thank God, you didn't die that day."

His lips curved upward, forming a slight smile. "No. I didn't. But you almost died last night."

He'd thanked God more times than he could count that she hadn't.

As soon as they had cleared the scene at Andino's place, Bravo had boarded R.I.S.C.'s private jet and got the hell out of Mexico and back to Dallas. After landing at Homeland's private airstrip, conveniently located next to the agency's medical facility, Zade and the others had insisted both Gabby and Sam be checked out more thoroughly.

Zade may have also talked Ryker, their Homeland handler, into ensuring the two women were admitted for observation for a minimum of one night.

Friends in high places came in handy.

"Zade, I'm fine. Really."

"I know you are." Keeping her hand in his, he rested a hip on the bed next to her covered legs. "But you need to know when I kicked that door down and saw you lying there, strapped to that fucking table..." His voice turned thick, and Zade had to clear the emotional ball away before continuing on. "When I saw Andino's knife and realized *you* were the one bleeding, and when it looked like Drake was going to shoot you, I..."

That time his voice cracked, and his nose began to burn. He looked down at their joined hands, the image blurring behind tears he had no hope of stopping.

Zade closed his eyes, sending those tears down his face and onto the stark, white sheet below.

"Zade," Gabby whispered his name again.

He looked up at her. She was lying in a hospital bed, her deep, red hair flowing around her shoulders. She had stitches in her arm and that damn bandage on her neck, and fuck if she wasn't the most beautiful sight he'd ever seen.

"I love you, Gabby. I love you more than I have ever loved anyone. I know we've already said it, and I know it's crazy given the short amount of time we've known each other, but I don't care. When I came into that room and thought I was going to lose you...baby, that scared me more than when I thought I was going to lose my own life that day in the car."

Because he loved her more than life itself.

Silver streaks ran the length of her cheeks. "I love you, too, Zade. The amount of time spent together, that doesn't matter to me. What matters is this." She held up their joined hands. "And what I feel here." She used her free hand to pat her chest, right above her heart. "What I feel for you...that's the only thing that matters to me."

Zade stood and leaned over her. He pressed his lips to hers and whispered, "What we feel for each other."

Gabby smiled. "That's right."

Someone behind him cleared their throat. Zade turned to see Jake McQueen, owner of R.I.S.C. and his boss, standing in the doorway.

"Sorry to interrupt. I wanted to come by and check on things." The former Delta operative walked into the room.

"Hey, Jake." Zade attempted to discreetly wipe his face dry before offering his hand to the other man.

His boss shook his hand in return. "King. And you must be the infamous Gabriella I've heard so much about."

"Hi." She smiled and held out her hand. "Please, call me Gabby."

"Gabby." His boss smirked. "Quite a grip you have there."

"Thanks."

"You doing okay? You need anything?"

"No, thank you." She glanced up at Zade. "I have everything I need."

Jake's gaze slid between the two. "I can see that."

"We appreciate you coming by, Boss, but you don't have to stay. Against much prodding on my part, we're going to head out soon. Plus you have that new baby at home. I'm sure you'd rather be at home with her and Liv."

"Actually"—Jake shoved his hands into his jeans pocket —"there's something I wanted to talk to you about."

"Oh." Zade looked at Gabby. "I'll be right outside if you need me."

"Both of you."

Gabby's brows scrunched in that adorable way they did when she was confused. Almost instantly, the skin on her forehead smoothed and she shook her head. "Zade did nothing wrong. He tried to tell me not to drink the champagne, but I didn't listen. If I had, I wouldn't have been drugged, and we never would've been taken to Andino's office, and—"

"Gabby." Jake put a hand up to cut off her cute as fuck rambling.

Jesus, she was trying to protect him.

"Sorry." She gave the man a chagrined smile.

"I'm not here to reprimand Zade."

Thank fuck.

"I'm here because I'd like to know your thoughts on joining Bravo Team in a more...professional manner."

It was Zade's turn to be confused. "You're offering her a job?"

"It would be an as-needed basis. You know as well as I do there are certain instances when having a female on an op is not only beneficial but necessary." The man's blue eyes shifted to Gabby's. "Alpha Team has Mac, but Bravo is an all-male team. Gabe and the others told me how cool you were under pressure, Gabby. Ghost and his men relayed the same sentiment. They all said you were quick on your feet, fell into an alternate persona flawlessly, and, other than maybe the part with the champagne, were as good as any seasoned operatives they've worked with in the past."

Holy. Shit.

"I'm sure you'll want to think it over," Jake continued. "Talk with Zade and your family, but just so you're aware, R.I.S.C. operatives are paid well for the work they do. We'll also make sure you get the proper field training." Jake paused as he studied them both for a few, awkward seconds. "From everything I've heard, you two make one hell of a team." He moved toward the door. "Think about it, and when you decide, let me know your decision."

With a nod, the man was gone.

"Holy shit." Gabby parroted Zade's thoughts.

He looked away from the door and back at her. "I know."

"I-I don't even know what to say."

"There's a first," he muttered teasingly.

"Hey!" Gabby smacked him on the thigh for his trouble.

Chuckling, Zade sat back down next to her and took her hand like before. "What do you want to do?"

"Honestly, I don't know. I hadn't thought past staying with you tonight. I mean, Sam's parents are supposed to be here soon. I think they were going to get a hotel room tonight and take her back to Chicago. She seems to be doing surprisingly well for what she went through, but I'm sure she's going to need some serious counseling over the next few months. If not forever."

On the plane ride back to the States, they'd learned Sam had been taken by a boy she'd recently started to date. Sam said it was still in the early stages and nothing too serious, which was why she hadn't mentioned him to Gabby or her parents. At least, she thought they were dating. In reality, he worked for Hector Andino.

He'd pick out a girl he thought could bring in good money, meet them somehow, and turn on the charm. After a few weeks of dating, he'd arrange to have them meet him someplace secluded, which wasn't hard to do in a city like Chicago.

The punk would drug them, put them in a van, and drive them to New Orleans for transport out of the country.

Homeland agents stationed in Chicago had already picked the asshole up, and the agency was working a joint investigation with the DEA and the FBI in order to bring down all of Andino's customers.

Most of the heavy hitters were caught and brought in the night of the auction. The others were well on their way to spending the rest of their lives behind bars.

See how you like it, fuckers.

"What about you?" Zade suddenly felt nervous. "We haven't really had a chance to talk about us or where we go from here."

"Well." Gabby sighed. "I guess that depends."

"On what?"

"On you."

"Me?"

She nodded. "I know *I* can handle it, but do you really think you'd be okay with me working side-by-side with you and your team?"

He blinked. "You're considering Jake's offer?"

"Why not? Champagne debacle aside, I think I did pretty well. Like Jake said, I can put on almost any mask I need to in a given situation. And, minus thinking Kole was dead and being strapped to that creepy torture table, I sort of…liked it."

"You liked it." The statement was one of disbelief.

One corner of Gabby's mouth rose. "Mostly I liked being with you." When he didn't say anything right away, she quickly added, "But if you don't want me to, I understand."

"No."

Disappointment crossed over her. "Oh. Okay. I guess that settles it."

"I mean, no, I don't *not* want you to."

"So you…do want me on your team?"

"I suppose having you there on an as-needed basis wouldn't be so bad."

Excitement flared behind her green eyes. "Really?"

"That look you got when you thought I didn't want you to join R.I.S.C. tells me you really want this."

"Yeah." She smiled wider. "I guess I do." Gabby sat up straighter, leaned in toward him. "There's something else I want even more."

"Oh, yeah?" Zade brushed his lips against hers. "What's that?"

"You."

Zade carefully cupped her head, watching so that he

didn't hit the bump there, and kissed her more thoroughly. The way a man kissing the woman he can't live without should.

When it ended, he smiled against her lips. "I bet you're wishing you hadn't made me that deal before."

"Deal?" Gabby pulled back in order to look at him more fully. "What deal?"

"You know, the one where once you become an official member of Bravo Team I get to boss you around."

Gabby's jaw dropped. "That doesn't count."

"I'm pretty sure it does. I have Kole as my witness. In fact, the entire Bravo Team, plus Ghost, Truck, Fletch, Coach, and Hollywood, were all listening, so—"

Gabby pulled on his shirt and kissed him again. Zade knew it was to shut him up, but he couldn't care less.

This time when the kiss ended, *he* was the one who pulled back enough to look into her eyes. He needed to be looking there when he said this next part.

With a little wiggling, he managed to keep hold of her hand and pull a piece of folded paper from his pocket with his other one. He smoothed it out on his denim-covered thigh and read part of it aloud.

"You gave me hope at a time when I thought there was none. I'll never forget that or you."

Gabby gasped. "That's the note I left you in Grand Isle."

"I kept it. I've read it probably a hundred times. Maybe more."

"You have?" She sounded stunned. "Why?"

"Because, Gabriella." He brushed the back of his knuckles down her cheek. "You did the same for me. I went to that island in search of something. I had no idea what until I met you. Like you said to me in this note, you gave me hope when I thought there was none. And baby, I will never, ever forget that."

"Oh, Zade." She was smiling, even as more tears fell.

"Marry me, Gabby."

She didn't hesitate. "Okay."

They laughed because neither one needed to take more time to think about it. Zade knew exactly what he wanted. What he needed. And she was right there, staring back at him.

His love.

His life.

My future.

EPILOGUE

Two weeks later...

"And then there was one."

Gabe Dawson glanced up at the figure walking toward him. The sun was behind the guy making his face appear dark and mysterious. He didn't need to see his face to know who it was.

"What's up, Ghost?"

"Not much, man. Wanted to come over and say thanks for inviting my team to this little shindig." The Delta Force operator took a seat in the empty lawn chair next to his.

"Least I could do after the help your team gave Bravo Team in Mexico."

"I'd love to take the credit for that, but if memory serves me correctly, we came to you guys for help."

"Oh, shit." Gabe smiled. "That's right. In that case, you're welcome."

Ghost laughed. "Thanks. I have to admit, our teams work pretty damn well together."

"Yes, we do. You ever get tired of living the easy life with Delta, I'm sure McQueen would take pity on you and put you with us."

"Not gonna happen, brother." Ghost grinned as he watched Truck and Fletch play a game of cornhole with Zade and Gabby. "They seem to be doing well."

"They are. Engaged, if you can believe it."

"I heard. Also heard they'd only known each other for a few days before all that shit went down in La Paz?"

"Yep." Gabe took a long draw from his beer. "Three days of fun there, three days of hell in Mexico."

Gabe looked over at the pair who were laughing hysterically at how forcefully Truck tried to throw the beanbag on his turn.

Ghost swallowed a drink of his beer. "Clearly it wasn't *all* hell. At least, not for those two."

"No." Gabe sighed. "Apparently not."

"I'd say three days isn't near enough time to be sure enough for marriage, but I pretty much knew after that first night with my Rayne that she was the one. Took my stubborn ass a little longer to admit it, but yeah. I guess when you know, you know."

"Yep." Gabe took another drink because, fuck. He did not want to delve into this particular conversation.

"What about you?" Ghost looked over at him. "You ever think about tying the knot?"

"Nope." He swallowed another gulp. "Like my life exactly how it is. Don't see any reason to change it."

Liar, liar, pants on fucking fire.

"I used to think that, too. But I'm tellin' ya. You have no idea what you're missing by staying single."

That was the problem. Gabe knew exactly what he was missing. He also knew he'd never find that kind of happiness with anyone else but her.

So he decided a long time ago not to even bother trying to look for it.

"Well, I think I'm going to call it a night." Gabe stood and folded up the lawn chair.

"Already?" Ghost looked at his watch. "Dude, it's not even ten-thirty."

"I know, but I was up late last night going over some intel on the next case Ryker wants us on. Plus I've got an early meeting at the office with a potential client McQueen wants me to meet. Some big, corporate guy, so I need to look sharp."

There was no intel from Ryker. There was no early meeting in the morning.

"Fun times." Ghost stood and held out his hand. "All right, man. Take it easy. Hopefully we'll get to work together again, soon."

"Looking forward to it." Gabe returned the gesture.

As Ghost headed over to the table to join a few of his teammates, Gabe glanced around at the others spread out around Kole and Sarah's large back yard.

The team had been spending more and more nights over here, lately. Between impromptu barbeques or having drinks and hanging out to watch a ballgame or race, there was one thing that had really started to gnaw at him.

The single guys were dwindling, fast. Now that Zade found Gabby, they weren't even dwindling anymore. Gabe was it.

And then there was one.

Ghost's words rang through him like a painful spur.

Not that Gabe wasn't happy for his teammates, because he was. He simply wasn't as good at hiding his other emotions as he used to be.

Whether it be his age and the fact that he found himself

reflecting more and more on his past, or just good old-fashioned jealousy, Gabe had begun to dread their off-hour get togethers.

And he fucking hated it.

He'd chosen this life. Chose his job and his duty over her. And he was perfectly fine with that decision.

Forget the pants, man. Your entire wardrobe just went up in a giant-ass ball of flames.

Ignoring that tiny voice, Gabe made sure the others weren't paying attention and snuck out of the party like a fucking coward.

By the time he got home, he was in an even more sour mood than when he left. Distracted by ghosts of his past, Gabe opened his door, almost missing the fact that the light he'd left on in his apartment—that he *always* left on so he had a clear view of the space when he returned—was off and the place was pitch black.

Almost.

In one fluid motion, he pulled his gun from its place at the small of his back and flipped the safety. After several years as a Navy SEAL and Bravo's team leader, the weapon was like an extension of his body. And even better than his American Express.

Never fucking leave home without it.

"I'm armed, and I will not hesitate to shoot," he warned whoever was there.

"I know," a man's voice rumbled low from the right side of his living room. "That's why I turned off your light."

"You picked the wrong apartment to rob tonight, my friend."

"Oh, we're not friends, Dawson." The man chuckled. "Not even close."

Gabe's lamp turned back on, and it took him a

millisecond for his eyes to adjust. Even then, he couldn't believe what he was seeing.

Sitting in his favorite recliner as though he didn't have a care in the world was the one man Bravo Team had been itching to find.

"Hello, Gabriel." Adrian Walker tipped his head. "It's been a while."

What the actual fuck?

Gabe's finger slid down to his trigger as he took a large, advancing step toward the traitorous bastard. "What the hell are you doing in my apartment?"

"Now that was almost *exactly* how I imagined this little reunion playing out."

Arrogant bastard. Gabe took another step closer. "I'm about two seconds away from putting a fucking hole in the middle of your forehead, so I suggest you cut through the bullshit and tell me why you're here."

"Ellena."

The name was like a physical blow. One that nearly sent Gabe stumbling backward. Terror for the only woman to have ever owned his heart filled his veins with an icy cold like none he'd ever known.

His trigger finger twitched. His voice held a deadly tone. "What did you just say?"

"You heard me, Dawson."

Walker pushed himself to his feet slowly. The second he did, Gabe took two, large strides across the hardwood floor, nearly covering the distance between them.

With his jaw clenched together tightly, Gabe's next warning came as a deadly hiss between his teeth. "Don't you fucking move, or I swear to *God* I will pull this trigger."

"Easy, Dawson." He put his palms up. "I'm not here to hurt you. On the contrary, I came because I have information that I know will interest you."

"Why did you say her name?" Gabe bit out sharply.

"Because she's in trouble. And the man after her, well…he plays for keeps."

Another unexpected blow.

"Why should I believe you? You're a goddamn traitor. A killer for hire, and you've aided in the abduction and near murder of *two* of my teammates' wives. Now you break into my apartment and try to tell me my—"

"Guilty on all counts." The man interrupted with a shrug. "I can assure you, it was pure coincidence that my professional path crossed with your teams on those other two occasions. This time, it's different."

"Different how?"

"The man after your Ellena? He's a special kind of twisted."

The ice in his veins melted as a heated fury took over. "I want a name." Gabe schooled his expression and swallowed that damn fear.

"Go to her, Dawson." Adrian ignored his question—and Gabe's gun—and started for the door. "The doc needs protection."

Mind filled with a whole slew of what-the-fucks, Gabe's reaction to the other man walking away was slightly delayed. He turned around, his gun following Walker's movements.

"I said don't move!"

"You won't shoot me." The cocky fuck was almost to the door.

"What makes you so sure?"

Walker sighed loudly, his body shifting to face him even as he was reaching for the doorknob. "One, you're a fucking Boy Scout. Yes, I'm in your apartment uninvited, but I haven't touched you or made any threats toward you. Hell I'm not even armed."

"My ass." No way a guy like Adrian Walker goes anywhere without at *least* one gun.

"Do you see a weapon?" The man smiled. "I know you, Dawson. You won't shoot an unarmed civilian. Not even me."

The fucker was right. *Goddamnit,* he was right.

"And two," Walker continued, "I still hold the answers to all those questions running around inside that brilliant brain of yours. Like how I even know about the gorgeous doc with the long, blonde hair and adorable dimples."

"You son of a bitch!" Gabe took a step forward. He'd never had to work so hard at not pulling the trigger as he did in that moment.

Walker glanced down at the gun now pointed at his heart and smirked. "See? I know you won't shoot me, because you're a smart man. As the great English writer, Samuel Johnson, once said, curiosity is one of the most permanent and certain characteristics of a vigorous intellect. And you and your team are some of the most vigorous men I know."

"Why bother to even come here if all you're going to do is speak in fucking riddles?"

"You a card player, Dawson? First rule of poker, never show the other players all of your cards." Walker opened the door and faced him again. "I give you everything now, you probably *will* kill me. At the very least, you'll turn me over to the authorities. Not that I could blame you. But either one of those happens before we talk again, you'll lose your chance at ever learning what I know."

"You've already told me someone's after Ellena. Why do I need you for anything else?"

Adrian's lips curled up into a smug grin. "Because I know who is after her and why. The knowledge she has will help you and your team stop them, but you need to get to her soon." He glanced at his watch. "It may already be too late."

The man vanished, leaving Gabe alone in his apartment to try to make sense of what had just transpired.

You let the asshole go. That's what happened.

"Fuck!" Gabe slammed the palm of his hand against the door, his booming voice echoing through the modest space.

He had him. He fucking *had* him. What the hell had he been thinking?

You were thinking about keeping Ellena safe.

From the moment Walker uttered her name, Gabe hadn't been able to think of anything else. His instinct to protect her had always been strong.

That same innate need to keep her safe had been the driving force in his decision to leave her.

If Walker was telling the truth—and Gabe's gut said the asshole was—Ellena was in danger. Again.

Gabe was well aware that this could all be part of some big, elaborate set-up to take him and the team down, but he couldn't think about that now. All he could think of…all he *cared* about…was the woman he'd spent the last three years trying to forget.

I need to call her!

Praying she still had the same number, Gabe shoved his gun back into his waistband and pulled his phone from his jean's pocket. Muscle memory took over as he dialed the number he hadn't called in ages.

It started to ring.

It rang again.

Come on, baby. Pick up!

It rang again, and then, "You've reached the voicemail of Doctor Ellena Dawson." Gabe's chest tightened, her sweet voice stealing every ounce of oxygen in his lungs. "I'm unable to come to the phone right now, but if you'll leave your name, number, and a brief message, I'll return your call as soon as possible. If this is a medical or mental health emergency, please hang up and call nine-one-one."

Gabe held his breath as he waited for the beep. He tried not to think about the fact that these would be the first words she'd hear from him since he'd left her years before.

"Take care of yourself, Elle. I'll see you in my dreams."

That's what he said to her the last time he'd seen her. He'd always said those last six words to her right before his SEAL team would leave for an op. That and... *I love you.*

Gabe hadn't said those three little words to her when he'd left for the last time. Not because they weren't true. They would always be true.

Until the day I die.

Gabe had purposely chosen not to tell Ellena he loved her right before he walked away. Mainly because he knew she no longer believed him.

Wrapped up in the particularly shitty memory, he nearly missed the beep's end. He swallowed hard and began to speak.

"Elle, it's me." He cleared the trembling fear from his throat and spoke quickly. "Listen, I know it's been a long time, and this is going to sound crazy, but I think you're in danger." God, he hated to just blurt that shit out. Mumbling a curse, he ran a hand over his salt and pepper scruff before continuing, "I'm sorry to drop this on you out of the blue, and I promise I'm not trying to scare you, but...I'll explain more when I get there, okay? I'm leaving Dallas tonight, and I'll call you as soon as I land. Do me a favor and don't go anywhere. Keep your doors locked, and don't answer them or the phone unless it's me. Call me when you get this." Because he knew how much she hated being bossed around, Gabe added a quick, "Please."

He barely got the message out before the phone beeped again, ending the recording.

Rushing down the short hallway to his room, Gabe began to frantically pack. Uncaring of how wrinkled his wadded-up clothes would be, he filled the large suitcase with enough to last a week, along with all the necessary toiletries.

He was zipping the suitcase closed when his phone began to ring.

Heart pounding, he snatched the phone from his mattress. He answered on the first ring.

"Ellena?" He was met with silence.

Frowning, he held the phone away and looked at the screen. The area code matched hers, but the call was from a number he didn't recognize.

Gabe put the phone back to his ear. "Hello?" He spoke a little louder that time.

"Uh, yes. Is this Gabriel Dawson?"

His heart sunk. The female voice on the other end of the call didn't belong to his Elle.

She's not yours, anymore.

Ignoring the annoying prick-of-a-voice, Gabe answered the woman. "That's me."

"Mr. Dawson, my name is Amy Hallowell. I'm an emergency room nurse calling from the Naval Medical Center in San Diego."

It was the same hospital where Ellena works. Except Ellena worked on the mental health floor, and this woman had said emergency room.

A ball of dread settled in Gabe's stomach. "Yes?"

"Sir, I'm calling because Ellena Dawson was brought in as a patient this evening, and you are listed in her chart as the person to contact in case of an emergency."

"Is she okay?"

"Sir, Ellena was in a pretty bad car accident. She's currently unconscious and listed in serious but stable condition."

Ah, God.

Gabe grabbed his suitcase from the bed and raced down the hallway. "I'll be there as soon as I can." Walker's warning ran through his head. "Do *not* let anyone other than hospital personal in her room."

There was a pause and then, "Sir?"

"Amy, I need you to listen to me. I am a retired Master Chief Special Warfare Operator." Because she worked in a Naval hospital, she *should* understand what that means. "Less than five minutes before you called, I was made aware of a threat to Ellena's life." He stepped out of his apartment, locked his door, and jogged to his truck. "I'm in Dallas now, but I'll be there as soon as I can. In the meantime, Ellena needs security posted outside her room. Do you understand?"

Obviously flustered, the woman attempted to respond. "I-I…um…"

Shit. He needed to make her understand. "Amy?"

"Y-yes?"

"I'm going to give you a phone number, and then I'm going to hang up. I want you to wait three minutes and call that number."

"Who am I calling?"

Gabe got into his truck and started the engine. Tires squealed loudly as he tore out of the parking lot and headed for Jake McQueen's ranch.

More specifically, the private airstrip located on his ranch.

"The number I'm giving you is a direct line to Agent Jason Ryker with Homeland Security. He will be able to verify who I am and that this is not a hoax or some type of prank. The threat to Ellena is very real, and I need for your hospital to take it seriously." He rattled off Ryker's number. "I'm going to hang up now, Amy. Please. Call the number. Ask for Agent Ryker."

"How will I know this man is really a Homeland agent?"

"Trust me. You'll know."

Another pause. "What exactly is your relationship to the patient? It doesn't say in her chart."

Gabe swallowed before answering, "Ellena's my wife."

ALSO BY ANNA BLAKELY

Other Books by Anna Blakely

Bravo Team Series

Rescuing Gracelynn

Rescuing Katherine

Rescuing Gabriella

R.I.S.C. SERIES:

Book 1: **Taking a Risk, Part One** (Jake & Olivia's HFN)

Book 2: **Taking a Risk, Part Two** (Jake & Olivia's HEA)

Book 3: **Beautiful Risk** (Trevor & Lexi)

Book 4: **Intentional Risk** (Derek & Charlotte)

Book 5: **Unpredictable Risk** (Grant & Brynnon)

Book 6: **Ultimate Risk** (Coop & Mac)

Book 7: **Targeted Risk** (Mike & Jules)

Want to read Kole & Sarah's story for FREE?

Click below to sign up for Anna Blakely's newsletter and receive your *FREE copy* of *Unexpected Risk-A Bravo Team Novella*

https://dl.bookfunnel.com/u3zicn7yhu

*Unexpected Risk was originally released as part of the Because He's Perfect charity anthology. It is now only available through this link, and brings you Kole & Sarah's trying experience while dealing with shocking news and a malevolent stalker.

ABOUT THE AUTHOR

Author Anna Blakely brings you stories of love, action, and edge-of-your-seat suspense. As an avid reader of romantic suspense herself, Anna's dream is to create stories her readers will enjoy and characters they'll fall in love with as much as she has. She believes in true love and happily-ever-after, and that's what she will always bring to you.

Anna lives in rural Missouri with her husband, children, and several rescued animals. When she's not writing, Anna enjoys reading, watching action and horror movies (the scarier the better), and spending time with her amazing husband, four wonderful children, and her adorable granddaughter.

FB Author Page: facebook.com/annablakely.author.7
Blakely's Bunch (reader group): https://www.facebook.com/groups/354218335396441/
Instagram: https://instagram.com/annablakely
BookBub: https//www.bookbub.com/authors/anna-blakely
Amazon: amazon.com/author/annablakely
Twitter: @ablakelyauthor
Goodreads: https://www.goodreads.com/author/show/18650841.Anna_Blakely

facebook.com/annablakely.author.7
twitter.com/ablakelyauthor
instagram.com/annablakely
amazon.com/author/annablakely

There are many more books in this fan fiction world than listed here, for an up-to-date list go to www.AcesPress.com

You can also visit our Amazon page at: http://www.amazon.com/author/operationalpha

Special Forces: Operation Alpha World

Christie Adams: Charity's Heart
Denise Agnew: Dangerous to Hold
Shauna Allen: Awakening Aubrey
Brynne Asher: Blackburn
Linzi Baxter: Unlocking Dreams
Jennifer Becker: Hiding Catherine
Alice Bello: Shadowing Milly
Heather Blair: Rescue Me
Anna Blakely: Rescuing Gracelynn
Julia Bright: Saving Lorelei
Cara Carnes: Protecting Mari
Kendra Mei Chailyn: Beast
Melissa Kay Clarke: Rescuing Annabeth
Samantha A. Cole: Handling Haven
Sue Coletta: Hacked
Melissa Combs: Gallant
Anne Conley: Redemption for Misty
KaLyn Cooper: Rescuing Melina
Liz Crowe: Marking Mariah
Sarah Curtis: Securing the Odds
Jordan Dane: Redemption for Avery
Tarina Deaton: Found in the Lost
Aspen Drake, Intense
KL Donn: Unraveling Love
Riley Edwards: Protecting Olivia
PJ Fiala: Defending Sophie

Nicole Flockton: Protecting Maria
Michele Gwynn: Rescuing Emma
Casey Hagen: Shielding Nebraska
Desiree Holt: Protecting Maddie
Kathy Ivan: Saving Sarah
Kris Jacen, Be With Me
Jesse Jacobson: Protecting Honor
Silver James: Rescue Moon
Becca Jameson: Saving Sofia
Kate Kinsley: Protecting Ava
Heather Long: Securing Arizona
Gennita Low: No Protection
Kirsten Lynn: Joining Forces for Jesse
Margaret Madigan: Bang for the Buck
Kimberly McGath: The Predecessor
Rachel McNeely: The SEAL's Surprise Baby
KD Michaels: Saving Laura
Lynn Michaels, Rescuing Kyle
Wren Michaels: The Fox & The Hound
Kat Mizera: Protecting Bobbi
Keira Montclair, Wolf and the Wild Scots
Mary B Moore: Force Protection
LeTeisha Newton: Protecting Butterfly
Angela Nicole: Protecting the Donna
MJ Nightingale: Protecting Beauty
Sarah O'Rourke: Saving Liberty
Victoria Paige: Reclaiming Izabel
Anne L. Parks: Mason
Debra Parmley: Protecting Pippa
Lainey Reese: Protecting New York
TL Reeve and Michele Ryan: Extracting Mateo
Elena M. Reyes: Keeping Ava
Angela Rush: Charlotte
Rose Smith: Saving Satin

Jenika Snow: Protecting Lily
Lynne St. James: SEAL's Spitfire
Dee Stewart: Conner
Harley Stone: Rescuing Mercy
Jen Talty: Burning Desire
Reina Torres, Rescuing Hi'ilani
Savvi V: Loving Lex
Megan Vernon: Protecting Us
Rachel Young: Because of Marissa

Delta Team Three Series

Lori Ryan: Nori's Delta
Becca Jameson: Destiny's Delta
Lynne St James, Gwen's Delta
Elle James: Ivy's Delta
Riley Edwards, Hope's Delta

Police and Fire: Operation Alpha World

Freya Barker: Burning for Autumn
BP Beth: Scott
Julia Bright, Justice for Amber
Anna Brooks, Guarding Georgia
KaLyn Cooper: Justice for Gwen
Aspen Drake: Sheltering Emma
Deanndra Hall: Shelter for Sharla
Barb Han: Kace
EM Hayes: Gambling for Ashleigh
CM Steele: Guarding Hope
Reina Torres: Justice for Sloane
Aubree Valentine, Justice for Danielle
Maddie Wade: Finding English
Stacey Wilk: Stage Fright
Laine Vess: Justice for Lauren

Tarpley VFD Series

Silver James, Fighting for Elena
Deanndra Hall, Fighting for Carly
Haven Rose, Fighting for Calliope
MJ Nightingale, Fighting for Jemma
TL Reeve, Fighting for Brittney
Nicole Flockton, Fighting for Nadia

As you know, this book included at least one character from Susan Stoker's books. To check out more, see below.

SEAL of Protection: Legacy Series

Securing Caite
Securing Brenae (novella)
Securing Sidney
Securing Piper
Securing Zoey
Securing Avery
Securing Kalee (Sept 2020)
Securing Jane (Feb 2021)

SEAL Team Hawaii Series

Finding Elodie (Apr 2021)
Finding Lexie (Aug 2021)
Finding Kenna (Oct 2021)
Finding Monica (TBA)
Finding Carly (TBA)
Finding Ashlyn (TBA)

Delta Team Two Series

Shielding Gillian
Shielding Kinley (Aug 2020)
Shielding Aspen (Oct 2020)
Shielding Riley (Jan 2021)
Shielding Devyn (May 2021)
Shielding Ember (Sep 2021)
Shielding Sierra (TBA)

Delta Force Heroes Series

Rescuing Rayne (FREE!)
Rescuing Aimee (novella)

Rescuing Emily
Rescuing Harley
Marrying Emily (novella)
Rescuing Kassie
Rescuing Bryn
Rescuing Casey
Rescuing Sadie (novella)
Rescuing Wendy
Rescuing Mary
Rescuing Macie (Novella)

Badge of Honor: Texas Heroes Series

Justice for Mackenzie (FREE!)
Justice for Mickie
Justice for Corrie
Justice for Laine (novella)
Shelter for Elizabeth
Justice for Boone
Shelter for Adeline
Shelter for Sophie
Justice for Erin
Justice for Milena
Shelter for Blythe
Justice for Hope
Shelter for Quinn
Shelter for Koren
Shelter for Penelope

SEAL of Protection Series

Protecting Caroline (FREE!)
Protecting Alabama
Protecting Fiona
Marrying Caroline (novella)
Protecting Summer

Protecting Cheyenne
Protecting Jessyka
Protecting Julie (novella)
Protecting Melody
Protecting the Future
Protecting Kiera (novella)
Protecting Alabama's Kids (novella)
Protecting Dakota

New York Times, USA Today and *Wall Street Journal* Bestselling Author Susan Stoker has a heart as big as the state of Tennessee where she lives, but this all American girl has also spent the last fourteen years living in Missouri, California, Colorado, Indiana, and Texas. She's married to a retired Army man who now gets to follow *her* around the country.

www.stokeraces.com
www.AcesPress.com
susan@stokeraces.com

Made in the USA
Coppell, TX
21 June 2022